The Wicker Tree

A novel by

ROBIN HARDY

Luath Press Limited

EDINBURGH

www.luath.co.uk

Extracts from 'I Tempted him with Apples' by Keith Easdale
reproduced by kind permission of Keith Easdale and JDC Productions.

First published as *Cowboys for Christ* 2006
This edition 2011

ISBN 978-1906817-61-9

The paper used in this book is sourced from renewable forestry
and is FSC credited material.

The author's right to be identified as author of this book
under the Copyright, Designs and Patents Act 1988 has been asserted.

Printed and bound by
Martins the Printers, Berwick Upon Tweed

Typeset in 9.8 point Sabon

© Robin Hardy 2006, 2011

For Vicky

Life can only be understood backwards, but it must be lived forwards.
Søren Kierkegaard, *Life*

Preface

NO ONE CAN SAY that a comedy, however 'black', need be devoid of meaning.

The Wicker Tree is a work of fiction and yet all of it is based on present reality or well documented fact about our Celtic ancestors in Scotland and in all of the British Isles. Much of their religion is still with us in the days of the week and the months of the year and, most particularly, in Christianity itself, especially Easter and Christmas.

While working on the film of *The Wicker Tree*, I was aware of how strong this ancient inheritance remains in Scotland today. I had recently seen the amazing Beltane festival in Edinburgh, where, on Calton Hill high above the beautiful city, a group of young people re-invent the ancient Celtic celebration which comes with each May Day. What can we know of it thousands of years ago before the Romans came? What matters to these young solicitors' clerks, students, artists and actors is that its inspiration is the same today as then. The sap rising in the blossoming trees, rising in their own bodies, inspiring them to make music and dance, to celebrate the renewing elements of nature: fire, water, air – the very earth itself.

Along with seventeen thousand other people I watched this joyous pagan masque unfold, while, below, the lights of the city started to twinkle and the spires and the domes of the great churches stood in bleak silhouette, as if besieged by fireflies. I had to have a version of this is my film and the perfect place for it is on the hill leading up to The Wicker Tree. For there the tree stands in for all the lovers in nature, for every evolutionary mating of every sentient thing. This is the climax of the film although not quite its ending.

In the transition from book to film we have kept the yearly drama of riding after the Laddie, a reality to this day in the little border towns where almost everyone seems to have a horse. All sorts of myth laundering cannot disguise how the most handsome young man, the cleverest and the bravest, elected by all as their Laddie each year, could never have been hunted over heather and heath simply to sit down at the climax of the chase for a cosy picnic of cup cakes, canned beer and tea.

The final reality, underlining the whole story, is the sinister presence of the Nuada nuclear power station, its threat implicit in the whole plot. While the book, of necessity, explains more of the apparent danger to our village of Tressock, we are re-publishing this story in the immediate wake of the ghastly nuclear disasters that have befallen Japan.

Some will see in this book or film a choice between two beliefs, the Christian and the Pagan. But in the end it is simply raising questions the answers to which are unknowable.

While we were making the film inspired by this story, the wicker tree left the forest and appeared amongst us, an icon, it seemed to us, every bit as potent as The Wicker Man that preceded it. Whereas The Wicker Man is an icon of death, The Wicker Tree heralds new life. The song says it all:

Wicker is woman and she is a tree.
With soft tendrils, tender and free.
Oh, wicker is man and hard wood is he.
Strong are the arms of the wicker tree.
They'll meet in the forest and passionate be.

For the fire that consumes them
Consumes all of we.
It licks and devours. So must we be.
Insatiable tree
Part he, part she,
Oh Wicker Tree – Wicker Tree – Wicker Tree.

The Wicker Tree song by Robin Hardy and Keith Easdale
© Tressock Films Ltd.

Robin Hardy, 2011

Beth's Awakening

BETH AWOKE THAT morning from a deep dream of peace and tranquillity, feeling blessed. In the dream, she had been singing in an empty auditorium. There was no band, no orchestra, no audience, no fans and, the biggest blessing of all, there was no microphone. Just her voice as she always heard it when no one was jigging around with it, playing it back with echo, with reverb, with the high notes tweaked, just her voice as it sounded in some inner ear of her own where nothing electronic ever penetrated.

This was a very special morning. It was, in a way, her first day of independence from 'the business' that had been her life since she was fourteen, a declaration of independence that had her father saying over and over, 'We made you fifty million dollars in seven years. All you had to do was go out and sing with that voice the good Lord gave you. Now you say this is not a career you "want to pursue." Are you crazy? What about a little gratitude? You're only twenty for Christ's sake. Haven't you heard about honouring your father and mother?'

Beth's answer, she knew it maddened him, was always pretty much the same.

'Fifteen per cent of my earnings would have been enough to keep you in booze and high-priced hookers for the rest of your life. But you've taken fifty per cent. Mom's dead and I've honoured you all I have to. Brother Kenny at the church told me so. And I won't have you taking Jesus' name in vain in this house. It's my house now. Get back to that palace in Dallas of yours. From now on I am doing my thing, my way. OK, Daddy?'

She knew he needed a drink real bad after she'd done telling him that again and he knew she didn't have a drop of alcohol in the house. So he hightailed it back down to Dallas. To his fancy chateau, on the corner of North Versailles Road and Stuart Avenue, where the bar had been copied from the Oak Room at the Plaza Hotel in New York City. She knew that he just couldn't figure how anyone in her right mind could turn down a twenty-gig tour paying all that loot.

But she knew, too, that he had really started to give up on her the previous fall. He'd been in rehab after her mother's death and Beth had refused to let him into the recording studio in Nashville. When he saw her at the launch bash for her new album she thought he might have one of those apoplectic fits. She'd let her hair go natural, sort of blondish but really very light brown. She'd given up on cosmetics altogether. All the specially created paints, creams and unguents her expensive consultants had prescribed to transform her pretty, slightly plump face into the lean and hungry blonde look favoured by Britney, Christina and the others – all had been thrown away.

It was for her wonderful to be seen as what she actually was at age twenty – but you would never have guessed it if you had seen the embalmed pop star that went by her name these last five teenage years.

Yes, it was a glorious day. Beth showered and dressed quickly, trying to think in an organised way about what she needed for her journey. But her excitement about her coming mission constantly distracted her. She had so much to look forward to in the next year. A chance to give some service to the Lord. To meet with some real needy people who were being literally starved of His word, His grace. Europe was like another world. Everybody she knew who'd been there said so. Whole countries there had pretty much turned away from the Lord. He who had given her that greatest of gifts – her wonderful voice – needed her.

She had started packing several days previously, trying to narrow down what would fit into two suitcases and a back pack. That was the most the Redeemers had told her she could take. She was an experienced traveller, as pop stars went, in that she normally packed just about all the clothes and shoes she possessed, knowing that the roadies would be handling all her luggage from one stop to another. That way she had access to any little thing she could possibly require just as if she was at home in Texas. As the star of the tour she naturally always had the largest suite at whatever five-star hotel existed in the town where the gig was being held. By arrangement with her publicity handler, she coped with the fan problem by living on room service, only going down to the lobby of the hotel to do a signing just before the gig. Sometimes it was arranged for her to go to a museum or a local beauty spot, but mostly she was hermetically sealed from the places through which she passed.

So, if you had asked Beth whether she was well travelled she would certainly have answered that for a little ole Texas gal from Walnut Springs she had done pretty well. Nine major tours of America that included virtually every important state and she had somehow fitted in two vacations, one in Hawaii and one in Puerto Rico. But the vacations had been working holidays, doing picture features for *Vanity Fair* and *Rolling Stone* respectively, staying in hotels indistinguishable from all the other Marriotts, Hiltons, Sheratons and Four Seasons that blurred together in her memory. She had even done gigs in Toronto and Montreal, Canada where many of the folks spoke French (although not to her).

Now she was becoming a missionary for a year. The Redeemers had given her a choice between several African countries and Europe, where Scotland was their target for the second year running. She had chosen Scotland largely because Steve had wanted to go there. That was the other great thing about this mission. She was getting to go with Steve. She was going to do work she just knew she was going to love. Telling people about Jesus. Explaining how wonderful it was to be born again. Sharing her joy in her faith. And doing it with the man she had loved ever since she was thirteen and they had both been eighth graders at Lyndon B. Johnson High School in Sasquahetta, Texas.

When she was at home in the simple colonial house she had always regarded as her mother's, now hers by virtue of inheritance, and in which no trace of her father remained, she liked to look forward to what she would make of it when she and Steve were married, when they had kids. That was a dream that always distracted her, but looking at her watch she realised she must concentrate. She'd read that Scotland could be cold, real cold, with snow and ice. She'd packed her skiing underwear and now she added several sweaters. Parts of Scotland, she was advised, were also plagued with midges, kind of miniature mosquitoes you could hardly see. She had already packed some insect spray. The news that the Scots' favourite food was sheep's stomach alarmed her and she checked that she had put the Imodium in her toilet kit.

Beth took a long last look at her living room, at all the familiar things she and her mom had collected. The very special collection of Tiffany glass on the illuminated shelves. The photographs of herself and Steve together when she had been elected Homecoming Queen. Her Grammy for Best Female Country Vocal Performance for 'Trailer Trash Love', her favourite song and the one for which her mother had written most of the lyrics. The gold and platinum album plaques had all gone to the palace in Dallas with her father. She didn't miss them.

Confident that she had forgotten nothing, especially her brand new passport, she gave a fond farewell hug to Vashti, her housekeeper, and carried her own suitcases across the porch. Beth detested flashing her money around and despised what her father had done with his. But a few luxuries she did allow herself. True to her career as a recording artist, she liked to travel by limo, and one was now and almost always sitting outside her house, like a beached white whale, waiting for her to do some shopping or to visit Steve at the Dragon x Ranch or to go to the Cowboys for Christ church at Osceola, off Route 171.

Benny, Vashti's husband, who drove the limo, was, according to his wife, 'the laziest nigger in Texas.' It always slightly shocked Beth to hear Vashti use that word. Beth regarded PCness as next to Godliness. But his wife's accusation just made Benny chuckle. Officially, he worked for a limo company with the grand name of Buckingham Livery and Hire, but when Beth was at home she liked to have him always available. Steve pointed out that it would be much cheaper to buy the limo and hire Benny to drive it.

'That would mean I had a chauffeur,' protested Beth. 'That's not me at all. This way, I just hire the limo when I need it.'

Steve seldom argued with Beth. Their friendship was based on being very comfortable in each other's company. It always had been. As kids they held hands a lot, not caring who laughed at them. Steve still lived with his pa, a widower and a working cowboy, a rarity now in Texas, who had originally been a hand on the LBJ Ranch when President Johnson and his wife, Lady Bird, were in retirement. Steve had somehow never been too dazzled by Beth's career. But he was proud of her voice and was one of the very few people around her who understood her view that it was her voice and not her career that was the more important.

Benny drove the limo at about forty-five miles an hour. He considered any speed in excess of that inconsistent with a Cadillac's dignity. Beth watched out the left-hand window as they started to approach Osceola down Route 171. The Church of Christ's Second Coming, recently renamed Cowboys for Christ (and part of a growing brotherhood of such churches) was located just two miles short of the little town. Now what she saw on either side of the highway was flat open country, just shrubs and occasional clumps of pine trees. Beth was looking to see if a rider leaving a long trail of dust from a track that ran parallel to 171 could be Steve.

She knew it should be, because when she phoned him, just before leaving home, he said that if Benny was driving at his usual speed, he'd beat them to the church on Old Johnson, his pa's favourite quarter horse. Sure enough, as rider and horse got closer to the road, she could see that it was indeed Steve, his hat laid back on his shoulders, his tousled blond hair all over his face so that he had to hold his head well back to see.

Now the church was coming into view, just off the road, nestling in a clearing of a small pine wood. It was built on the classic log cabin principle, only the logs looked Wal-Mart shiny and new. There was a corral close by where some cowboys were just finishing a morning of showing off their ropin' skills. Further on was a car park with several hundred vehicles, everything from old, rusty pick-ups through heavily chrome-plated Humvees and SUVs to fancy European automobiles and even occasional Fords and Chevies. Steve had joined the road now and was riding beside the Cadillac, shouting down at Beth through her open window.

'Looks like we're the last to get here. What are you singin'?'

'The Magnificat.'

'Yeah? Do I know that?'

'Maybe not, Steve. But I think you'll like it.'

'What happened to Amazing Grace?'

'This is my new deal, honey.'

'OK. So do the band know this piece?'

'Not doing it with the band. Holly Dempster – she'll play piano for me. Like I said, this is my new deal. I am just going to use my voice.'

'Can the folks stomp and holler?'

'Don't think they'll be inclined, Steve.'

'Well you go for it, girl. Pa came on ahead. He's got my bag and my passport and my ticket. This trip of ours got him all worked up. If he could come too, he'd be there in a New York minute.'

Steve clapped his heels into Old Johnson's flanks and the horse took off towards the church, leaving the long white Cadillac alone to make the majestic arrival for which it had been designed.

Benny would not have dreamed of letting Beth walk from the car park, which she would much have preferred to do, so he drove straight up to the church's main door, reserved usually for funerals and weddings. Beth sighed as she saw the outside broadcast truck of a local TV station, its lines already hung up to the church, its auxiliary generator humming. The video guy was wandering around looking, Beth always thought, like some weird mutant of the human race that had great black cameras growing out of its necks and shoulders.

There were fans crowding in as she got out of the car but, thankfully, Big Bill Marlowe, the guy to whom she (and her father) owed so much, was there to greet her and take charge.

'C'mon guys, give Beth a break,' he said in a voice that was not that loud but nonetheless penetrated the hubbub around them. 'This is a church service, not a gig or a concert, you know. The service will be on your car radio, on TV. Anyone being a regular worshipper at this church will hear Beth inside.' He lowered his voice. 'How many will you sign, Beth?'

'Twelve,' she said. She always said twelve. It was her lucky number.

Two minutes later they were inside the church and she was being greeted by Brother Kenny, the pastor. He took her and Big Bill into his little office. Worshippers were still streaming in to be met by a couple of elders who kept the tally of who was or was not a bona fide member of the congregation. Some serious fundraisers for the President had taken place at this church. He'd even been there himself and said a few words when he was still Governor of Texas. Even so, it was probably not an obvious target for terrorists but, since 9/11, people liked to see real good security wherever they went.

Beth sipped some hot coffee that Brother Kenny had waiting for her and listened to him with the attention she had always given to anyone producing or directing her, whether for a live gig, a music video or a recording.

'Beth, we're real glad you are agreeing to go – and take Steve with you – on this Redeemers' mission. Ever since this church became associated with the Redeemers we've wanted to encourage young people to go out and preach the word of God to heathens everywhere. To have you go to Scotland is such a fine example to other young people. Because you could've just given money – and I know you've done that too.'

Beth felt what he had just said was a tad redundant. She knew all that, so did Big Bill. Where was she to sit? When was she to sing? Where was Holly so she could have a last word about the music? Where was Steve going to be sitting? She wanted him near her. At what time was the Redeemers' bus coming by?

Kenny might have read her mind because he just smiled and produced two photocopied sheets giving the Order of Service and the seating plan of the church. The bus was scheduled to come by in an hour and a half's time. Beth had the grace to look apologetic. She leaned forward and briefly squeezed Brother Kenny's hand. It was a little gesture her mom had taught her. Warm, intimate, friendly, but not in any way sexy. Useful.

'Holly will come and fetch you when it's time for you to sing that hymn of yours,' said Brother Kenny, leaving to start stage-managing the service.

She was alone now in the office with Big Bill, who looked like he had something special he wanted to say to her. He got up to his feet, hesitated, then shut the door, drowning out '*I'm riding down the trail with Jesus, yes I am.*' Then he sat down opposite her and looked at her with that special look of his, head on one side like an old hound dog, eyes a little bloodshot but serious, sincere. Although he was no more than forty or so, still he seemed pretty old to Beth, who'd always called him Big Bill, cause her mom had started it to distinguish him from Beth's father, also a Bill. Her Daddy was small and round. Folks called him Fat Billy, though not to his face. Whereas Big Bill was tall and lean and dignified, built like a true cowboy, except he was really a venture capitalist born with more in his trust funds than you'd find in the treasuries of many a foreign country. She respected Big Bill as much as she despised her father.

'Just thought we'd talk about this trip of yours, Beth. Of course, I agree with Brother Kenny. You are doing a wonderful thing here. But I'm not sure you realise the risk you're taking. Sure, I know you got Steve to look out for you, but he's just a kid too.'

'We're not kids, Bill,' said Beth sharply. 'Kids our age are ready to fight for our country.'

'That is my point exactly. There's a war going on out there. I checked with the Redeemer people. They had to admit, valuable as you are to them PR-wise, they do not plan to detail anyone to act as full-time security guard for you like you'd have on a tour.'

'Bill, I discussed all this with them. I do not want a guard. I do not want any publicity once the main gig in Glasgow is over. Steve is my special guy. You know that. He'll take good care of me. We'll just be two young people, me and him, over from Texas with this message of hope for these poor people who have seemingly lost their faith.'

'Have you any idea what Europe is like these days?'

'Sure. The Redeemers gave us a whole lot of info about the Godlessness in Scotland, the strange beliefs they have, like we're all descended from animals and slimy things out of the ocean. A lot of Yankees believe that stuff too you know, even folks in this state. They really do. We know we got a real big hill to climb with these folks.'

'Did they tell you what the Reverend Pat Robertson said about the Scottish people? He said too many of those poor lost souls are gay, wearing those skirts and all... Do you know something? My dear grandma used to sing songs from a book called *Gay Ditties*. They've stolen that lovely word from us. God help me, I do resent that.'

'They're called kilts. Have you ever been there, Bill? To Europe?'

'I have not. Like President Nixon said: "I don't care what religion a man has, as long as he's got a religion." In Europe religion is mostly dead. They're lost people. To be frank with you, I don't want to spend

17

any of my precious time on earth with lost people.'

'Bill!' Beth cried. 'You're trying to discourage me? You of all people. You gave me my start. You paid for my dad to take me to Nashville and for those first recordings. I just can't believe this.'

'You're throwing away your career,' said Bill sadly. 'I'm not saying this just because I invested in you. I think you know that. But because you've been doing great. You're on a roll now. Go away for a year and maybe it'll be, "Beth who?" Aren't you at all scared of that?'

Beth wasn't scared at all. Although she had kept this to herself, she had decided to re-invent Beth, the singer, in the service of her voice. Maybe this was the moment to start breaking this to Bill. She leant forward and put her hand over his big hairy paw and squeezed gently before withdrawing it.

'You are a very dear man, Bill. I love you like I was your own daughter. When I come back, after Steve and I get married, I'm going to sing like you'll hear me sing today. Maybe there won't be no more Grammy awards. But I think people will pay to hear my voice. And if they won't then I'll sing for my little old self and Steve and, I hope, you Bill, and my other real good friends.'

The door to the office had opened a little and Holly was peering through.

'Oh, excuse me,' she said and stood there speechless for a moment. She recognised Bill as the rich, legendary drinker and womaniser who had been saved by Jesus some ten years ago and was now seldom out of the society pages of the newspapers. Holly wondered for an instant about him and Beth, and if she was interrupting something.

'I'm supposed to fetch you now, Beth. Is that OK?' she said hurriedly, as if she'd suddenly remembered her errand.

'Sure, we're all through here,' said Big Bill, rising to his feet. It sounded a bit abrupt, although he was smiling. But Beth had remained seated. She tugged for a few seconds at the hand she had squeezed.

'Bill?' her voice had lowered and he turned to her quickly while Holly went back out the door to wait in the passage.

'Yeah, what is it Beth?'

'I don't owe anyone anything, do I? My dad's paid off. You recovered yours some time ago, I guess. The label... Well I fulfilled my contract. The option to continue was open. I've let it go... I told them I'll come back to them if they still want me in a year's time. They didn't like it. But I'd say they were smart, they were cool. They gave me a nice six-figure kiss goodbye. So who do I owe?' She raised her voice: 'I'm coming Holly.'

'No one, Beth. No one I can think of,' said Bill.

'Right, except the Lord. I'm doing this for Him,' said Beth.

It sounded melodramatic but Bill recognised that it was true.

Brother Kenny was about to start his address when she sat down just behind him on the stage next to Steve. The band had left their instruments behind, but Holly had already seated herself at the piano. The collection was in progress: two women passing black ten-gallon hats down the rows of worshippers. Beth reflected, not for the first time in this church, that the pastor ought to get up one day and ask the Lord to help him put the whole congregation on a diet. Most of the men out front were dressed in cowboy clothes; boots, silver-decorated belts and hats which they wore on their heads, except of course during the saying of the Lord's prayer. Beth loved them. These people were, for her, the salt of the earth. Good, kind, God-fearing people. Her people and Steve's people. But she thanked God that he was a real cowboy, not just a suburbanite dressed up.

Brother Kenny took the microphone from its stand by the lectern and started to stride across the stage.

'Lord,' he said, 'this is a special day for this church. Because two of our young people, Lord, will go forth from here to do Your work. Like St Paul in the olden times they are goin' forth to preach Your word, Lord…'

Beth only half listened to what Brother Kenny was saying. She, herself, was trying to get used to talking to the Lord as if He was a next-door neighbour, chatting over the hedge from his back yard. Brother Kenny was good at it. But for her it had never been easy. She tried to think of the friendly approachable Jesus, but the vengeful Jehova of the Old Testament tended to materialise. Now, however, Brother Kenny was referring specifically to her and to Steve. She focused her attention on his pacing figure, his slightly theatrical but effective gestures, his lean, expressive face under his cowboy hat.

'We are gathered today to say Godspeed to two of our Redeemers who are going to give a year of their young lives to Jesus,' he was saying. 'They are going to bring His message to the poor people of Scotland. This is the second year the Redeemers Choir have been over to their Christian Music Festival. But I got to tell you folks that our Missionaries, going door to door to bring the good news – they've found it real tough going. Some of these dear Scots don't even believe in angels, and some are hardcore atheists.'

Brother Kenny had stopped by Beth's chair and placed a hand on her shoulder.

'Beth,' he went on, 'I want you to know we are all real proud of you, because we all know you only gotta raise your little pinky to go right on being a truly great singin' star. Steve, you take good care of this lovely lady, d'you hear? You are one lucky son of a gun to be goin' with her, but you know that. God bless you both and bring you back safe and pure to us here, and we will give you the wedding of the year. And that's a promise. Amen.'

The church was suddenly filled with the noise of cheering, clapping, stomping people, which only subsided as Beth stood and signalled to Holly to start playing. A hush fell almost instantly as Beth handed a slightly surprised Brother Kenny the redundant mike, stepped forward to the edge of the stage, and started to sing.

'My soul does magnify the Lord
And my spirit does rejoice
In God, my Saviour
For He has regarded the lowliness
Of his handmaiden
For behold, from henceforth
All generations shall call me blessed
For He that is mighty has magnified me
And holy is His name.'

The piano, underscoring her voice, carried the melody that Johan Sebastian Bach had written for this canticle more than two hundred years earlier. But, even he, who must have heard some of the greatest singers of his age, could not have failed to be moved, exalted even, by this wonderful instrument that was Beth's voice.

'For He has shown strength with his arm
He has shattered the proud
In the imagination of their hearts
He has put down the mighty from their seat
And He has exalted the humble and meek
He has filled the hungry with good things
And the rich He has sent empty away.'

Steve, who had never heard her sing like this before, was dazed by the beauty and wonder that she had created in the church. He applauded along with the congregation, who not only had never heard a sound like hers before, but had never heard a hymn (let alone a canticle) without the backing of guitars, drums, accordions, xylophones and the like. Steve guessed that Brother Kenny, applauding with the rest, was relieved that Beth's magnificent sound was not going to disrupt the church's traditional cowboy music. At least not for another year.

The bus carrying the Redeemers Choir to the Dallas/Fort Worth Airport stopped to pick them up from the melee of fans and well-wishing members of the congregation. As they emerged from the church, Steve saw his pa being interviewed by Buz Dworkin, a reporter for one of the local TV stations.

'So it's your boy, Steve, is it, going with Beth?'

'Sure is,' said his father proudly. 'They been promised since eighth grade. His ma, she found them playin' "I'll show you mine, you show me yours". Made them promise. Wait till they're wed. She's gone now, rest her soul. Still, before she went, she had them make a commitment. They're members of that – they call it the Silver Ring Thing. The ring says they won't have no screwin' around – just no sex no-how – till the day they're wed...'

Steve was more embarrassed by this revelation of pa's than was Beth. Sitting next to each other on the plane, with the twenty-strong Redeemers Choir all around them, Beth and Steve held hands. Both were lost in their own thoughts as they took off, bound for Great Britain. But both of them were thinking pretty much the same thing. The commitment they had made to avoid sex until marriage had worked pretty well as long as they were both living apart and taken up with their separate busy lives. Now they were going to be together, day in, day out, and all the time they must keep to this commitment. Beth thought it would be very hard. Steve was afraid it would be impossible.

As for the dangers that Big Bill and many others had warned them about in Europe, they had long since discounted these. In addition to service to God, this was an adventure. And what was adventure without some element of risk? People they knew had been to Europe and returned with nothing worse than astonishment at the price of everything.

Pretty soon they slept.

Tressock Castle

SCOTLAND'S SPRING COMES later than England's, but on the Borders between the two nations it is well advanced by mid April. The kitchen gardens in little towns like Kelso, Coldstream and Tressock are already full of fruit blossoms, and the rough winds that blow across the bare, heather strewn countryside do not wait for the darling buds of May but are already scattering a torrent of petals around the sturdy stone houses of these borderland Scots.

Tressock Castle rises like a cliff face from a rocky promontory where the River Sulis, a tributary of the Tweed, provides it with half its moat. Its towering stone flanks are surmounted by an odd jumble of turrets, mansard roofs, domes and pinnacles. It is a Scottish baronial collage of a building. Somewhere its innards are mediaeval, sometime courtyards long since enclosed as great airy Adam-decorated rooms and everywhere, on the lower floors, huge windows have been punched into the cliff-face walls, to let in the precious light, work done in the seventeenth century when the possession of lots of valuable glass was a mark of conspicuous consumption.

On the dry side of the castle, as it were, lawns and parterres, reflecting pools and fountains, immaculate glass houses and a well-stocked, walled kitchen garden all attest to this being the home of people who care about their surroundings and can afford to do so. Only the topiary, which forms a kind of honour guard from the castle's porte cocher, past its stables, to the great gates that lead to the little town of Tressock, is so unusual as to be condemned in local guide books as 'odd'. Foreigners, unused to British English, do not always realise how severe a censure this adjective implies, for the carefully pruned yew trees that parade along each side of the drive suggest rows of jaunty phalluses.

On the comparatively rare occasions when the sun penetrates the grey, purple cloud cover over the Tressock hills, it waits until it has risen high enough for its warmth to seep through, casting pale shadows on the castle's lawns. But just occasionally it surprises by rising clear and bright over the heathered hills at dawn.

On such a day, Sir Lachlan and Lady Morrison found themselves awakening in their Tressock Castle home to great shafts of blinding sunlight coming through the windows of their bedroom and penetrating the half drawn curtains of their huge four-poster bed. Four broad-bosomed, bearded hermaphrodites, carved in ebony, supported the canopy above the awakening couple. Lady Morrison closed the bed curtains hastily, shutting out the sun, and thought, perhaps for the thousandth time, how she hated the hermaphrodites and how extraordinary it was that Lachlan admired them.

She watched her husband slowly awaken. In the fifteen years of their marriage she had become accustomed to the unexpected from Lachlan, save in a small number of foibles and habits where he was as consistent as a well-oiled chiming clock. Unusually for a Scot, he never took a bath, subjecting himself to freezing showers instead, and he shaved with a cut-throat razor that had belonged to his great-great-great-grandfather, Sir John Morrison (VI of Tressock), who had served with the Coldstream Guards at Waterloo under the Duke of Wellington. It lived, this razor – actually there were several – in the long-dead soldier's leather travelling kit. The sound of it being sharpened on its stone slab always put Lady Morrison's teeth on edge. So she had bought Lachlan a state-of-the-art electric razor as a May Day present. He thanked her with his customary civility and suggested she use it on her legs.

But now he was completing what, for him, was the ritual of becoming totally awake. His eyes stared at her, unblinking, unwavering for at least thirty seconds – a long time, at any rate. It was as if some battery inside him was slowly activating and then, suddenly, startlingly, he was again the vivid presence that filled her days, her life. He was speaking to her, speaking urgently.

'Delia, I want you to be ready to go to Glasgow tomorrow early,' he was saying. 'This wretched concert is so late this year it gives us very little time to do what must be done.'

'But I've still got the feasts to plan,' said his wife a little plaintively. 'Unless you think we could persuade everyone to celebrate May Day a little later… well, people do it with birthdays.' She had seen the expression on his face and knew at once the absurdity of her suggestion. 'I'm joking, of course,' she added hurriedly.

At breakfast, Lachlan's mobile cell phone rang repeatedly. Beame, a tall, corpulent butler with a mincing walk poured coffee while Lachlan fended off a series of business calls. Delia took the phone from him so he could finish his breakfast. It rang again almost at once and she answered it.

'This is Lady Morrison. My husband is having breakfast, Mr Tarrant.' She put her hand over the phone and looked questioningly at Lachlan. He scowled and stretched out his hand for the phone. By the time he spoke his voice was quietly composed:

'If you want a statement from me in reply to your article – in the *Echo* was it? Yes… you can have one. Call my office and make a time to come in, Mr Tarrant. It's Magnus isn't it? I am always anxious to be completely open with the press, you know that… Well you should. I'm away for a few days. But as soon as I get back… I look forward to it, Magnus.'

Lachlan has been studiously polite with a journalist whose hectoring tone could easily be imagined by Delia, who had met the man more than once.

'Does all this fuss they're making over the water worry you?' she asked.

'No. Why should it? Every nuclear power station in the country, probably every one in Europe, has the local press cooking up stories about dangers to the local population. If it's not radiation, it's the hazard of some terrible accident. Nuada is no exception. Our accident was quite a while ago, and it wasn't as serious as it might have been. They never seem to quite accept that.'

'Well it affected those fish in the river,' said Delia

'They only ever got to photograph that one mutant fish out of the Sulis. But what real damage it has done they simply can't figure out. Listen, they'll keep on trying to get another story out of it. And we've got to keep on showing we've nothing to hide.'

Beame had meanwhile reappeared.

'The Glee Club have arrived, sir,' he announced. 'I've shown them into the music room. Coffee is already there, ma'am, so if I may be excused?'

For a moment Delia looked puzzled. Then she remembered the task for which Beame needed to be excused.

'Of course, Beame,' she said.

The sound of the Glee Club singing drifted through the open doors of the music room, up the marble Jacobean staircase with its heavily carved balustrades and into the room where Delia was putting the finishing touches to the public uniform worn by most Scots women of her kind: sensible shoes and a heathery tweed suit over a pale purple cashmere jersey, a string of good pearls and a brooch of enamel and gold, framed in modest sized diamonds, in this case representing the arms of the Black Watch, a Scottish regiment to which a former husband had briefly belonged before she left him for the far more interesting and, it must be said, challenging Sir Lachlan.

Delia lifted the house phone to call Daisy, the cook, but got no answer. She knew that Daisy, while unusually good at cooking anything but vegetables and a conscientious member of Alcoholics Anonymous, tended to fall off her wagon as the heavy responsibility of preparing the May Day feasts approached. Delia was about to hurry down to the kitchen when she was detained by her mirror (a seven-foot-high Victorian looking glass which reflected the whole six feet of her), not simply to confirm that her lipstick was on straight or that her tights showed no wrinkle at the ankle, but to check that the Lady Morrison face and figure, celebrated in paintings by Hockney and Annigoni, had not somehow faded away overnight.

No more vain really than most people, Delia had originally believed she was cursed with being beautiful, because she had learnt to suppose that both men and women found it was her single most important characteristic. Perhaps some even thought it was her only real asset. It came, she thought, this mild paranoia of hers, from her observation that people simply stared at the few other beautiful women she knew, rather than listening to what they had to say.

She paused again in her hurried journey down to the kitchen, at the open doors to the Music Room. Lachlan was playing the piano and intermittently conducting the Glee Club in the Amen section of Handel's *Messiah*. How unnecessarily long-drawn-out that Amen always seemed to Delia, who loved the music but cared nothing for the words. Lachlan was not at the moment singing, but of course would be in Glasgow Cathedral tomorrow. She was slightly disappointed. His singing voice always thrilled her. The Glee Club, a dozen local men from Tressock and six of Lachlan's employees from the Nuada nuclear power station, had their backs to her as they sang, but she recognised most of them.

Delia never ceased to marvel at how Lachlan held the loyalty and respect of so many diverse people. In a Scotland where deference of any kind was long since banished, and lairds, like Lachlan, were very often distrusted as effete and too English sounding, he held his neighbours' and his employees' esteem. They continued to accept him as their leader, she believed, because he had always included them in his project, in his adventure. His seemingly effortless authority was perhaps part political, part priestly but really defied analysis. Whatever. It worked. She had waited for a moment, just in case he sang, and was rewarded, because Lachlan was now delivering Handel's last great crowning Amen in his glorious, deep bass voice. In Delia, this always produced a melting inner throb, as if from an intimate caress. She gave a little shiver of pleasure and hurried on down to the nether world of the castle's great kitchens.

On one side of the long, wide passage that bisected the basement lay the main kitchen and another huge room, which was almost always locked. On the other side were the still room, the laundry, the larders, the freezers, the now defunct dairy, the sewing room and what had once been the servants' dining room and the cook's and butler's parlour. Where, sixty years ago, there had been twenty-five servants at Tressock Castle, the place was run now with a staff of five: Daisy, the cook, Beame, the butler, and three women who came in daily to clean the twenty-odd rooms still in more or less constant use. Half a dozen major modern appliances made the cleaning no more than a repetitive chore. The roaring whine that Delia heard as she reached the basement passage came not, she at once realised, from one of these machines but from Beame's workshop in the defunct dairy.

Daisy was standing outside the door to the dairy encouraging a slightly tearful young Heather, one of the cleaners, to mop up a spreading pool of blood that was seeping under the door and onto the flagstones in the passage.

'The door's locked of course,' said Daisy. 'I keep shouting at him to stop a minute but he canna hear me over that machine of his. Please be careful where you step.'

Delia was relieved to see that her cook was perfectly sober and immediately wondered why Heather had her apron and hands covered in blood.

'I slipped in it, ma'am. The blood is that sticky.'

'Well go and wash yourself, Heather,' said Delia. 'And get out of those soiled clothes. Daisy, find her something else to wear. Give me that mop.'

As the two other women hurried away, Delia started to mop up the blood. Just as she did so, a great splash of gore hit the farther side of the frosted glass panes set into the dairy door and started to trickle viscously downwards. Under the door, a fresh crimson flood streamed outwards while the howling, whining mechanical sound continued louder than ever. Delia hammered furiously at the door and shouted Beame's name at the top of her voice.

After a few seconds, the sound behind the door stopped and there was silence. Then Beame's voice, cautious, suspicious: 'Who's that?'

'It's me, Beame. The blood is flooding out into the passage. You've got plenty of room in there. Move what you're doing away from the door.'

'I didna realise, ma'am. Sorry.'

'It's quite alright, Beame. Carry on the good work. We're off to Glasgow tomorrow early. Hope you'll be finished by then.'

Delia and Lachlan

DELIA'S CONFERENCE WITH Daisy over the May Day feasts was assisted by the fact that there were plenty of precedents. They had been planning for May Day every year for more than a decade and were used to catering for the whole little township when the celebration was at its peak. As usual, Delia detailed what would have to come from Glasgow, which she herself would bring back. Suckling pigs, for instance, were always hard to find locally. Daisy listed what she knew she could buy at the local supermarket.

At nine o'clock, Delia and Lachlan walked into the castle's entrance hall, ready for their journey, to find Beame waiting for them with a curious air of expectancy that puzzled Lachlan.

'Beame and I have planned a little surprise for you, Lachlan,' said Delia. 'We thought that truly magnificent Imperial you culled deserved some lasting recognition.'

Beame at once turned his gaze from his employers and looked up at the wall above the great oak door. There, the noble head of a stag with sixteen points to his huge antlers gazed glassily into the hallway. But his nostrils seemed to be sniffing the air as if he sensed the nearness of his enemy.

'The colour of those glass eyes is no exactly right, sir. But I can fix that later…' Beame was waiting for their reaction.

'You're an artist, Beame. That's what you are. I think it is splendid. And it looks perfect up there, my dear,' Lachlan added, turning to Delia.

'I really don't know where else we could have put it,' she laughed, looking around at the serried ranks of stuffed game's heads on the entrance hall's walls. Buffalo, moose and deer of different breeds and sizes, a white rhino, a Bengal tiger, a wild boar and even a giraffe, they were all the trophies several generations of Morrison lairds had brought back from a now defunct British Empire, where they and their relations had once played their small part in ruling a quarter of the world.

Beame, pleased at their reaction to his artistry, had already hurried out to open the door to the big Phantom III, the 1936 model with headlights that looked like silver soup tureens, in which he was to drive them to Glasgow. For Beame, being a butler was playing a role, one in which, however suitable his costume, he was always slightly uneasy. Being a chauffeur was simpler, a peaked hat sufficed, but he still thought of it as a role and the flourish with which he opened the car door was one he had seen in an old Hollywood movie. Only in his capacity as a taxidermist was he truly in his element. Working for the Morrisons, he had occasion to do really interesting taxidermy, and his roles as chauffeur and butler were not all that onerous. Beame was a relatively happy man and Delia, who made a practice of observing everyone who worked for her and for Lachlan quite closely, believed that he was incapable of any lateral thinking whatever. She therefore trusted him and urged her husband to do the same.

The back of the vintage Rolls had a cocktail cabinet in a burled walnut case, into which Lachlan had installed a sophisticated Danish sound system. There was also an elaborate contraption by which the passengers could communicate with the chauffeur on the other side of the glass barrier. This had not been used since before the Second World War. When communication with Beame was called for, Lachlan simply shouted.

Driving through the rolling countryside they soon crossed a mediaeval stone bridge over the River Sulis and passed into one of the region's rare forests. Huge beech trees, under which very little but ferns and wild mushrooms grew, towered on either side of the road. Deer grazed here unconcerned by any passing traffic. The herd belonged to Tressock Castle and only Lachlan or one of his gamekeepers was authorised to cull them, this being done usually in anticipation of the May Day feasts. As the Rolls emerged from these woods, the huge smooth deciduous trees giving way to meaner spruce and fir, they were suddenly in an enormous clearing, where the river had snaked back to meet them.

Upon the other side of the Sulis, monstrous in its scale, hideous in its utterly functional cacophony of steel pipes and concrete blocks, stood the Nuada Nuclear Power Station. Armed police idled outside its gates while two of the utility's own security guards came up to greet the Rolls and to escort Lachlan into the guardhouse, where one of his executives and his secretary were awaiting him for a brief conference.

Delia remained in the car, allowing herself to think about the problems Lachlan faced as chairman of Nuada – and doing this to distract herself from the prospect of what must very soon be done in Glasgow. Chernobyl was a word no one ever actually mentioned in relation to Nuada. But the melt-down at the Soviet Russian power station in 1986 was a disaster that would probably always haunt the whole nuclear power industry. Since then, not only the press, but the public at large, tended to view nuclear power stations as accidents waiting to happen. Gazing out at the vast complex of buildings dominated by the cooling towers and encircled with walls topped with razor wire and punctuated with watchtowers, Delia thought how threatening it all seemed. Lachlan, on the other hand, enjoyed the game of protecting Nuada from all who conspired against it; the press, the Greens and quite often the government itself. On the rare occasions he had time to watch television, he tried to catch *The Simpsons*. He loved this series and pretended to identify closely with Mr Burns, the president of the nuclear plant, applauding every machiavellian scheme he cooked up. Delia was not amused. She hated and feared the always looming crisis at Nuada, reassuring herself only with the thought that it had loomed for ten years, since the accident, but had never materialised – so far.

Lachlan finished his brief conference and they then headed for what is sometimes called Scotland's Second City, after Edinburgh – but which Glaswegians claim to be the first in both commerce and enterprise. Recently, encouraged by its nomination by Brussels as a European City of Culture, some have called it 'the Paris of the North'. For Beame, the Thai massage parlour on Glasgow's Portcourtauld Street provided as much international culture as he felt he needed or could afford.

Cocooned in the rear section of the Rolls, Delia tried to feel insulated from that part of her life with Lachlan that most excited her, but which sometimes induced an odd kind of fear. She thought of it as a form of stage fright.

'I will be alright on the night,' she repeated when Lachlan reproached her for looking tense and nervous. He started to stroke her hair, as one might that of a fractious, nervous cat, while humming a refrain from the *Messiah*. She suddenly felt one of her rare attacks of irritation with him.

'It's alright for you,' she said sharply. 'The gods or your mother forgot to provide you with nerves. You behave as if we were on a trip to choose wallpaper for one of the guest rooms.'

Lachlan ignored her and put the tape of Handel's *Messiah* on the sound system in the old cocktail cabinet. As its sound filled the well-upholstered rear of the Rolls, he prepared to sing along with the Vienna Boys' Choir.

'Hallelujah! Hallelujah! Hallelujah!' the boys were singing in their sweet treble voices and Lachlan, counting beats with his fingers tapping on Delia's knee, found his cue and launched his great deep basso profondo voice to echo, 'Hallelujah! Hallelujah! Hallelujah!'

When the singing briefly paused for the orchestra to work up to the next crescendo, she said: 'Did you know that those Redeemers are coming again this year? I had hoped that they'd send the Mormons or some of those wonderful black Gospel singers.'

'So what difference will it make?' Lachlan asked.

'There's Orlando, the new young policeman you met with Lolly. She says she thinks he's quite sharp. Peter, at the Grove, agrees. We know what he has been sent to do and it worries me.'

'He struck Peter as a nice, average young policeman, very Glaswegian,' said Lachlan. 'Tressock will seem like a foreign country to him. He's nothing we can't manage.'

The crescendo of Hallelujahs had arrived, heralding the end of the *Messiah*. Lachlan placed his left hand over Delia's, turning to sing to her. She did not snatch her hand away but slowly removed it.

'Everything will be as before,' he said reassuringly, and then sang:

'As it was in the beginning...
Is now and ever shall be
Wo-orld without end
Ah – ahmen! Ah-men! Ah – ah – ah men!'

The Peace March

THE FLIGHT OVER had provided only a slight preparation for the foreignness of Scotland. The air crew had those British accents you hear in movies, usually from upper crust bad guys. They called Beth 'madam' instead of 'ma'am'. Both she and Steve reread the pamphlet provided by the Redeemers about the Scottish people. *Mostly white, speaking a sometimes hard-to-understand version of English, but usually friendly to visitors*, it said. *Known to admire America and Americans for achievements like Hollywood, Marshall Aid, Disneyworld, Jazz music, The American Constitution and*, for some reason the pamphlet did not explain, *everything to do with the late President John F. Kennedy and his family. Their knowledge of Dallas is confined to the TV series of that name and, for some older people, the place where Kennedy was shot.*

To someone as accustomed to hotel living as Beth, the Grand Hotel was, at first sight, unusually old for a five-star establishment. However, it belonged to a familiar American chain which had done a good job of modernising it. There were Gideon Bibles in the side-table drawers and, an unusual innovation, little foot-baths alongside the toilets in the bathroom. It was, for Beth, pretty much like a home from home.

Steve thought his room, across the passage from hers, was like something out of an old European movie and just terrific. She had been given the Royal Suite, usually reserved for star football players, what you call soccer players in America, they'd told her. She had never seen so much chintz all in one place in her life but the TV was huge and the bed imperial-sized. Beth had considered it very cute of Steve to point out to the folks on the reception desk downstairs: 'That's my fiancée in that poster over there,' in case they didn't recognise her in the huge picture of the Redeemers Choir under the headline: 'This Year's Christian Choral Concert. Country Star BETH BOOTHBY Leads The Famous Redeemers Choir.' Steve was sometimes naïve, that was for sure. But she preferred to think of his occasional naïveté as purity of heart and plain old faith in the Lord and the God-given things.

In the morning, they decided to walk to the church where the Glasgow Festival of Christian Choral Music was being held. The Organisers had telephoned to urge them to travel by the limo they were sending, but Steve had persuaded her that it would be fun to walk. He had seen, from his bedroom window, that some kind of street festival was going on.

'If we're goin' to preach the Word of God to these folks, we best get to know somethin' about them,' he said.

That made sense to Beth. So she told the Organisers they had 'made private arrangements.' The Organisers would think some local celeb or 'high net worth' person was taking them in their own limo. That way they wouldn't send over the security folks. Beth was a veteran of what she called 'the organiser wars'. 'Keep 'em guessin'.' That was her motto.

So that was how, on a chilly spring morning, Beth and Steve were set to leave the Grand Hotel to walk the half mile to the church the local folks called the Cathedral, armed with a map provided by the kilted concierge. This guy did not look gay to Beth. He certainly looked at Beth in the way she was accustomed to guys looking at her, registering the fact that she was a beautiful woman. A gay guy could register that too, but there would be a subtle difference in his look. The Bible was full of great truths. Beth had been raised on the King James Bible and believed every word of it. But she was smart enough to know that lust was what those horny old Elders were feeling when they watched Suzanna taking her bath. The way the doorman looked at her was simply what the Bible meant when it said 'and she was good in his sight.'

Of course, the Rev. Pat Robertson was unlikely to be wrong on the subject of these Scottish guys in kilts mostly being gay. She'd watched his TV show and it was clear that he actually talked to the Lord every day like they were on cell phones, maybe more often than that, just like Beth spoke to Steve and he spoke back to her. When she'd asked the guy at the reception desk with the crossed keys on his lapels about kilts and why she hadn't seen many since she had arrived, he had said, 'Up north, madam. More men wear them up north.'

'Is it true what they say about guys that wear them?' she couldn't help asking him.

He had looked genuinely surprised at this question.

'Do you mean that they wear no underpants? Probably depends on the weather. Anything else I can help you with, madam?' he had asked.

So you couldn't fault the Reverend Pat! But she was relieved to be saved from a response, for at that moment Steve tugged at her arm, anxious to go out and see what was going on in the street fair outside. She left the puzzled concierge with a flash of her best, for fans only, dazzling smile, which she knew was a tad excessive for everyday but which looked great in photographs. Where were those paparazzi?

They'd been right there in the lobby a little earlier.

Then she and Steve were out in the street, walking in the midst of that horde of people. Some beating drums or playing bagpipes, others carrying street-wide banners that read AMERICA'S WAR, NOT OURS. Still others carried placards with messages for politicians in far away London and Washington DC, saying NOT IN OUR NAME or NO THANKS YANKS, KEEP YOUR TANKS, WE WANT PEACE. It made both Steve's and Beth's minds reel, and now they knew where the paparazzi had gone. They were all around them like little old mice round a piece of cheese, darting in and out with their cameras, shouting things like:

'How d'you like our demo, Beth?'

'Are you marching for peace, Beth?'

'Who's the cowboy, Beth?'

She could tell that the reporters were going to let the photographers tell most of this story. They could see Beth was in shock. Her face told it all. Far from the state where almost every lapel carried a little enamel American flag and almost every stoop and car radio mast had Old Glory fluttering away, where somehow everyone believed that Saddam Hussein had personally ordered the 9/11 atrocities, Beth wondered what possible objection any sane person could have to going to war. How could these dear people (Beth was determined to go on thinking of them that way) be so misguided? They seemed to be of all ages and both sexes and there were quite a few, well, ethnics; not Mexican but dark brown or Chinese. Some looked richer and some poorer, but no one looked real under-privileged. All seemed cheerful, like on a kind of company outing. How could they look so normal and think these terrible things about America?

Steve, for whom politics and politicians were a 'pool of shit,' was less shocked. His old man was a Democrat who thought old George Bush's boy was a couple of dozen steers short of a herd. Still Steve liked to think of himself as a patriot and certainly didn't care for the anti-American tone of the placards and the chanting. It was starting to make him real angry. He was wearing his usual hat, the hat he had worn since he was fifteen. It was a stained and a tad crushed looking cowboy hat, with a hole in it where his Daddy had shot at it. Now he used the hat to try and brush the paparazzi away from Beth like they were a bunch of pesky flies. He wasn't goin' to hit nobody. There was no occasion for that. But he was struggling real hard to contain his anger.

Suddenly, the photographers were all pointing at a nearby placard and asking Beth to look at it. It read:

RICH MEN'S FRIEND
OIL MEN'S WHORE
BUSH HAS SENT
HIS LIES TO WAR

She grimaced and two dozen cameras clicked and popped.

But Steve had grabbed the placard and was about to break the shaft of wood over his knee.

'No Steve, please don't!' Beth grabbed his arm.

He looked over his shoulder at her. She was pleading with him. She was right. Vile though the insult to the President certainly was, it would be a lousy start to their ministry. The nerdy guy whose placard he was about to trash looked kind of scared, and the rest of the crowd seemed just curious – hoping perhaps for some drama to unfold. He gave the placard back and, taking Beth's arm, hurried her through the crowds towards the cathedral.

The Arm of the Law

THE GLASGOW POLICE force is a constabulary that serves a community with sharp sectarian and ethnic divisions. These rivalries are an acknowledged fact, but they are hardly unique to Glasgow. They are no greater than in New York and Chicago or other British cities like Manchester and Liverpool. They are nevertheless institutionalised rivalries that all Glasgow's politicians lament but no one seems able to completely cure. The regular football matches between Glasgow's nominally Catholic team, Celtic, and their rivals, the supposedly Protestant Rangers, are often the more bitterly contested because of these tribal divides between their fans and supporters.

But Glasgow is a melting pot, with many minority communities. Fortunately for them, the quasi religious rivals who together form the majority reserve nearly all their hostility for each other. For the West Indians and Asians, the Scots have an easy tolerance, having taken to curry as virtually their national dish. There is a certain respect for the Jews, as a race the Scots consider nearly as canny as themselves. For the English, there is the same kind of resentment that exists in a marriage where divorce is contemplated but has had to be indefinitely postponed. This leaves others, but principally the Italians. Around this small but prosperous minority a mythology has grown up that accords these ice-cream manufacturers, restaurateurs, lawyers, civil servants, teachers and merchants a touch of the romance and glamour that clings to all things Italian.

Detective Constable Orlando Furioso had known from the start that he had a bright future in the Glasgow Constabulary. The chief constable, who belonged to the same Masonic lodge as Orlando's father, had welcomed him into the force and eased his way from the very beginning. Being an effective fly half in the force's rugby team had done him no harm. His promotion from the uniformed branch to the rank of detective constable had happened, Orlando knew, rather faster than he really deserved. Detective Inspector Rory McFadden and Detective Sergeant Murdo Campbell, to whose section he had been assigned, were already in the middle of an extremely complex investigation involving alleged corruption and embezzlement at the headquarters of one of Scotland's leading investment agencies, Caledonian Inward Investment. They needed an inside informant and their young recruit faced his first test. Orlando was always to remember with pride how easily he had been able to talk his way into a job at Caledonian's cost control department, passing himself off as a trainee accountant working to pay for his after-hours tuition.

His real after-hours work started when the cleaners arrived and Caledonian Inward Investment's overstaffed offices were otherwise empty. Hidden deep in senior executives' computers he found details of secret transactions involving millions of pounds – the final step on a paper trail DI McFadden and DS Campbell had begun following through off-shore accounts and trusts. When the indictments were finally being prepared he was told that he was likely to get a commendation if and when the case came to court.

The Caledonian inquiry had played to Orlando's strengths. He was fairly well educated, highly computer literate and blessed with a certain boyish charm. Coupled with the physique of an effective rugby player, these assets made him popular with men and attractive to women.

Years later, Orlando remembered his work on the Caledonian Inward Investment case as a watershed in his early career. His success as an undercover detective had led his superiors to choose him for an assignment that really required a far more experienced and certainly older police officer than Orlando. But, for him, the success or failure of that assignment soon dimmed in importance beside the fact that it led him to fall hopelessly, almost fatally, in love for the first time in his life. Indeed, it led him to the love of his life.

This new case was, from the start, known officially and confidentially as the Tressock Inquiry, but unofficially it was codenamed Operation Borders Cult. A series of troubling anonymous letters to the Secretary of State for Scotland (by-passing the Scottish Executive in Edinburgh) had complained that a heathen cult existed in the Tressock area of Roxburghshire that ought to be investigated. Tom Makepiece, the local police constable, had been asked to conduct an investigation that revealed nothing more serious than a perfectly legal pagan ceremony that had taken place in celebration of the sun at the summer solstice. The report recorded that Tom had never actually seen people worshipping the sun and didn't believe it was likely that anything illegal had occurred. He recorded that a man with a speaking disorder had talked of the ritual quite eloquently, indeed in verse, but firmly refused to make a formal statement to the police. Had he written the accusing letters, which certainly weren't in verse? Tom doubted he was the letter writer. He could read poetry of every description, but there was no record of his ever having written even a brief note. The letters had been typed on a computer and he did not possess one. Worshipping the sun is not a crime in Scotland although it is certainly unusual, not least because the life-giving deity (if that is what it is) is more often than not shrouded in mist or just hidden by clouds. So, at first, no official action was taken.

Then the tabloid newspapers started running a completely unconnected story about Devil worship in the Orkney Islands. Lurid accounts of Satanic rites by a group of middle-aged housewives and two Presbyterian ministers were attested to by a woman who later turned out to have absconded from a psychiatric hospital at Cork. But by the time her accusations had been proved totally false the Secretary of State's department had already asked the Borders Constabulary to investigate the Tressock rumours and make a confidential report. This had coincided with the sudden illness and subsequent death of Constable Makepiece; people said from cirrhosis of the liver. Since he had no close relations and was a bachelor this was never confirmed, but was easy to believe for those in Tressock who had drunk with him over the years.

The Borders Police, robbed of their local informant, appealed for one of Scotland's big city forces to send them a detective from an experienced crime squad. It fell to the Glasgow Constabulary.

The McFadden/Campbell team, riding high in the authorities' esteem, was assigned the case while still in the laborious process of handing over all the Caledonian Inward Investment evidence to the Procurator Fiscal. To gain time, therefore, DI McFadden recommended that Orlando be sent to Tressock as Tom Makepiece's replacement. Tom had never risen above the rank of a uniformed police constable. He was one of the very few PCs left as a small town or village policeman when the force was centralised on the larger towns. Rapid response to calls for help in outlying areas would bring police in small Ford and Vauxhall cars, whimsically known as Pandas, to the scene of the crime. McFadden was given to understand that Tom had stayed at his post only at the request of a local landowner, Sir Lachlan Morrison, who also happened to be the chairman of the nearby Nuada Nuclear Power Company.

So it was agreed that Orlando don once more a PC's uniform and take Tom Makepiece's place, although in the eyes of his colleagues and employers he would secretly remain and be paid as a detective constable. Orlando's mission was to gather information while posing as the new friendly neighbourhood cop. If his reports suggested some urgent action was required, DI McFadden and his superiors would decide on an appropriate strategy for effective and immediate action. The assistant chief constable of the Borders informed his good friend

Sir Lachlan of these arrangements, making light of the anonymous letters as being almost certainly the work of some crank. Lachlan expressed his appreciation.

'All I care about,' he said on the telephone to the ACC, who secretly feared Lachlan and his political connections, 'is that we can all sleep safely in our beds at night. There is simply no substitute for the cop on the beat. The policeman who knows everyone and everything about them is the best guarantee against crime. I know you agree. Any sensible man would. So why successive governments of all parties have allowed the bean counters and the pen pushers to decree that the police be huddled in cheap-to-manage centres, well away from where most crime now occurs – well, I simply cannot conceive.'

'I wish you'd tell them, Lachlan,' said the ACC.

'Me?' Lachlan was incredulous. 'I'm just another business man in a country where we are an endangered species.'

Orlando was pleased enough with his posting. A city dweller all his life, he regarded the whole of Scotland, beyond the densely inhabited belt stretching from Edinburgh to Glasgow, as almost terra incognita. In these out of city areas the indigenous inhabitants of Scotland were still to be found – Scots his father rather disrespectfully referred to as the natives. With their many tribal costumes: kilts and Highland regalia for gala occasions; the elaborate tweedy uniforms of the shooters of game; the pink coats of the hunters with dogs; this to him was a postcard Scotland, picturesque but not to be taken too seriously.

In a way, he regarded his new assignment as an opportunity to indulge in his hobby. It was only a little later that he fell in love, putting hobbies entirely out of his mind. He had been a keen body-builder at college. But senior beer-bellied colleagues in the force tended to mock that sort of thing. Now there was an opportunity to catch up on his training and work on his pecs. So he'd packed all his sports gear ready to take with him to Tressock. He really looked forward to the next few weeks. It seemed inconceivable it would take much longer than that to learn all there was to know about Tressock, its deepest secrets and all. If it harboured some cult, he was sure to discover it.

Orlando's only slight regret was leaving Woman Police Constable Morag McDevitt behind in Glasgow. He had met her first at Police College when her hair was the raven's wing black that goes with pale skin and china blue eyes, a combination you sometimes find among the Scots and the Irish. Just before her graduation, however, she had gone Madonna blonde. Orlando, who had agreed with his fellow cadets in finding her almost threateningly beautiful but curiously un-sexy, now suddenly thought her – well, desirable. Where WPC McDevitt had seen admiration, without lust, in her male colleagues' eyes, she now saw what any woman would have recognised as that sly biological urge. Being a sensible girl she decided, almost at once, to choose one out of the pursuing male pack and send the rest off in search of other game.

She chose Orlando because he was unquestionably the best-looking police cadet on the course. Coming from the Gorbals, a neighbourhood now moving up towards gentrification from appalling poverty, she liked the fact that he had some extra money in his pocket, didn't get vomiting drunk, shared her enthusiasm for the movies, and appeared to have the conservative approach to sex that she knew she preferred. If she had been completely honest with herself then, as she became later, she could easily have done without the sex. But it was expected of a girl by her steady boyfriend. Her girl-friends would have thought it a bit freakish of her if she had said what she thought: 'He pounds away, pants like an exhausted cocker spaniel and when he comes, that noise of his, that gurgling moan, as if he was drowning, well it just makes me want to laugh.' But she remained silent on this. She liked his company, felt his trophy value at parties and down the pub. Mercifully, love had never been mentioned. However, she might not have been so pleased to know what Orlando really thought of her.

While he liked her Madonna blondeness – it was acceptably flash and other blokes stared – he worried about the fact that she seemed a complete stranger to what he vaguely imagined as romance. Having decided one night after seeing *When Harry Met Sally* together at the Arts Theatre re-run cinema, that sexual prevarication was both crazy and a terrible waste of time, Morag took Orlando home to bed, a first for them.

'You're no the first man I've opened my legs for,' she told him. 'And don't think you'll be the last,' she added, as without further preliminaries she laid herself out on the bed as naked as a piece of hake on a fishmonger's slab. Her undressing seemed to have taken five seconds during her visit to the bathroom. One minute she was a formally dressed police person. The next she seemed to expect to be an object of torrid desire.

Orlando, who had been suitably moved by her undeniably lissom, generously breasted body, was transfixed by her bush. It reminded him, he couldn't get the image out of his mind, of Adolf Hitler's moustache. An oblong black tuft of hair, as smooth as a cat's pelt. It was so totally unexpected, halfway down to her toes from her luscious Madonna blonde curls, that he had to think hard of Mai Ping at the

Thai massage parlour before he was able to do what was so evidently expected of him. He learned, only later, that turning the female bush into a form of topiary was a lucrative new service provided by the hair salons of Glasgow. Popular shapes included four leaf clovers (Celtic supporters), St Andrew's Crosses (for international away games) and something called 'the landing strip', which was what Morag had selected, unaware of its likeness to Hitler's moustache.

So it wasn't that he expected to miss the ritual encounters in bed with her, when she lay like a relatively soft log and he toiled away, wondering why people thought this such a wonderful way to spend their time. 'Very nice,' she would say afterward, like an amiable aunt congratulating her little nephew on his finger-painting. He could very easily do without sex with beautiful WPC Morag McDevitt. It was the thought that, as soon as he was gone, someone else would almost certainly move in on his trophy that disturbed him. He already worried that she found him inadequate. After all, if he found her wanting, surely she must feel the same about him. He reflected, as many men in his position do, how fortunate it is that women represent half the human race. Where he was going, in the rustic borderlands, women who would be dazzled by his looks, his Glaswegian sophistication and his uniform would surely abound. Mai Ping, at the Thai massage parlour, had stroked his tender ego. There was nothing to worry about. She had, she assured him, rarely met a man as well endowed, as energetic, as strong as he. As a pollster of these matters, Orlando reflected, considerably re-assured, Mai Ping had more credibility than most.

Before leaving Glasgow, he took Morag to an informal dinner the police rugby team had organised to see him on his way. It was a raucous evening and Orlando was among the first to leave, explaining that he still had packing to do. Morag was deep in conversation with the only other woman at the party, Inspector Jill Meander, a jolly, older woman built on generous, Junoesque lines with close-cropped, carroty-coloured hair and twinkling brown eyes.

Morag looked up at Orlando as he came to say goodbye to her, gave him her most winning smile and offered her cheek for him to peck.

'Don't forget to e-mail as soon as you're settled in,' she said. 'And take care,' she added kindly.

'Yes, you take care, Orlando,' laughed Inspector Jill Meander. 'They hunt laddies like you down on the Borders, they really do.'

Concert at the Cathedral

DELIA SAW THEM arrive. It could only be them because the boy was wearing a cowboy hat and the girl had the kind of brave glow that Delia had observed before in some artists when they were approaching a performance. It was not totally unlike the aura of fear, tempered by defiance, she had witnessed years before when she had accompanied the earlier soldier-husband to watch an execution in Aden, in the last days of colonial rule. The American girl's lack of any artifice surprised Delia. Nothing to label her 'pop star'. No make-up. A plain navy-blue turtle-neck jersey and black trousers clothed a good, understated figure. No jewellery, not even earrings, but a pretty belt decorated with small silver and turquoise medallions. A country girl, thought Delia, so confident that she needs no props. One indication of what had made this girl a star.

As the bud of almost any flower or blossom first leaves the carapace of enclosing green, the texture and colour it shows the world is of a delicacy and freshness that is lost almost at once as the bloom develops. The female human face goes through this phase for a very short time and, while it varies immensely from person to person, one can occasionally glimpse it in its most sublime form. Too soon, and it can be spots and oily skin. Too late and the beautician's art may be needed. But Beth possessed, at this very moment in her life, the loveliness that only youth can confer and it made men and women alike stop and stare. Delia had recognised it across the crowded nave of the cathedral. Knowing she had once possessed it herself and what an incomparable gift it had been, she felt slight pangs of regret and envy.

Delia and Lachlan had just been greeted by the Reverend Byng McLeod, the most fashionable and clubbable divine in the Church of Scotland, beloved of television talk-show hosts and his congregation alike. He wore his prematurely snow white hair as Oscar Wilde once had, long and carelessly wavy, as if he judged it his crowning glory. Behind him, musical sounds from an assorted collection of instrumentalists came from the specially erected stage in front of the sanctuary, where all was in place to receive the full orchestra. From both his tone and his manner the Reverend McLeod exuded the self confidence that confirmed that in this cathedral, on this occasion, when presenting this musical programme, there was no impresario, no authority higher than he.

'Sir Lachlan, Lady Morrison, welcome indeed!' He spoke with a diction so musically cadenced, so successful in using the softer felicities of Scottish English, that one half expected him to burst into song.

'We are absolutely thrilled, Lachlan, that you are giving us that solo of yours again this year. I saw your Glee Club rehearsing a little earlier, but I fancy they are now wetting their whistles around the corner at the Silver Thistle. Singing is such thirsty work. Don't worry. I've got the lovely Adelaide looking after them and she'll have them back just now I have not the slightest doubt...'

Looking confidently around, the Reverend McLeod saw Beth and Steve advancing a little hesitantly up the nave. Delia, who had been watching the couple, thought she heard a little neigh of excitement as he tossed his locks from one of his eyes and led her and Lachlan to meet the Americans.

Beth, who had already met with the Reverend, braced herself for the wave of Scottish or British (what was the difference?) effusiveness that she knew was now coming.

'Now Delia, Lachlan, I want you to meet our American star Beth Boothby. If you were sixteen, Delia, you'd already be swooning, I assure you. She is the wonderful new soloist with the Redeemers Choir. And a successful recording artist. Gold and platinum platters, eh Beth? I expect you'll remember the Redeemers from last year? Beth, meet Sir Lachlan and Lady Morrison. He will be singing with you in the Oratorio.' Steve hung back while Beth's hand was shaken but Delia was sizing him up.

'And who is this?' she asked. Steve, still wearing his hat, seemed ill at ease.

'This is Steve Thomson,' said Beth. 'I guess you'd call him my fiancé. Right Steve? We've made like a commitment.'

'To help fund a mission? Is that right?' the Reverend McLeod was clearly unsure.

'No sir,' said Steve. 'Our commitment is – well, we've promised to save it for marriage. We call it our Silver Ring Thing.' They both smilingly held up their hands to show their rings, looking at the slightly surprised faces around them. 'Tough huh? But we're both Redeemers you know. Like the Choir. Only when they go home, we're staying behind to like spread the Word.'

The conductor had now appeared on the stage and was signalling to the Reverend McLeod that he was ready for Beth. Glad to be at last able to regain her own medium, she smiled her farewells to the Morrisons and the Reverend, planted a light kiss on Steve's cheek and hurried across to the stage.

The Reverend excused himself to Lachlan and Delia and, taking Steve by the arm, led him to a chair in the nave where he would have a good view of the rehearsal. On the way, he gently removed Steve's hat from his head and handed it to him.

This left Lachlan gazing admiringly after Beth's retreating form. The organist was floating chords out into the enormous nave while small rehearsals or meetings of musicians were going on in various parts of the cathedral.

'What a very beautiful girl,' said Lachlan. 'Another Redeemer you see. What a little star. If she can really sing.'

'A country girl, I'd bet,' said Delia. 'Yes, she is beautiful in a cornfed, apple-cheeked way. I bet she smells of the dairy. A musky bush, milky tits and just a hint of warm cow's dung behind the ears.'

'Does that mean you approve of her?' asked Lachlan, amused.

Delia was laughing now. 'And that poor Steve, waiting till his wedding day. It's another world over there in America, isn't it? Oh look, they're fixing up a microphone for Beth. None of these pop people can really sing.'

But even as the orchestra warmed up and the conductor conferred with Beth she was quietly indicating that the microphone should be removed. The Glee Club were drifting back from the pub, being chivvied along by a tall lady with wiry, iron-grey hair and an imperial bosom, 'the lovely Adelaide'.

Lachlan had drifted off to gather his Glee Club for their pre-performance pep talk. Delia remained standing in the middle of the aisle watching Beth, almost willing her to be less than was clearly expected by the Reverend McLeod and hyped by the media. Now Beth had stepped forward. The conductor, his baton raised, glanced from Beth to the leader of the orchestra and back to Beth. His hands gave the signal. Delia saw the huge breath she took. Now came the voice:

'I know that my Redeemer liveth…'

The sound was literally enormous. The purity of the voice. The richness of tone. The absolute mastery of the long drawn-out phrase. There could be, Delia knew, no corner of that great building that had not heard with absolute clarity the exquisitely conveyed message: *Beth is certain her Redeemer is alive.*

Apart from the voice and the orchestra, total silence had fallen on people in all parts of the cathedral. Delia who, not for nothing, lived with a man whose chief aesthetic pleasure was music, was aware that for Handel the impact of the first performance of the oratorio at St Patrick's Cathedral in Dublin was the stuff of musical legend. But she found it hard to imagine a greater impact then than the sound of Beth Boothby singing it now in Glasgow Cathedral.

Delia saw Lachlan turn from staring at Beth, to look across the nave at her, to signal to her the importance of the moment. It was rare to see astonishment on his face. But she saw it now. She knew what he would be thinking. Beth was the one they must have. But how?

She wondered, as she walked towards where Steve was seated, whether Lachlan had really registered the young man, so impressed had he been with the young woman.

She sat down quietly beside Steve, briefly touching his hand to make her presence known. She saw peripherally that he turned his head and studied her profile and noted how absorbed he was in Beth's singing.

'A truly wonderful voice,' she whispered.

'Yeah, my pa and me,' he whispered back, 'we always say she sounds like an angel.'

'Of course. That's what she reminds me of. An angel.'

'Hey,' Steve was so delighted that he forgot to whisper. 'You believe in angels?'

'Doesn't everyone?' responded Delia in a surprised tone.

The conductor was rapping with his stick and the orchestra had stopped playing. Beth was waiting patiently while he addressed the string section.

Delia rose now and turned to Steve.

'I hope we'll see you later,' she said.

He half rose for an awkward handshake. As she walked away Steve marvelled that anyone could talk quite like she did. It was one of those Brit accents you heard in movies, usually old historical movies. He'd watched quite a few of those on TV because they often had great horses in them. Stunt riding was one of the things he'd always thought of doing. Delia had reached close to where the tall, exceptionally British dude, her husband, was hanging out with some guys who were all studying some sheet music. Her husband leant towards her to listen to what she had to say over the racket coming from the orchestra. Then they both looked over to where he, Steve, was watching them. They smiled and both gave a small wave before continuing their conversation. He waved back. These people were weird alright, but, in their own way, he thought, they were probably OK.

Orlando's Revelation

FOR ORLANDO, TRESSOCK was something of a revelation. The streets lined with trees and white washed houses, with their brick framed windows and porticos, their brightly coloured front doors and decorative skylights, were quite festive in his eyes. Used to the sombre, manse-like Victorian houses in the shabby genteel part of Glasgow where he had been raised, he discovered in this new place a quality he had never seriously considered before, a certain charm.

The little mews house that had long served as the Police Station lay at the end of Main Street where it curved to meet the great gates of Tressock Castle. This vantage point meant that he could, from his bed-sitting room's lace-curtained windows, survey the movements of the townspeople and their comings and goings from the Grove Inn, while, from the big window in his office, by the Police Station's front door, he could see the gates to Sir Lachlan's castle and monitor all who visited it.

He was less pleased with the interior of his new home, which seemed to have been preserved just as Tom Makepiece had left it, like some grungy shrine. The bed-sitting room was spacious enough but so crammed with heavy Victorian furniture and stuffed birds that it made Orlando wonder whether the late Tom's aim was to create a mortuary out of an aviary, or maybe vice versa. A sizeable bathroom adjoined it on one side while, on the other, there was a door that led directly to the Police Station office. This was convenient in its way, but forced him into an unaccustomed tidiness in his living quarters.

His cleaner, old Mrs Menzies, fitted perfectly with Orlando's idea of a crone or witch, and had become his first suspect as a possible member of a cult. She seemed to have a life contract to come in three days a week to redistribute the dust and make sure that everything was still as dear old Tom had left it. Orlando's suggestion that the stuffed birds might find a happier home elsewhere shocked her deeply. He learned from her that apart from Mr Beame, the butler up at the castle, Tom was considered the finest taxidermist in Tressock, a place renowned for this ancient craft. This seemed to make Orlando the fortunate custodian of a precious collection. He tactfully tried to sound impressed, but the truth was that the birds depressed him deeply. Everything from a golden eagle, through barn owls and jackdaws to sea birds, like sand pipers and terns, had given their lives for this, in his view, pointless hobby. If Orlando had been a countryman he would have belonged to the 'if you can't eat it, don't kill it' school of shooting and hunting.

The Police Station office got most of Mrs Menzies' professional attention. She liked to linger with her bucket and mop while Orlando dealt with routine police business on the phone. Tom had obviously indulged her curiosity about every small misdemeanour committed in Tressock, letting her know by whom it was done and with what consequences. On the day that Orlando received a large poster from headquarters, with the faces of some forty missing persons upon it, to be placed on the public notice-board, she gave him the favour of her opinion on all indigent or transient persons, young and old.

'It's a chronic waste of your time looking for the likes of them,' she said. 'Most of yins are cracked, and should be in with the loonies and moonies. But the young yins are away to the sinbins and fleshpots of London, and good luck to them.'

Orlando had arrived in March, while snow flurries were still skittering down Tressock's Main Street, and the folks at the Grove Inn had welcomed him with some hot rum toddy and a game of skittles. Their friendliness seemed real enough, but he guessed it was just cordiality to a foreigner, with maybe a bit of keeping in with the law thrown in. 'Any help we can give you,' said Peter McNeil, the innkeeper, 'just let us know.' The crowd of younger men in the bar chorused their assent and Orlando found himself with yet another drink in his hand. Happily, like him, the Tressock men all followed the game of rugby, both in the papers and on the television, rather than soccer. This meant that however doubly foreign their new cop might be, both Glaswegian and Italian, they all had a strong interest in common. At least this was true for the men.

There were, of course, often women in the bar, who tended to ignore the rugby, but mostly they were the girlfriends or wives of the male drinkers. No new female appeared on Orlando's horizon to diminish his memory of Morag's beautiful face. His e-mail correspondence with her was chatty; police force gossip, some tittle tattle about mutual friends, but very little in the way of personal news.

An officer becomes a regular customer at a particular bar or inn at his peril, said one of the manuals on Public Contact and Awareness that Orlando remembered from police college. He knew this was a sensible warning, so he kept his visits to the Grove occasional and brief. With Peter, the innkeeper, he managed to cultivate a slightly closer relationship than with the others. But that, both of them knew, was part of their professional duty. An inn may at any time have need of the police and it is useful for the latter to have friendly access to a place where so much of the drama of life in a township like Tressock is played out. Or, as another bromide from police college put it: *An officer's effectiveness is only as good as the intelligence he has managed to gather.*

He had copious notes, in particular from his interview with Jack, the curly-haired little man who frequented the bar and stared fixedly at people with his unblinking eyes. Orlando was intrigued by this probably aspergist Englishman who was guardian of the ravens, a mysterious job he had been given by the Laird himself. It involved regular feeding of these rare birds, apparently unique to Tressock. He lived a rather precarious existence, tolerated by his neighbours in spite of his nationality and his tendency to make bizarre pronouncements as if he thought of himself as some latter day prophet. When asked by Orlando what he did when not feeding the ravens, he said (and the detective carefully noted):

'Sometimes I seek for haddocks' eyes
Amongst the heather bright
And make them into waistcoat buttons
In the silent night.'

This answer was obviously a silly lie and certainly not a prophecy. But re-reading the notes he had taken of the Englishman's statements (conversation with him was very hard to achieve), there was nothing that really seemed to point to cult-like activity.

One day towards the end of April, soon after his arrival in Tressock, and well before the Morrisons' trip to Glasgow, Orlando was comparing his notes with the possibly relevant articles he had culled from local newspapers, filed at the Tressock public library, when he heard the loud clattering of horses' hooves on the cobbled road outside.

Through the window overlooking the castle gates, he saw a woman galloping towards him on a mount which seemed dangerously out of control, certainly very over-excited and frisky. Not far behind, a man riding a much larger, black horse, seemed to be trying to catch up with her.

Orlando was still at his desk when the riders disappeared from view. They were now too close to the Police Station's front door to be seen from the desk and were creating an ever more alarming amount of noise. As he moved hurriedly towards the window for a better view, a series of terrific staccato bangs shook the door. A man's deep voice was speaking loudly, but reassuringly:

'Dismount Lolly! She'll calm down if I grab the rein.'

Orlando now quickly opened his front door to find a bucking, prancing horse's rear facing him, its lethal hooves coming dangerously close to his face. The rider had slid from the saddle and was holding a rein close to the animal's head, trying to calm it with a caressing hand on its neck. She was murmuring the soft words one might use with a fretful child. The man, tall in the saddle of the huge black horse, held the other rein. Seeing Orlando at the open door, he shouted:

'Watch her hooves, man! Close that bloody door!'

The police are not to be shouted orders by mere civilians – that might have been Orlando's first reaction. But he could see that, in this case, the man knew this horse. Where horses were concerned this man was to be obeyed. His door was already bearing the marks of a powerful kick which had splintered wood and shattered paint. Orlando closed the door and went to the window. The woman was succeeding in calming the horse. The man had dismounted and was waving reassuringly at him through the window.

'Alright to open the door now, officer,' he shouted finally.

Orlando did so and found himself facing the two deeply apologetic riders. She suppressed a laugh as she said:

'I am so sorry about your door, officer. The Laird and I had planned to call on you soon after you arrived to welcome you to Tressock. But we've been very busy…'

'Needless to say, it wasn't our plan to come and kick down your door. We'll have someone come over and fix it right away…' added the tall, distinguished-looking man who was obviously Sir Lachlan, the Laird.

'I'm PC Furioso, sir. Tom Makepiece's replacement,' said Orlando.

'Welcome to Tressock, officer. We were told you'd be coming by your ACC. I'm Lachlan Morrison,' said the Laird. 'And this is Lolly, who is our head groom, my right hand person and much else besides…'

Throughout this conversation, indeed from the moment when he first saw her just beyond the prancing mare's backside, Orlando had been conscious of a gloriously attractive woman. He remembered his instantaneous reaction long afterwards. Here was a radiant sun of a face that quite eclipsed poor Morag's beautiful but pale moon of a countenance. The suddenly enchanted Orlando's mind was fogged of all else but Lolly. Only she was in sharp focus, particularly her face. It was, he thought, a work of nature formed by what, in geography class at his school, they had called *the agents of denudation*. Sun, wind, rain, frost. Her tousled, tawny hair, her laughing grey-green eyes, creased at the corners from squinting through all sorts of weather, skin that had the russet blush that some apples have when ready to be picked...

'Officer Furioso.' It was Lolly's voice, breaking into his reverie. A little husky, that voice, but it had a bell-like tone.

'As I was saying,' added a smiling Sir Lachlan, 'we're taking the horses back to the stables now. But if you can spare the time, Lolly would like to show you around the estate. Then perhaps Constable Furioso will join us for a glass of sherry, Lolly, in the gun room.'

He gave Orlando the inquiring stare of someone whose suggestions rarely, if ever, meet with refusal.

'That's very kind, sir,' said Orlando. 'It would be useful for me to have a clear idea of the lay of the land, so to speak. I was anyway thinking of coming and asking for such a tour.'

Orlando had been told to handle Sir Lachlan with great care when their paths crossed. His wide net of political connections was given as the reason. Scotland, he knew, might no longer be a nation where people were deferential to class. But deference to power and money remained strong and Sir Lachlan had both. Orlando loathed sherry and guessed, correctly, that on these favoured occasions the help on the estate got a dram of whisky and real guests received champagne or whatever they wanted. Who else got sherry? The local councillors probably (correct again), Sir Lachlan's solicitor (a borderline case). He wondered these things while watching Lolly mount her now calmed little mare. The neat, sweet posterior on Lolly (what a seductive name!) as she swung it deftly into the saddle made him think of an old Kiwi rugby song: *She has freckles on her – butt – she is nice.*

Not much hope of ever detecting those particular freckles, if they exist, he thought, rather gloomily. But there he was wrong.

Seduction in a wet climate has a long tradition of inspired improvisation. One has only to think of bundling, a Scots innovation where two young lovers were placed together in an open box but, to preserve their virtue, a wooden plank divided them from the chin down. This had given way in recent years to a custom imported from America, which was lending them the keys to dad's car. Virtue was no longer the aim. Stopping them mooning around the parental home while staying out of the ubiquitous rain, that was the point.

In the case of Orlando and Lolly, things moved at a pace he could hardly have imagined possible were it not for the fact that, later that day, she gave him an eloquent guide to Sir Lachlan's topiary. As they were proceeding up what the locals called the Willies Walk, she recalled for Orlando the genesis of this wildly erotic avenue: a whim of Sir Hamish Morrison (third of Tressock), the trees represented just some of the infinite variety of male organs that the French writer Rabelais had thought worth mentioning in his satirical fantasy, *Gargantua*. The topiary trees, she explained, were exceedingly ancient but greatly cherished by the Laird and his gardeners. In the wide variety of their shapes and attitudes each phallus had its own unique character.

'Reflecting a universal truth,' said Lolly. 'One never sees even a really similar one twice, does one? Well of course you wouldn't know. You're fairly obviously a hearty. But almost any girl would agree with me,' she concluded, as if quoting Germaine Greer rather than an old French satirist.

'Really?' said Orlando. Not a question. Playing for time. Feeling a sudden shiver of Scots Puritanism at the sound of the words issuing from Lolly's lovely unpainted mouth, that too-big humorous mouth quoting Rabelais. This talk, that mouth, this fabulous woman, that feeling Orlando had never felt before. If, impossible if, she will have me, let me make love to her, nothing, he thought, will ever be the same again. He decided he must, in spite of the turmoil going on in his mind, somehow keep up his end of the conversation. 'Odd though that they should all be more or less erect, don't you think?' he was slightly surprised to hear himself saying, then adding: 'I like the notion that they only assume these positions when you, Lolly, walk up this drive.'

Lolly stopped in her tracks and faced him, taking both his hands in hers.

'Oh PC Furioso, I know I'm going to like you. A lot. What a delectable thing to say. But there are some quite flaccid, pathetic ones halfway up the drive. You'll see. I'm afraid my presence leaves them quite unmoved.'

Direct though she could be, most of the time, Lolly possessed at least one of the ancient wiles of born coquettes – a talent to fashion useful surprises; to make the male caught in her web flounder a little.

'If I was a dress designer,' she was saying, 'I would bring back the cod-piece. It would make the fashion houses' fortunes. Think of all the precious materials and jewels a man would be prepared to have lavished on his cod-piece. There would be pin-striped ones with discrete silver clasps for businessmen. Imagine a pop star's, all glittery jewels and maybe a line of little tinkly bells which would sound like a tiny carillion when he got excited. Now this is the west wing. The body of water over there looks like a river, but is not. It is actually a reflecting pool and is only about two feet deep.'

Never having heard of cod-pieces before, it had taken a moment or so for Orlando to realise that she had not suddenly switched to Scotland's favourite North Sea fish but was still on the subject of the male member, though the context seemed obscure to say the least. They had emerged from the topiary, somewhat to Orlando's relief, and Lolly had started to describe those parts of the estate through which they were now passing. He noted that the castle would be very hard to burgle except by a really agile cat burglar, for all the great Georgian windows seemed to be on the upper floors whereas, at ground level, there were only heavily barred apertures dating from the castle's past role as a fortress. One exception to this lay on the south side of the building where a series of tall French windows opened out onto a flag-stoned terrace strewn with terracotta pots planted with herbs. One of these rooms was heavily shuttered from within, but, as it was dusk, Orlando noticed a rosy pink glow peeping through cracks in the shutters.

'What happens in there?' he asked Lolly.

For the first time, Lolly – who had expounded on the usefulness of the ha ha in keeping the deer away from the roses, on the rarity of the five pine trees ringing the lawn, each imported from a different continent, and on the hideousness of the Henry Moore sculpture of a disembowelled mother and her headless child – was suddenly perceptibly silent for a whole long moment.

'Mm?' she murmured, as if she hadn't quite heard his question.

'What happens in there?' he repeated, pointing to the windows.

'Nothing really. It's a ballroom that is almost never used.'

'Someone's left the lights on,' he said, just as he felt her arm slip through his.

'Guess so,' she murmured, steering him back towards the front of the castle. Her sudden closeness banished the room with the eerie pink light completely from his mind.

Sherry in the gun room was not what Orlando would have expected if he had had any grounds or previous experiences to lead him to expect anything in particular – except of course sherry. This was as nauseatingly sweet and sticky as he remembered it from the time when he had, as a child, secretly sipped the dregs from some left-over glasses after one of his mother's whist parties.

Lachlan dominated the conversation from the start with a series of penetrating questions about Orlando's opinion on the rules of rugby.

'Drop kick goals, Orlando – and I hope I may call you that?' said

Lachlan, assuming that anything he hoped was instantly fulfilled and getting a smiling nod from his guest. 'Don't you find it absurd that they should be worth three whole points? I'm referring of course to our match against Italy. Or was it Iceland?' He looked to Lolly for the answer:

'Close. The Faroe Islands.'

Orlando knew they were both wrong but saw no point in saying so. Lachlan went on as if rugby was almost as important to him as nuclear power or choral singing. Orlando, who guessed that Lachlan had not been above doing a little research into his background, was nevertheless flattered. More so, when the Laird reported that he knew, thanks to the ACC, of Orlando's key role in the Caledonian Inward Investment affair.

'No one in Tressock knows that you are not an ordinary Police Constable,' Lachlan informed him, rising after about half an hour to indicate that *Sherry in the Gun Room* was over. 'And of course no one will hear it from Lolly or me,' he added. 'I just wanted to assure you of that.'

Having made a polite but rather formal farewell to his host, Orlando walked part of the way home with Lolly. He left her making her way to the stable block above which she evidently had a flat. The shock of learning that someone, presumably quite high-up in the force, had told the Laird of his real mission at Tressock had been eclipsed by what had happened after, that magical moment when Lolly kissed him boldly on the mouth before leaving him.

Poetry was not a part of Orlando's life. He had never bought a book of poetry, but at school he had been subjected to a certain amount of verse and a few snatches of it, here and there, had stuck. Now, closing his battered front door behind him, shutting out the suddenly less than cruel world, verse came to his lips. He found himself almost singing it aloud to his stuffed aviary.

'To see her is to love her
And love but her for ever
For nature made her what she is
And never made another.'

He even knew that Rabbie Burns wrote that and that the poet was thinking of a unique girl. God knows Lolly was as unique a girl as he was ever likely to meet. She had promised to come out with him. When she gave him that memorable kiss on the mouth she had said: '*See you soon sweet constable.*'

Going to bed that night, he thought only of her. What else was there to think about?

Shaving, the next morning, he found himself re-reading several times the elegant little embossed card she had slipped into his pocket. He had stuck it into the frame of his shaving mirror:

Loelia (Lolly) Morrison, BA
PO Box 521, The Stables
Tressock Castle
Roxburghshire

it read, before providing telephone, fax and e-mail details.

He had to admit that he found the Bachelor of Arts slightly intimidating. His own two A levels had got him into the police college, from which he had graduated very creditably. But a BA labelled her, in his book, an intellectual. Someone must shag intellectual women, he assumed, but he hadn't imagined himself doing so. It was a slight set-back. While it no way made her any less gorgeously desirable physically, there were bound to be gaps in between their lovemaking when conversation was inevitable and one thing he really couldn't talk to her about was his undercover work. But then again, perhaps that was the advantage of the ACC having told Sir Lachlan what he was doing in Tressock, and Sir Lachlan having informed her of it.

Starting his day in the Police Station, checking out the new missing persons lists, filling in the voluminous report forms required for almost every misdemeanour he had encountered in Tressock, and fortunately there weren't that many, his mind returned to Lolly and planning his first date with her. There was a cinema at Kelso. He checked what was showing and what the reviewers in the Sunday paper had said about the films. During his lunchtime break he went up to the Grove and consulted Peter, the publican, who provided a list of local restaurants in what the credit card leaflet blurbs call the 'fine dining' category.

He telephoned her as soon as he got back to the station. She was out but he left a message with a giggling girl – one of Lolly's under grooms, he supposed. Lolly called back almost at once.

'Is it a police matter?' she asked.

'No. I just wanted to ask you out to dinner. Go to the cinema perhaps. If you're free sometime. One evening. Whenever you can make it.'

'Oh Orlando. I'd love to. But not this week.'

'Not this week?' It was Tuesday. Did she mean Saturday? Did she mean next Monday?

'The blacksmith's here all week. Lachlan and Delia are away. They'll be back on Monday. Next Monday?'

Think of all the hours we'll be sleeping apart till then, Orlando wanted to yell down the phone. How can you bear it Lolly? But he said:

'Monday then. About six o'clock? Great!' he hung up, fondly believing he had sounded like Mr Cool, with five other girls to call now she had said 'wait'. But in Tressock, where everyone seemed to know everything about everybody else, he realised that she probably knew the truth. Five – six days to go. Meanwhile there was always the bloody cult to investigate.

At the Grand Hotel

WHEN THE LIMO finally returned them to their hotel after the concert, Beth and Steve were both in a state of elation, the high that comes after performing or witnessing a hit show. '*The Redeemers' Messiah and their lead singer Beth Boothby's sublime voice blew the capacity audience in the cathedral away,*' reported the BBC radio news programme. Steve would never forget the excitement of that colossal standing ovation at the end. Beth was still feeding upon it, that power to move people so much. She only worried slightly that her plain black dress was not quite adequate for the occasion. Steve just couldn't wait to get out of his formal suit and tie.

Terry Buckhauser, the Redeemers' co-ordinator, over from Texas just for the concert, had talked to them both in their limo as it was taking them to the Dome, the Grand Hotel's real fancy restaurant where Lachlan and Delia were giving a reception for Beth. Terry told them how terrific the concert had been and how good for America's image it was to have something other than war to export right now. 'Not that I am suggesting it is anything but a just war,' he said hurriedly, adding: 'God certainly wants us to punish those evil-doers out there. But right here in Scotland you'll be facing, when you start going door to door, preaching God's word, probably a very different reaction. You mustn't think you're going to get quite the reception you got in that cathedral. But I know you're brave people. You'll find some hostility, no doubt. But these Scottish, they're basically kind, decent folks. You'll find that too. I'm sure of it.'

When she entered the small lobby of her suite, Beth found banks of flowers, in baskets, pots and wrapped in fancy paper; all tributes for her performance. Steve was waiting for her, watching the television coverage of the reception from which she had just come, which was still going on down below. Breathlessly excited, she ran towards him, and he, equally excited, caught her in his arms, swinging her off her feet.

'Steve, I just cannot believe how those folks can talk,' babbled Beth. 'I mean they're just so kind and enthusiastic but like so totally polite… it's awesome… in that amazing accent of theirs.'

Steve, dressed now in jeans and a T-shirt, laughed at her slightly incoherent babble. 'You're just used to kids, honey. Fans that are kids and teens.' He was looking at the television showing the milling crowd, and a presenter interviewing Lachlan and Delia. 'Those dudes are old.

But boy did they love you. Wow!'

'So how about you, cowboy? That singin' gal is the new me. D'you still love me?'

For answer he grabbed an open bottle of champagne he had been drinking and took a gulp of it from the neck. He put his mouth to hers, letting the champagne flow in. Beth went slightly pop-eyed as she tried to gulp it down, and they were both spluttering and laughing and falling on the bed, Steve on top of Beth. Suddenly they were both following their strong instinct to make love to each other, his hands on her thighs, her open mouth hungrily seeking his. Steve whispered teasingly: 'I loved you when you had braces on your teeth. And I love you now you're the most beautiful and talented woman in Scotland.'

Beth's dress was up to her waist now. She suddenly wrenched herself away from him, sitting bolt upright, stretching her legs to plant her feet firmly on the floor again. She grabbed his silver ringed hand in her silver ringed hand, and thrust them close to his face.

'Silver ring, Steve!' cried Beth. 'Silver ring, honey!'

Breathless, Steve's response came slowly.

'Sometimes I don't think I'm ever – ever goin' to get used to...'

'Abstainin'?' Beth whispered, distracted, because in the backgound she could now hear her own voice singing in the cathedral.

They both leaned forward to watch the television as the presenter wrapped up the programme against a clip of Beth finishing her performance.

'Well that was the new Beth Boothby bringing the Word of the Lord to us sinful Scots. Now let's take a last look at the old familiar Beth singing her greatest hit...'

Another clip of Beth filled the screen. This time she was dressed in hot pants and in the full pop princess costume. Her body undulating, she was making love to the microphone as she sang a breathy, sexy ballad.

Beth grabbed the TV control gizmo and tried to switch herself off, but pushed the wrong button and the image kept bouncing back. Furious, she pointed the gizmo at her image like a gun.

'I just hate her!' she cried.

'But she's you, baby,' said Steve.

'Not any more she isn't.' Beth finally achieved a blank screen. Meanwhile Steve had gathered up his sneakers and was heading for the door. Beth darted in front of him.

'Where you goin' Steve?' she asked sharply. She put her arms round him and gave him a languorous kiss on the mouth, to which Steve, sulky and frustrated, only half responded.

'My room, honey,' he said.

The telephone by the bed started to ring. Beth hesitated, her attention on Steve. She suddenly sounded very serious and earnest.

'I promise that – when we're wed – you're goin' to know you married a real lil' ole Jezebel.'

She turned away to pick up the telephone while Steve waited an instant to see who was calling.

'Delia!' Beth assumed her best, socially-friendly tone. 'Yeah, that reception was so wonderful. You and Lachlan were so kind... No... Steve has gotten a whole lot of maps. But thank you. Yeah, we got your numbers. If anything comes up we'll call... Sure. We'll let you know how it went... Really appreciate it, Delia... Good night.'

While Beth was talking Steve snuck up behind her and kissed the nape of her neck and immediately left the room. Beth turned to see Steve had gone. She touched the back of her neck, sighed and smiled a little ruefully.

The Mission

THE MORNING BROUGHT the news on both Beth and Steve's bedside phones that their chauffeur, Mr Beame, was waiting for them as soon as they were ready. The further news that it was ten o'clock in the morning made them both leap from their beds, shower, dress, gather up some of the pamphlets Terry had given them and hurry down to meet him. To their relief, he had entrusted the Rolls Royce to the kilted doorman, and was enjoying a hearty breakfast.

'It is maybe the only true good reason to have a Rolls Royce,' he told them in his rich Glaswegian accent. 'No doorman can resist looking after it for you. You double park outside their hotel, throw them the keys and tell them if they play their cards right you may allow them to clean it.'

They drove first to a section of the city called the Gorbals.

'When I was a bairn this was my home. Mordaunt Street. You'll find more honest to God sinners here than in any other part of town. But now it's all changing. See, over there? Big new blocks of flats for nobs. Pricey.'

'Nobs?' asked Steve.

'Aye. Solicitors, insurance salesmen, doctors. That class of person. One of the best known taxidermists in Scotland lives in that block.'

'Taxidermists?' Beth was curious this time.

'They stuff... well animals. I do a bit of it myself. Stags, foxes, rare owls. You know what I mean?'

'Oh sure,' said Steve. 'My pa's got an old stuffed mountain lion my grandaddy shot up in Arkansas. My ma, she hated that thing. Said it was full of vermin.'

Beame made no comment on this revelation. To his mind it sounded typically American. No respect for a science and art form that was as old as the pyramids of Egypt, or so the Laird had once told him. But his wife had given him his orders and he was almost as frightened of her as he was in awe of her husband. These young Yanks had to be handled just right.

When Beame dropped them off where his native Mordaunt Street met the avenue of smart new blocks of flats, they had agreed a plan. First the flats, then Mordaunt Street. They found a nice familiar Starbucks on the corner and, having decided their opening strategy, settled down to discuss tactics.

'I thought Terry was a tad pessimistic about how folks will receive us,' said Beth. 'We got to go to each door thinking – these people are going to be real pleased to see us and when they hear what we have to say why they'll just be one hundred per cent receptive and interested. Don't you think?'

'Are you forgetting that march yesterday?' Steve reminded her. 'All those folks dumping on the war, and on the President. I guess they're goin' to know real quick that we're Americans. I never knew that I had an accent till I realised that Mr Beame has as hard a time understanding us as we do listenin' to him. That's one fence we're goin' to have to climb wherever we go.'

'Folks back home, Big Bill for one, think these Europeans – they're anti-American. That's wrong. They just hate Bush.' Beth was all sweet reason. 'I've met a whole lot of Yankees who hate Bush too. They just don't understand what a great Christian the guy is. He came back from being an alcoholic, and some real doubtful business deals. Then he found the Lord. He gave himself to God and that's all I need to know about him. He's a genuine born-again Christian gentleman and our President. But whatever these folks think of him, haven't they shown us nothing but kindness? If we can teach them that God loves them, each and every one of them, they may start to think of our President as like their big brother in Christ. 'Cause that's what he is. God bless him. Know what I mean?' Beth remained sunnily optimistic.

They were lucky in that their first call to a homely little lady with a Pekinese went well. She lived in the first block of apartments where there seemed to be no doorman, just a row of bells and an entry phone. It turned out she'd seen the concert on the local TV and couldn't wait to make them tea. It helped that her normally fierce little dog, which answered to the name of Chang, seemed to like Steve. It allowed him to rub its tummy while Beth helped make the tea and talked about the Lord. The woman kept their pamphlet and asked Beth to sign her schoolgirl daughter's autograph book.

So far, so successful. But they knew that recognition of Beth had helped. It wasn't to happen again. School was in and the few kids they were to meet were playing hooky. The next apartment where someone answered the bell was probably the janitor's because it was on the ground floor and smelt of cats' piss and disinfectant. A very old man opened the door. At first he didn't seem to notice them, but that was because he was bending to pick up some milk bottles. Then he looked up and saw them. He seemed nervous but he smiled at them nevertheless, showing a large expanse of badly-fitting false teeth.

'Good morning, friend,' said Steve. 'Do you believe in Jesus?' He handed the old man a pamphlet, which was accepted by a trembling, liver spotted hand.

'I'm Labour, old Labour and proud of it,' he said. 'My wife, she doesn't vote. Doesn't hold with it. Says you're all liars.' He cackled with laughter at what he had said and peered at them through weak, red-rimmed eyes to see how they were taking it.

An old woman in a pinafore had appeared behind him, taking the milk from his hand, steering him away from the door.

'Not today. Not today. Thank you very much,' she almost shouted. 'There's no election, dad. They're just a couple of Jesus freaks. I'm sorry but that's what we call you round here,' she added shrilly, as she shut the door in their faces.

Disappointing. But the man had held on to the pamphlet, and Steve thought that mildly encouraging.

'Suppose he keeps the pamphlet in the toilet. Reads a bit every time he's spending some time in there. One day he gets the message. Then he's telling her about the Lord all day long till she just like gives up, falls on her knees and is saved. Hallelujah!'

'You've got an amazing imagination, Steve,' said Beth admiringly. 'For a cowboy,' she added teasingly.

The next bell that responded was for the penthouse apartment of a building that overlooked the river and had been well converted from a warehouse. The middle-aged woman who came to the door this time was wearing an expensive looking robe and looked as if she was not long out of bed.

'If you could spare us a few minutes, lady. We'd like to talk to you about Jesus,' said Steve, holding his pamphlets prominently in his hands. Beth gave her winning smile.

The woman took a perceptibly long time to answer during which her face was a blank. Then she suddenly summoned up a bleak smile.

'Actually I'm a Buddhist,' she said. 'You would be too if you knew anything about it. Anyway, why don't you come in and give me your spiel? Maybe I can critique it for you. I know the market round here pretty well.'

Steve and Beth followed her into the apartment, a huge, luxurious loft conversion which was largely open plan, the kitchen-dining area being closest to the front door. On an island kitchen counter, a bottle, newly opened by the look of it, sat next to a half full glass of white wine. The woman took two glasses from an overhead rack and placed them beside the bottle.

'My name is Constance,' she said.

'Constance, my name's Beth and this is Steve, and we don't drink, don't normally drink alcohol. At least I don't.'

'Well poor old you, Beth. Anyway here's some for scrumptious Steve.' Constance was already handing him a well-filled glass and looking him up and down. Beth had never seen a woman undress a man with her eyes like that. Of course men did it all the time to women. God made men that way. Admiring a neat pair of buns from the rear was OK in her book, but this was embarrassing.

'We're here to talk about Jesus, Constance,' said Steve firmly. 'And it's real kind of you to offer. But I never drink when I'm…' He paused. Was this work, he was wondering.

He returned the full wine glass, sliding it across the counter back to Constance. She stared at it for what seemed an unnaturally long time. Then she stretched forward awkwardly to take the glass, knocking it over, so that it spilled, rolled and smashed on the floor. She surveyed the mess, but made no move towards it. Instead, she stared at Beth, managing the wintry smile. Steve had stooped to pick up the pieces.

'You're wrong Beth,' said Constance at last, speaking carefully in her posh Scottish accent, as if at an elocution class. 'Quite wrong. Wrong technique. You want to get people's attention? What you should be saying is: "My name is Beth." Then you turn to him… you introduce him. "This is JESUS," you say. Now you've got their attention. So here is the grabber… now you say: "I want to talk about YOU." Who wants to talk about anyone else?'

Beth had a visceral dislike of anyone who revived memories of her father's alcoholism.

'Steve,' she said quite sharply, 'I think we are intruding on this lady. Let's just leave our little pamphlet with her. Food for thought, Constance! When you're not too busy, honey. OK?'

Constance's nervous system was already in delayed-action mode. Surprise now completely immobilised it. She just stood there, her wintry smile still painted upon her face. As Steve made to follow Beth, she reached out to touch him but – missed. She staggered but did not quite fall. They closed the door behind them.

'I guess she's very lonesome,' said Steve as they hurried on to Mordaunt Street, the next target on their map. 'I feel sorry for her.'

'So go back and comfort her,' snapped Beth.

'Are you kidding?' Steve was appalled, not so much at Beth's words as at her tone.

It took a little while for Beth to examine what she had been feeling when she said that. It was just so un-Christian, she knew that. She told herself that Jesus loved Constance and, God help Him, loved even her shit-faced Daddy. So somehow, she would never understand how, she must love them too. Meanwhile she was walking as fast as she could. It had started to rain. Steve, trying to check their position on the wet, wind-tossed map, had a hard time keeping up with her. Suddenly Beth stopped and flung her arms around him.

'I am so sorry Steve. I can be such a bitch sometimes. You are right. Of course she's lonely. She could have been pretty once. Now she's all puffy and blotchy, smelling of booze and borderline crazy. Who would want to spend any time with her?'

'Beth, are we here to try and help people like her? You tell me! I mean all those guys with couches charging a hundred dollars an hour, don't they do that?'

'They don't tell people that Jesus is the answer. Sure we could have maybe helped her. But I just couldn't stand to spend one more minute with her. That's my problem, Steve. I admit it. She was reminding me of my Daddy.'

It was Steve's turn to pause and take this admission in.

'Well that sure is a human reaction,' he said finally, and deciding that was as judgemental as he was prepared to be, went on: 'Mr Beame suggested we start on the right-hand side of this street. Thought we might find some likely prospects there.'

The owners or tenants of the first eight houses they tried didn't answer their bells or knockers. The ninth was opened by a big beer-bellied man in a T-shirt and jeans. He laughed when Steve asked if he believed in Jesus.

'If she'll come and sit on my face I'll give it a go, mate,' he said with a lascivious chuckle.

They hurried on down the street, missing out three doors in order to be well away from the further genial obscenities the man was aiming at Beth.

The next house had a freshly-painted front door and clean glass in the fanlight above it. The man who opened the door was polite and friendly. He shook hands when they offered theirs and said it was Jenny, his wife, they should be after.

'I'll take a pamphlet for her,' he said. 'She believes but I don't. I once said to her, "Do you really think the world was created in seven days?" She said, "Well the Bible says so." So I said, "What about the dinosaurs?" "What about them?" she said. So now we just let it go. But I'll give her this,' he added, putting the pamphlet on the hall table.

'Thank you sir,' said Beth. If a man had heard or read the word of God and didn't believe it, what more was there to say? But she gave him her special smile. To their surprise, as she and Steve were just turning to go on up the street they heard him say: 'Stop!'

Looking back to see what was the matter, they saw that he had stepped back into his doorway and was gesturing for them to come closer.

'I wouldn't go no further up this street if I was you,' he said, keeping his voice low, although there was no one else around to hear him. 'I think someone's planning to take the piss, big time.'

'You mean someone who knows we're comin'?' asked Steve, astonished.

'No comment. Isn't that what they say? Listen. Unless you got some magic tricks for dealing with dogs I wouldn't go no further.'

'Dogs?' Steve was as used to them as to horses. He'd had gun dogs for hunting all his life. 'You got a back yard? I could use a stick.'

'You haven't seen this dog,' said the man. 'But be my guest,' he added, pointing the way to the back of the house and the yard.

While Steve was looking for a suitable stick among the bushes in the tiny but well kept garden, Beth vented her curiosity about what made some people in this street so hostile. The man hesitated. She wondered if he was feeling guilty about tipping them off about the dog and felt to say more would make him really treacherous.

'You're foreign,' he said thoughtfully. 'There are some people here, in this street – not all by any means – but some – who hate foreign. Yanks, yes I'm sorry, but they do. English too, oh particularly English. If there weren't English there to hate, we'd have to invent them. I'm sorry but you got a fleesome task ahead of you.'

'But, Jesus?' she asked. 'What is there to hate about him?'

'Ah, that's territorial. Jesus can invade their territory. To let him in makes them look soft to their mates. They're mortally afraid of that. I'll be frank with you. I know the feeling.'

Steve had come back with a good stout stick about three feet long. He thanked the man, who went inside and shut his front door. Steve rang or knocked at the next three doors, telling Beth to stay well behind him.

At the fourth door, number 94A Taggart Street, there was a voice answering from within. Beside the voice there was the sound of a dog giving a deep growling bark followed by a curiously high pitched growl.

'Yeah? Whatisit?' A deep, glottal slur of a voice it was.

'We're Redeemers, sir,' said Steve. 'We'd like to talk to you about Jesus.'

For a couple of instants Steve and Beth stood waiting, with Steve trying to push Beth behind him. Then just audibly the voice hissed, 'Gettem Tyson!' The door opened with a bang and a huge mastiff came hurtling out with one snarling leap, straight at the stick held out for him. Unfortunately, just behind the stick Beth, turning away, inadvertently presented her rear and he bit into it before Steve managed to force the stick into his jaws, getting him to bite deep into the wood. The moment his teeth had sunk into the stick Steve was swinging him into the air and hurling him back through the door, where a burly, tattooed man with arms like lamp posts tried to catch him but got the full force of the flying mastiff in his face, knocking him to the ground. From behind the shouting, whining mass of dog and man writhing on the hall floor, a fierce little woman in an apron darted out into the street, closing the door behind her.

'Serve you right, you creepin' Jesuses!' she shouted. 'Who the hail are you Yanks to come here and tell us what to do? What did your God ever do for us?' She was reaching behind her to re-open the door.

'Run like hell, Beth!' shouted Steve. She ran. He followed.

Looking round as he did so, he was relieved to see that Tyson was still inside, probably resisting any attempt to take his prize stick away from him. At the end of the road, they managed to flag down a bus going they knew not where, but well away from Tyson.

Lolly Day

THAT BLESSED MONDAY (*Lolly Day* as he had written on his calendar) had arrived for Undercover Detective Constable Orlando Furioso. He filled time while waiting for six o'clock to arrive with writing a report on what he had gleaned from Jack. Looking back on the interview, he now thought he had gone on too long, frustrated as he was by the interviewee's endless recourse to irrelevant verse. When he pressed the poor man very hard on the subject of some kind of ritual animal sacrifice (referred to in one of the letters) Jack had stiffened and croaked more than spoken in his sepulchral voice again:

> 'When seeking an abstraction
> You'll get no satisfaction
> From an ugly rumour too,
> Too bizarre to be a clue,
> Yet of truth a vulgar fraction.'

As he was trying to make some sense of Jack's words in his report he glanced up and saw Lolly walking up the street from the castle gates, heading for his front door. She was wearing a dress. Gone were the slightly mannish riding clothes she'd worn before, that so accentuated the lovely woman inside them. The dress looked, from a distance, as if it was made of loose leaves that partly clung to her form and partly fluttered around her long legs, caught in the breeze. She was very early. He was still in uniform. He went to the door to greet her, planning to give her a – what? – he couldn't serve a drink in the Police Station…

On opening the door he saw that she was still twelve paces away. Her face, still thoughtful at that instant, still in shade, saw him, burst into a great sunburst of a smile and she was running, yes running, straight at him, throwing her arms around his neck, kissing him full on the mouth again.

'Orlando!' she cried, 'I know I'm early, but I just couldn't wait.'

Almost in shock, Orlando could see, in his peripheral vision, half a dozen passers-by, good citizens of Tressock, glancing up at them and smiling.

'Come in. Come in. I can't be seen kissing you in uniform,' he said, leading her inside, shutting the door behind them. Lolly clung gently to his neck, cleaving her body to his, her mouth slightly open, her tongue ready as if she was about to lick some cream from his taut, embarrassed face. But she didn't speak, only searched his face with her eyes as if she were, ever so benignly, inspecting her prey.

'I've reserved seats at the Odeon; it's the multiplex on the Kelso Road,' he said, feeling he was losing the initiative. 'They're showing the new Schwarzenegger movie. I'm that glad you're early because we can have a nice leisurely drink at the Slug and Lettuce first – they do real ale there. Good wine too. No rot gut. The lads at the Kelso cop shop recommended it highly. Then I've reserved a table at... I hope you like curry... the British Raj restaurant in Kelso. I thought I would surprise you... Is all that OK with you?'

She was staring at him as if she hadn't heard a word he had said. It was the inquisitive stare of a woman who sought to look through his little torrent of words at what might lie behind them.

'Would you like a – a cup of tea – while I go and change?'

'Tea? No, Orlando. At the end of this evening you have so sweetly planned for us, don't think I am not grateful and flattered, what do you hope for as a finale?'

Once again the element of romance seemed to be slipping away from Orlando, but somehow this time he felt he could trust Lolly to... what?

'Make love?' he said hopefully.

'Thank heavens for that!' she said. 'Tell me this. After goggling at Mr Schwarzenegger's pecs for an hour and a half will I want to make love to you more than I do now? After swilling real ale and wonderful cop-shop approved wine will you be a better lover? Will either of us, rumbling and farting with British Raj curry, be much of a treat for each other?'

'So?' It had suddenly occurred to Orlando that in just a matter of minutes he could have skipped a long evening of expensive anticipation and be doing what the characters in a popular American sitcom call 'it' – more or less right away. 'So?' he repeated.

'We can do what you planned and skip the finale. Or go straight to the finale and make it...'

'The main event?'

By way of assent she kissed him again, this time quite chastely. Then she was walking through to his bed-sitting room while he was frantically locking the front door, pulling down blinds, drawing curtains and finding the *Thai Opening Lotus* condoms Mai Lin had given him as a farewell present.

'Won't that old witch allow you to get rid of the birds?' she asked as she shrugged off the leafy looking dress, which seemed to be made of some gossamer material, revealing only the essential Lolly underneath.

'So you think she's a witch too. Can there be white witches?' he asked as she helped him fling off his clothes.

'Of course,' she replied. 'One day, a thousand years from now, I will tell you all about them.'

From outside the Police Station a soft, warm light shone through the blinds of the bed-sitting room. Inside, Lolly and Orlando were slowly entering that breathless, post-coital quiet zone which is particularly poignant if, as on this occasion, all has gone very well. It was Lolly who broke the spell.

'Or-lan-dooo!' she almost yodelled his name. 'What a fantastic lover you are. Is it being Italian, do you think?'

'Sorry, Lolly, but that's bullshit,' he replied. 'Reckon I'm almost as Scottish as you are. My ma's pure Scot. My da's a Scot on his mother's side. It's just my grandad. He came over to sell ice cream after the war. So just a wee bit of me is Italian.'

'Well, I think that must be the bit that was so fantastic,' said Lolly, giving him a languorous hug. 'And I wouldna call it wee. Let's do it again. Not exactly the same thing of course. I want to learn something new from you. Some wild, wicked Italian thing. Cover me with double virgin olive oil. Think of me as a Caesar salad.'

'This is a Police Station, Lolly, not a delicatessen. But do you really think I'm a fantastic lover?' As he was saying this, Orlando had raised himself to kneel beside her on the rather precarious sofa-bed they were sharing, looking down into her eyes, those eyes that always seemed amused, as if she was nursing some cosmic joke he would never be able to share. Yet, in spite of this, there was something completely open about her. She always seemed to say exactly what she was thinking and say it at once without any calculation or hesitation. Her openness inspired him to be equally unguarded.

'I could fall for you, Lolly. Really fall for you, and that's a fact.'

He didn't know what he expected her reaction to be. But, in the event, it really surprised him. She seemed quite taken aback.

'Oh no! No, no, no!' she was saying. 'Please don't say that, my lovely Orlando. Don't you see, I just like doing *it*? Particularly with someone who does *it* as well as you do. I never, ever fall in lerve.' She pronounced it rather self-consciously, as if it was not really part of her vocabulary. 'And Orlando, not that anything so silly would ever occur to you I hope, I am never, ever anybody's exclusive woman. Nor do I expect exclusivity in any man. Is that OK with you?'

Orlando managed to laugh, but his mind reeled at what she had just said. She loved doing *it* with him, but she didn't want to be his girlfriend. What kind of an arrangement was that?

'OK with me? Since you put it like that, Lolly, I guess it'll have to be.'

'Thank heavens, another free spirit!' she cried. 'If I can use your shower, perhaps you'll join me and we'll think of something really wonderful for Act Two.'

He wanted to believe she had really found him a wonderful lover. But he knew she had steered him away from what, before, had always been slightly mechanical. She had created a sort of theatre of the erotic in his bed. Into his ears, she had whispered urgent cues; conjured up wild allusions; invented roles for him and assumed others for herself.

'Let's imagine,' she had urged at one point, 'that you are the last man left on earth, and that I, among all the millions of women that remain, have won you in a lottery for this one night only. After this, I shall have to remember how you made love to me for the rest of my life... there can never be an encore.'

Meanwhile, joined together in the shower, another highly imaginative act was starting and this time he, remembering the boastful talk he had shared with his team mates in the communal bath at their Glasgow clubhouse, couldn't resist reminding her that: 'This is number three, Lolly.'

'So it is,' said Lolly, thoughtfully. 'You know a compatriot of yours, one Caesar Borgia, bet his father the Pope that he could do it five times with a poor little virgin princess on their wedding night. He had five horsemen waiting under the window of their bridal chamber and each time he came he shouted out to another horseman to ride and tell his father. If he could do that with some poor whimpering little lassie, straight out of a convent, just think what you could with me!'

A lot later Anthea McWhirter, a stable hand who worked for Lolly, was walking back from the Grove after an evening rehearsing May Day songs when she heard some sharp cries of pleasure coming from the Police Station. Wondering idly to herself what a person who is not a voyeur but a listener is called she paused long enough to hear Lolly give a triumphant shout of: 'Orgassissimo Orlando! Orgassissimo!'

Walking Wounded

THE GLASGOW ROYAL Infirmary has the usual complex parking system most hospitals support and Delia was anxious to arrive there before Beth was discharged. Beame was reassuring about her injuries. He'd spoken to the dog owner and reported that it was a simple bite in the girl's bottom, regrettable but not serious. Delia left the Rolls Royce, with Beame still hunting for a parking spot, and hurried into Accident and Emergency. Steve was sitting in the waiting room. Delia hurried over to him, her beautiful face a mask of concern and compassion.

'Steve! How is she? Poor love! What a dreadful thing to happen. I am so glad you called me.'

'She'll be OK I guess,' said Steve. 'They already gave her a tetanus shot. Right now they're putting a few stitches in her butt.'

'Butt? Oh you mean her bottom. Poor old thing. Where is she..?'

Steve pointed to a cubicle off to the right of a passageway, murmuring that he'd been asked to wait outside. But Delia wanted to make contact with Beth as soon as possible and was convinced no 'please wait outside' request could apply to her. She therefore invaded the cubicle just as a nurse was completing putting a dressing on Beth's upper thigh. A young woman doctor was there too.

'D'you wear a bikini?' she was asking Beth.

'Never have. Why?' asked Beth.

'It could leave a bit of a scar,' said the doctor.

'My vanity doesn't extend to my butt,' laughed Beth, not noticing Delia standing just inside the cubicle.

Beth thanked the doctor and the nurse, wondering why no one had yet mentioned insurance or credit cards.

'Take this to the pharmacy for your medication,' said the doctor.

'Try and keep the dressing dry,' added the nurse.

And they were gone. It was then that Beth saw Delia smiling sympathetically at her.

'My dear Beth. You have been in the wars. I'm so relieved it is nothing worse than, as Steve puts it, a bite in your butt.'

'Thank you so much for coming, Delia.' Beth was really grateful. Some of these Scottish people were so kind and thoughtful. Others were – well you'd find them in Texas too. She knew that, and added: 'Terry, our teacher, said there'd be days like this.'

Beth had slipped on her clothes while Delia went to find Steve. On their return she was delving in her handbag for her credit cards.

'So where do we pay?' she asked.

'Pay? You don't pay. No one pays,' Delia told her. 'Now listen you two. Lachlan has this terrific idea. We want you to come home with us. We have some wonderful raw material for your mission. You never saw as many heathens as we have at Tressock, our place on the Borders. Lachlan, for one.'

'Lachlan is a heathen?' Beth was astonished.

'Lachlan's religion is music,' said Delia. 'If he weren't the chairman of a big company he would like to have written an oratorio like Handel. Call him agnostic if you like. Buddhism, Hinduism, Zoroastrianism are all one to him – manifestations of the Life Force. Christianity too of course. But, as I said, you'll find better missionary material within twenty miles of our home than in Papua New Guinea. Not like the lot you saw this morning. Nice people. People who probably deserve to be saved – starting with Lachlan. Me too perhaps.'

'Sounds good to me. No mad dogs?' asked Steve.

'Friendly dogs,' smiled Delia. 'We specialise in horses actually, Steve. Beautiful horses. Do come. We'll invite the whole of Tressock. Our little town.'

But Delia could see that Beth was unconvinced. She wondered whether the girl had a bit of a martyr complex and really wanted to suffer for her cause.

'You and Lachlan are both just so sweet to think of doing that,' said Beth without a great deal of conviction. 'But right now I think I'd feel I was running away from the challenge right here in Glasgow. Don't you, Steve?'

'No I don't. To be honest with you I figure a country soul is as good as a city soul any day. Let's go save some.'

'But Steve, those poor city folks... OK so they called us Jesus freaks... but we haven't hardly started...'

'Those city folks just hated our guts as soon as they saw us. A soul is a soul, Beth. Now maybe we got a real chance to save some, thanks to our friends here.'

'Steve's right, Beth,' added Delia. 'Our people may be a bunch of heathens, but they'll hear you out, that I promise you. But we'd like to take you home with us tomorrow – quite early.'

Beth managed a wan smile at them both. Then suddenly her usual ebullience reasserted itself.

'OK, OK!' she cried. 'I'm being obsessive. You guys are so kind.'

And suddenly she was hugging a rather startled Delia and giving a pleased and relieved Steve a kiss.

Introducing Sulis

THEIR DEPARTURE FROM Glasgow next morning was, as a result of their hosts' anxiety to get home as soon as possible, rather hectic. Beth was starting to see the virtue in the small amount of luggage she had been allowed. They took a limo to the airport to say goodbye to the Redeemers Choir, who were heading off to Austria to give another concert, this time with the Vienna Boys' Choir.

At the airport, the Morrisons' Rolls Royce awaited them. While Lachlan was showing Beth a review of the concert in the *Scotsman* newspaper and Delia was supervising Beame in the stowing away of the luggage, Steve found himself examining the car. He had assumed it was a Rolls Royce, but the silvery lady on the radiator looked wrong. There were enough Rolls Royces around Dallas for him to be familiar with the classic radiator and the winged lady leaning forever into the wind. This lady seemed to be rising from a silver stream. Lachlan noticed him examining the little effigy and smiled.

'You're very observant, Steve,' he said.

Beame came forward to elaborate.

'Normally, sir, that figure would be the Spirit of Ecstasy,' he said. 'That's what the Rolls Royce people like to call her. But this here is our Goddess Sulis. The Laird,' he nodded towards Lachlan, 'had her made special.'

'Sulis is our Celtic name for her,' added Lachlan. 'The Romans, when they were here, called her Minerva. She doesn't suffer fools gladly. Among her many roles, she is the goddess of the bright, intelligent people we like to think we are.'

The car threaded its way through the city of Glasgow before entering rich farmland as they headed south east.

For Beth, the rolling hills and woodlands of Scotland on that sunny day were like a fairyland revealed. It was the kind of landscape the Disney people had used in heart-warming movies with the likes of Julie Andrews singing her great British heart out. Little sheep dotted around small fields on either side of the narrow, hedge-lined roads on which undersized cars sped along as if racing against the clock. The greenness of everything was broken only by brilliant white clumps of early May blossom.

The air was so clear after the showers of the previous night that as every prospect revealed itself, it was like the Lord had suddenly given Beth the power to see all the way to what her camera's guide called infinity. Whatever that turned out to be. Of course Beth knew it was just a camera term, but she liked to think it was somewhere like the end of the Yellow Brick Road. And if, come to think of it, Lachlan and Beame were almost as weird as the Lion and the Tin Man, they certainly seemed just as friendly. While Delia, who sometimes looked as if she could play the Wicked Witch of the West quite convincingly, nevertheless smiled and smiled and smiled as if she knew the best joke in the world but wasn't telling.

They talked first about the concert and Beth's voice. Lachlan wanted to know how she had trained it and why she had chosen to change the way she used her voice so radically. Beth explained how it had dawned on her only slowly how much bigger her voice was than the tasks it had been given. She started listening, at home, to recordings of great singers like Maria Callas and Joan Sutherland and buying the scores of operas she liked.

'One day we were doing a gig some place, I think it was Kansas City,' she recounted. 'At the end the kids screamed for more. So I thought let's give them that great song Carmen sings in the tobacco factory. I put aside the mike and told the guys to kill the sound system. And I gotta admit I sang it real sexy – well that is what it is. The reaction was awesome. At first there was a minute of total silence. Then they just roared. Wanted me to do it again. But my dad, who was managing me at the time, he had them kill the show lights, put on the house lights and led me off the stage. He just hated it. Scared the hell out of him.'

'A voice like that is a gift for the gods,' said Lachlan with a sigh.

'The Lord God gave me my voice, that's for sure,' said Beth. 'You talk about gods – plural. Are you really a heathen like Delia said? You're kidding us. Don't you think they're kidding us, Steve?'

'He must know what he is, Beth,' laughed Steve. 'Talkin' of voices, what about yours, sir? That's some sound you've got there. I thought that Hallelujah thing you sang with your Glee Club – wow – that was awesome too.'

Lachlan was hunting for a cd on a rack inside his fumed oak music centre.

'Don't start him,' complained Delia, but Lachlan was already inserting the disc.

'These are a couple of our Scottish songs. They were written by someone you might call a heathen. We'd call him a pagan,' said Lachlan. Both Steve and Beth recognised the songs instantly, and the voice. It was Lachlan himself singing 'The Foggy, Foggy Dew' and then 'The

Homebody's Song'. But he had the volume turned fairly low and talked with them while the cd was playing.

'These old folk songs. In a way they're our hymns, our anthems, our spirituals,' he said. 'Because they celebrate life.' Lachlan paused so they could hear the chorus, turning up the volume.

'She jumped into bed boys, making no alarm,
Thinking that a drover lad could do her no harm
And she wished the short night
Had been seven years long.'

'Really Lachlan!' said Delia. 'Don't you think that's a bit raunchy for our young Redeemers?'

Beth laughed. Now was not the time to preach. With luck, if these folk kept their promises, there'd be plenty of time for that later.

'The Devil has all the best tunes, they always say,' she declared politely.

The Inquiry Develops

IT WAS AN unusually bright spring morning in Tressock when the telephone started to ring inside the Police Station for the third time since nine o'clock, its normal opening time. It went on ringing as one of the blinds was pulled up and the bleary face of Orlando peered out at the world. He was wearing a terry towel bathrobe and made his way unsteadily to his desk to answer the telephone.

'Tressock Police Station,' he croaked and then held the phone well away from his face as if he was hoping to avoid the person at the other end.

The severe voice of Detective Sergeant Murdo Campbell reminded him of the time of day and the fact that he had failed to answer three previous calls and that his mobile appeared to be switched off. Orlando visibly pulled himself together, painfully straightening his body from a stoop to standing more or less at attention.

'Morning to you DS Campbell!' Orlando just managed to sound crisp and welcoming of this unexpected call. 'I haven't heard the telephone ringing. Not repeatedly. Not at all. Must be a problem at the exchange. I'll report it. As for mobile phones. They don't work too well down here and that's a fact. Sir Lachlan, the big cheese up at the Castle, doesn't like seeing those booster towers around here. This place is a wee bit feudal. Not so much Shangri-La, more Middle Earth...'

'Not so much what as what?' bellowed DS Campbell, startling Mrs Menzies who was just letting herself in to start one of her futile attacks on the Police Station's grime of ages. 'You're making no sense laddie,' the sergeant was still shouting, 'have you gone native down there or what?'

'Just the way a source I was interviewing last night described this community, DS Campbell,' replied Orlando, managing to sound quite calm. 'It'll all be in my next report. Anyway, this was your call. How can I help?'

Campbell's voice had returned to normal. He was inquiring about certain missing persons.

'Tad and Lucy Mae? Sound like Americans,' mused Orlando, spotting their names among the mostly young people listed alphabetically with their pictures and ages on the back of the door. Lucy Mae stood out. A beautiful girl with flame red hair.

'What would Yanks be doing here?' grumbled Mrs Menzies loudly. 'Unless it's to come and see the Willies Walk? Disgusting, I call it!'

She habitually and shamelessly eavesdropped. But hitherto Orlando had been tolerant of her. This time he lifted a heavy stapler from his desk, waving it as if about to throw it at her.

'Och, you wouldna?' she squeaked and fled into the bed-sitting room.

'Who the hell's that? DC Furioso?' DS Campbell could be heard shouting, for Orlando had put down the phone in order to shut Mrs Menzies into the bed-sitting room.

'That was Mrs Menzies, my cleaner,' he now replied, as calmly as he could. 'She's about 109 and slightly crazy. But she knows everybody and can be a useful source. That's the only reason I haven't got rid of her. Yes, those two you mentioned are on my list. I'll make enquiries. As for the witchcraft thing. It's tricky. As you probably know, a few people all over the country are involved in Wikka. A kind of pagan revival. Its all on the web and quite harmless. I've raised it with people here and none of them have ever heard of it, and I believe them. But I do sense that there really is something else going on that I can't yet identify. What it needs, as you and DI McFadden said before, is solid police work, elimination of suspects, following up all leads, and that's what it is getting. I was interviewing someone last night who may turn out to be a very good source. It was necessary to at first gain her confidence. Pretty soon I think she'll talk.'

There was a squawking sound from the detective sergeant that Mrs Menzies couldn't decipher, close though her ear was to the bed-sitting room door. What she did hear quite clearly was this:

'I know what you're saying. They want some results soonest. Leave it with me.'

The Road to Tressock

HALFWAY THROUGH THEIR journey to this small town called Tressock, which Lachlan spoke of as if he owned it, Beth was surprised to see the countryside interrupted by a huge industrial complex; somehow not the sort of thing you expected to find in this corner of little old historic Europe. Armed police, the first she'd seen since they'd left the airport, stood outside the gates of what a sign proclaimed as the Nuada Nuclear Power Station. Nuclear! That was a shock. Where Beth came from, you could be Republican, Born Again, a Member of the Silver Ring Thing, anathematise Charles Darwin and still be quite green when it came to nuclear power.

Beth and Steve, therefore, exchanged a surprised glance, but said nothing because Lachlan was being saluted by one of the police, who seemed to want to hold traffic so that the Rolls could enter the plant. Lachlan wound down the window and leant out to speak to the cop.

'Afternoon Hamish,' he said genially. 'I'm not coming in right now. Going home.'

'Oh very good, sir,' said Hamish, this time directing the traffic so that the Rolls could immediately continue on its way. Whereupon a motorcycle cop appeared, his siren blaring, and led their car through the Nuada plant's home-going commuter traffic. They cleared the vicinity of the power station, crossed an old stone bridge, and then the road led into a section of thick forest, where the motorcycle cop stopped at the roadside and waved them on.

'You seem to be quite the famous guy round here, sir,' said Steve, smiling.

'What makes him famous is that everyone works for him. He's the chairman of the Nuada board,' said Delia.

'Infamous, more like,' laughed Lachlan. 'When things go wrong, I'm usually the villain.'

'So is nuclear OK here?' asked Steve politely

'Not with everyone,' answered Lachlan. 'But one day oil and gas will run out or become just too expensive. So we're working on making nuclear cost effective. When I was a boy, my science teacher held up a golf ball. Unleash the atomic energy in this object, he said, and you could drive the Queen Elizabeth liner to New York and back on that power. So far it hasn't worked out quite like that. But your American submarines, and ours, are circling the globe running on nuclear and hardly needing to refuel.'

'Do you think your God approves of nuclear?' asked Delia rather unexpectedly.

'That's a tricky question, darling,' said Lachlan, almost reprovingly.

'Well, He disapproves of quite a lot. We're here to learn from Steve and Beth. So, if you don't mind,' Delia said this with a smile, 'I would like to know.'

'*When asked tricky questions,*' Beth remembered Terry saying, '*keep real cool. Never risk telling a lie, even if what you are saying seems likely to be true. To be caught out in a lie is to devalue your whole mission and possibly destroy it. Remember the Bible holds the answer to everything. If you are asked something you cannot readily answer go check it out in the Good Book and make sure you tell the questioner what he or she wanted to know before you go to bed that night.*'

'Delia, I just cannot recall the subject being mentioned in the Bible,' Beth said, after a pause. 'So I guess it is probably OK. But I will check and let you know. '

To Beth's relief, and as she thought she heard Delia murmur, 'I'm not sure I can stand the suspense,' this was the moment when a diversion appeared in the shape of a young woman on a beautiful black horse. They had left the woodlands behind and were once more in open country with the outskirts of a small town appearing ahead. 'Tressock Welcomes Careful Drivers,' a sign said.

Steve was staring hard at the young woman, who Beth thought was certainly borderline attractive, her hair blowing and cheeks reddened in the chilly wind and all. She looked to Beth as if she pretty much lived on that horse. She knew the type. There were plenty of them that hung out by the cowboys' stables at the Dana Ranch where Steve had worked at one time. More fixated on the horseflesh than the cowboys, to hear Steve tell it. Beth rather doubted that. Lachlan had lowered the window and shouted across to the young woman as she galloped her horse parallel with the Rolls.

'Hullooo Lolly! And how's my Prince today?'

'He's been missing you.'

'Lolly, Delia and I are giving a rather special party on Sunday – up at the castle,' said Lachlan. 'Everyone is invited, so spread the word. Beth here will be our very special guest. She is a famous American singer. Lolly is our head groom, Beth.'

'Hi!' Beth said, and gave her the smile. Lolly waved her riding crop in reply.

The Rolls had slowed as it reached Tressock's 30 mile an hour speed limit area and Lolly trotted alongside. She was returning Steve's stare.

'What a beauty!' said Steve.

'Steve!' Beth's reaction was one of surprised irritation.

'The horse, Beth. Did you ever see such a beauty? And rare too. You don't hardly see black horses like that.'

'That's right, Steve,' confirmed Lachlan. 'Quite rare. I collect black horses for the Queen's household cavalry. Apart from those, you don't see many. I'm sorry... and this is Steve. He's from America too,' he glanced sideways at Steve. 'How'd you like to ride him?'

Lolly, still taking in the rugged attractions of young Steve, pretended to think Lachlan's question was addressed at her.

'I'd like it fine,' she said, laughing. 'But I expect yon Beth would kill me first.'

'And you'd deserve it,' said Lachlan severely. 'I'm asking Steve. Would you like to ride Prince?'

'Ride that horse? You bet.' Steve suddenly looked more energised than he had all day.

'Then you shall, Steve. Preaching is hard work I've no doubt. But you must have a little recreation while you're here.'

Lolly was cantering ahead into Tressock, Prince's hooves echoing sharply from the macadamed street as the whitewashed row houses with the brick-lined windows and doors started to appear on either side of the advancing Rolls.

Beth was wondering why she had thought that Steve had to be staring at that woman, when it seemed to have been the horse – well of course it was the horse – all along. How dumb of her. Not that she felt entirely comfortable with the thought that he might get to go riding with Lolly. There was something slightly suggestive about that name. She trusted Steve absolutely, she told herself. Being lovers was a bond with a man, there was no denying that. But it wasn't what the Lord wanted, so other ways to bind must be found. Working together in this alien atmosphere would help. Although Lachlan and Delia were being so friendly and helpful, Beth knew that Steve shared her sense of isolation when everything around them, every new encounter, was so – so foreign.

Lolly was practically obscured from view for a few minutes by a wheeling, cawing mass of black birds.

Tressock

TRESSOCK IS DESCRIBED in the very short entry it gets in the *Michelin Green Guide to the United Kingdom*, under Local History:

> *Tressock is located close to the border between Scotland and England. Founded sometime before the departure of the Romans from a still Celtic Britain, its inhabitants had originally been British speakers; the language that still survives in the Principality of Wales. Some place and family names are still evidence of this. Myth and History are mixed in the local custom collectively called the Border Ridings which extends to neighbouring towns too. Each town has its special ritual, but they generally involve the election of a king for a day who is hunted over hill and dale, ending with his presiding over a feast. Tressock's is known as the Riding of the Laddie.*
>
> *Tressock's history has been closely linked to the castle and the steeple of its now ruined church of St Ninian is inhabited by a rare branch of the Raven family (Corvus Corax). These birds, which elsewhere do not live in colonies, have for centuries been cared for at the expense of the Morrisons of Tressock Castle. A Guardian is appointed to feed the birds which are carnivorous. Similar to the legend attached to the ravens at the Tower of London and the apes at Gibraltar, it is believed that were the birds to depart then the Morrisons of Tressock would be no more. The river which flows through the town, a tributary of the River Tweed, is still known by its pre-Roman Celtic name Sulis.*

Had Beth and Steve been conventional tourists and had they read the admirable French guide book they would probably have been particularly pleased to find that they had arrived in Tressock just as one of the ritual feedings of the birds was taking place. This was a twice daily rite and was timed to coincide with 'opening time' at the pub. Michelin didn't mention the fact that, in parts of Scotland, bars open for business very much at the convenience of innkeepers rather than customers, and that to have them open at all after 10 p.m., in parts of the kingdom, is but a recent innovation.

Lolly had cantered through the town well ahead of the Rolls, and all those citizens who happened to be on the streets then dematerialised almost at once into the inn or their nearby homes. As she passed the inn, the feeding of the ravens was sufficiently interrupted by the clattering of Prince's hooves for the birds to take off in a wild fluttering, whirling flight before settling down again outside the inn's front door where their feeder patiently awaited them.

A small man with tight curly fair hair had a flat baker's basket on his arm, upon which appeared to be dozens of blind baby mice. They wriggled and made squeaky, mewling sounds as he threw them one by one into the air for the wheeling, flapping ravens to catch in their lethal yellow beaks. It was as this process occurred that the Rolls pulled up outside the inn's front door.

Beame, clearly used to the ravens, could be seen braving the still fluttering, excited birds, taking Steve's case out of the trunk of the Rolls and handing it to him. Beth had also got out of the car, but her luggage had not been fetched. Lachlan held the door open and Delia remained in the car.

'So when do I see you?' said Steve to Beth, unaware of dozens of faces watching them from inside the pub and through the windows of adjacent houses.

'You can see her any time you like,' said Lachlan, answering for Beth. 'She'll be just down the road. Tomorrow you'll both have to rehearse how you're going to handle the prayer meeting on Sunday.'

Beth did not care for this separation at all. Nor, she knew, would Steve. So she leant back into the car to address Delia:

'Couldn't I stay here at the inn too?' she asked.

'Of course,' said Delia calmly. 'But Mary Hillier's house is where the girls mostly hang out. Staying there will give you a chance to meet some of the young women you may want to convert.'

'Delia has been to a lot of trouble,' interjected Lachlan, 'to arrange things with your mission in mind.'

Steve's expression was really troubled, but Beth climbed back in to the car, deciding that it was too early on this gig to start arguing with the organisers. 'It's cool Steve. That's a great idea, Delia. Thank you,' she said.

Steve was left standing outside the inn as the Rolls drove off. He paused for a minute, fascinated by the man feeding the ravens. He thought them ugly birds, a little like vultures with their balding heads. Curiously, the man seemed equally intrigued by the sight of Steve, who thought it might be because of his cowboy hat. He'd noticed quite a few folks here stared at that. The man's basket of food for the birds was now empty and the birds were flying away, up to the church tower, except one particularly shiny black fowl that sat now on the basket as if hoping for seconds, his head wobbling sideways as he eyed his feeder. Then the man spoke. He seemed to be addressing the bird, but his quick side-glances showed that he was aware of Steve watching him.

'"Prophet," say I, "thing of evil! Prophet still, if bird or devil!"' The man's voice was sepulchral, theatrical, his accent not Scottish.

'"Whether tempter sent, or whether tempest tossed thee here
    ashore,
Desolate yet all undaunted, on this desert land enchanted –
On this home by Horror haunted – tell me truly, I implore –
Is there – is there balm in Gilead? – tell me – tell me, I
    implore!"
Quoth the Raven…'

And then an astonished Steve seemed to hear the bird, the raven itself, in a croaky, unearthly voice, say:

'Nevermore.'

'It's just ventriloquism,' Steve heard another, this time Scottish, voice beside him say. He turned and saw the smiling face of a youngish man with a bristly red moustache and horn-rimmed glasses. He was reaching for Steve's case.

'So welcome, Steve. We have been expecting you. Come on in. Your room's ready if you want to rest up after your journey…' He turned to the man with the raven. 'If you're coming in Jack, will you please leave that bird outside. We're tired of cleaning up after it.' He grabbed Steve's hand. 'I'm Peter McNeil by the way. Anything you need here, just give me a shout.'

The room they entered was a spacious saloon which, in Steve's eyes, looked to be very old with great big beams across the ceiling and a long mahogany bar with a zinc top. He had not seen the great number of people who had watched his arrival through the big windows of this bar, but right now there were maybe twenty in the room, mostly men standing in groups, drinks in their hands. Upon his entry they were all silent, turning to look in his direction, most smiling and welcoming. He smiled right back, but something about the people in this bar made him feel uneasy. Perhaps because he had never, in all the times in his young life that he had entered a bar, back in Texas, been greeted like this. Peter McNeil was introducing him – like he was someone real important – and that seemed strange too.

'This is Steve, everyone,' said Peter. 'He's Sir Lachlan's guest and he's here with his fiancée who is staying with Mary Hillier and the girls. As you probably heard she is Beth Boothby, the well-known singing star from the good old US of A.'

'I'm mighty glad to be here,' said Steve loudly, 'thank you all.'

He followed Peter up a big staircase that led off the far end of the bar, next to a small band-stand with an upright piano, drums and a jumble of other musical instruments. His bedroom, which seemed to have no key, looked out on the street. It puzzled him that it was still quite light out there. Just how far north was this place? No one had ever taught Steve any geography, but having crossed an ocean to get here he wondered, for the first time, exactly where he was. He knew that normally if you wanted to know a thing like that you went to a travel agent. His ignorance of this and so many other things he'd seen or heard in the last twenty-four hours made him feel particularly vulnerable. Putting aside his mission, something he knew he would be able to share with Beth, there was so little here that was familiar. Prince, and the promise that he should ride him, was reassuring. He knew horses. He was sure that anywhere on God's green earth, horses would always be his kind of people. But when it came to human people he couldn't think of anyone that he'd met here to whom he could easily relate. Back home you would class Lachlan and Delia as like toney, up scale Yankees, except their voices were all wrong. As for Jack, the guy with the ravens, what a weirdo he was! At least Peter McNeil was normal and friendly. One person did stand out. That Lolly. What a heck of a lot of woman she was. Steve thought how he would like to... and then he remembered Beth.

The Men at the Inn

THE BAR DOWNSTAIRS wasn't that different from a half dozen he knew in and around Fort Worth. As he descended the stairs he found the atmosphere now much more reassuring. Conversation, lively chatter even, had replaced the eerie silence that had greeted him earlier.

A guy dressed in a suit came up accompanied by three others wearing jeans and working clothes. He guessed them to be just a few years older then he.

'I'm Danny,' said the suit. 'This is Carl, he's Paul, and he's Dawcus.'

One of Steve's great gifts was a most charming smile, which showed up perfect teeth in a well-tanned face, under his tousled mop of butter coloured hair. He looked like a Scot's idea of what a cowboy ought to be like. Even without his hat, although he rarely took that off, so it was never put to the test. He shook the other men's hands and they all moved to the bar where he was offered a drink on the house by Peter, the innkeeper.

Steve had promised Beth that, at least for now, until their mission was well established, he would be dry. He looked around the bar at the rows of Scotch whisky bottles (he just loved Scotch, more than Bourbon even, and he had a real taste for that) and his mouth felt so dry. He looked at the beer on tap, but he'd heard they served it warm and he didn't care for the idea. Beth must be thinking of him, so vividly did he feel her influence.

Every drop of drink accursed
Makes Christ within you – die of thirst.

Beth'd sung that old Salvation Army hymn at their last Redeemers meeting back in Texas. And then a scene from an old Bob Hope movie he'd seen real late one night came into his head and made him almost laugh out loud.

'So what will you have, Steve?' repeated Peter, while the others looked on expectantly, politely waiting to place their own orders.

'Don't suppose you guys ever saw an old Bob Hope movie called *The Road to...* I guess it was *Alaska*,' said Steve. 'Bob Hope comes into this saloon full of real tough lookin hombres – like Jack over there.' Everyone looked at Jack and laughed. 'And there's this, like, total silence while they all stare at Bob. And he asks for a lemonade. Yeah, a lemonade. Then he sees they're all looking like they're goin' to throw him out into the street. So he adds: "A lemonade – in a dirty glass!"'

The laughter was real.

'I'll have a Coke please,' said Steve.

Some musicians had gathered by the upright piano near the staircase. Steve thought it would be good to hear something other than religious music again and immediately felt guilty for thinking it. He noticed, too, that Jack was standing at the end of the bar, staring, not directly at him, but once again at his hat. It made Steve a bit nervous so he took it off and put it on the bar in the hope that Jack would look away. He did. Steve then asked Danny in a quiet voice to tell him about Jack.

'Is that all what Jack does, look after those birds?'

'Find him a bit strange do you, Steve? Did he quote poetry at you? The Edgar Allan Poe piece?'

'It was about a raven. He made like the bird spoke to him. I gotta admit – it was like weird. His accent was kind of different from your Scottish accents. So I couldn't quite get it.'

'He's English and maybe has a condition called Aspergers – much less serious than autism, but one of those things that affects the brain from childhood. His parents were killed in a car accident when he was a teenager. His dad was a nuclear physicist working up here for Nuada, so Sir Lachlan arranged for him to be well supported and he's ended up with this job looking after the ravens. He had a very bad stutter as a kid so someone tried teaching him verse – made him try to sing what he had to say. It's a recognised treatment for stuttering. His singing is really terrible, so we managed to cure him of that part. But he is always sort of reverting to verse. He has this amazing memory for poetry. Poor Jack can be a real pain. But some people treat him as a kind of oracle…'

'Oracle?' Steve thought he knew about autism. Dustin Hoffman in *Rain Man*. But what was this?

'A bit like a prophet,' said Danny, and saw the astonishment on Steve's face. 'Well not really a prophet. It's just that since you can't have a real conversation with him – he makes statements. Sort of oblique they are. He makes them sound like prophecies. The Laird has called him a fortune-cookie prophet and insists that he can hold a conversation with you if he really, really wants to. Still it's usually in verse even then.'

Steve decided to ignore Jack's stare and chatted on with the crowd at the bar. He learned that Danny had a senior job as Head of Personnel at the Nuada power station. Carl, a good-looking, heavily built, athletic man who reminded Steve of a guy who had played line back for the Carolina Panthers, was watching a rugby game on the TV set above the bar. He explained the rules to Steve, who was a tad incredulous that the only protective gear the players wore was a 'box' to preserve what Carl called 'their testimonials'.

A youth with long spatulate hands had started to play the piano. Steve turned to watch and listen. The drum slipped rhythmically into sympathy with the melody while, a few bars on, a penny whistle gave a little sobbing sound and started to weave its way into the tune, just a beat before the pianist's voice came in too:

'Will you go, Laddie, go
To the braes o' Balquiddher
We'll crown the lass your Queen
We'll feast the night together.'

At Mary Hillier's House

BETH HAD SPENT less of her life in female company than most women of her age. Her fame, her consequent riches and her beauty tended to keep people like her female high school classmates at a distance. Some went out of their way to show they were unimpressed, some were frankly jealous, while the majority were somewhat awe-struck and a few girls had shown all too embarrassingly that they had a crush on her. In spite of this, she had found a couple of close woman friends. Her make-up artist, who had been so wonderfully supportive about her decision to give up using cosmetics altogether, was one. She was a real close friend. There was also one girl from the same grade at school who helped her with the long gaps in her studies caused by tours and special gigs. These two kept close through lengthy telephone calls in which they shared the minutiae of each other's lives.

Boys had been easier. They accepted that she was Steve's girl and he handled his role as the alpha male in that pack in the typically relaxed, cool way that made her love him so much.

So, the warm welcome she was to find in the house of Mary Hillier, where four other young women seemed already quite at home, was a slightly novel experience.

It might have surprised Beth and Steve to recognise the same song that was being sung at the inn was also being sung at Mary Hillier's house. As Beth entered the big comfortable living room, the four young women either had their heads bent over some needlework or were carefully guiding cloth through a couple of sewing machines.

'Will you go, Laddie, go...' the four girls were singing in unison, apparently unaware of Beth's presence.

'Girls...' Mary began to speak. But Beth put a restraining hand on the older woman's arm. They'd been introduced outside, by the car. Lachlan had said that Mary had once been the school mistress, but the nearest school now was ten miles away, so she co-ordinated the May Day celebrations, taught singing and ran the Tressock library.

'Please Mary,' said Beth. 'I'd like to listen for a moment. That is just such a lovely song.'

'It's a May Day song. One of many we sing in Maytide...'

The girls, one by one, noticed Beth's presence and stopped singing. They stood, smiling, and, putting their dressmaking aside, immediately came across the room to greet Beth with outstretched hands.

'Hi, I'm Bella,' said a dark-haired girl with ivory white skin and deep brown eyes.

'I hope our singing didn't sound too awful. We're longing to hear you sing. I'm Chloe, by the way,' said a tall fair-haired beauty with eyes as pale blue as a kitten's.

'This is Sweet Sue…' said Mary Hillier, laughing, clearly an in-joke.

'…Who would much rather be called Sensible Sue,' said a stockily built young woman with thick pebbled glasses that enlarged smiling eyes over dimpled cheeks.

'And I'm Deirdre. I think it's only fair to warn you – I'm a witch.'

'Don't believe her,' laughed Sue. 'What she is just rhymes with witch. But we love her just the same.'

They all laughed, even Deirdre. Another in-joke, thought Beth, but she felt comfortable with these women. They seemed relaxed with her. They were friendly. She liked them.

Deirdre had just finished the dress she was working on and she held it up for Mary to inspect. Beth was fascinated by it. Much more than a mere party dress, something a girl would go out to a dance in, or wear at a prom, or as a bridesmaid at a very fancy wedding, this dress was like a costume for a festive scene in an opera or in a classical ballet. It had a clinging under-garment made of pale mauve satin. Embroidered upon the gauzy material a profusion of blossoms seemed to cascade from the shoulders, nestling around the bust, which the dress held high, like in those Jane Austen television plays Beth had seen on public television.

As if they read her mind, the four girls begged Beth to try it on but Mary Hillier seemed doubtful.

'It's the Queen's dress,' she said. 'We don't normally…' she began. But a chorus of protests made her hesitate.

'Well, if Beth would like to try it on,' she said eventually. 'Let's take her stuff up to her room and she can slip it on there, in front of that tall mirror.'

Beth was genuinely delighted. How right Lachlan and Delia had been to have her come here and get to know these girls. No way they'd have been as relaxed and comfortable with her if Steve had been there too. Now, when the time came to talk to them about the Lord, they would be already on the way to becoming friends. They'd promised Delia and Lachlan that she and Steve would wait for their signal as to when it would be appropriate to start their mission in Tressock. The party they were being given up at the Morrison's place was apparently to be the venue. Some kind of castle it seemed; she'd just glimpsed it as they were driving into town. Steve, who'd had a better view, had said, 'holy shit!' and then, 'wow,' before she managed to give him a gentle kick. She hadn't wanted the Morrisons to think they were hicks.

By the time Mary and the girls had crowded into her cute but definitely small bedroom, Beth had taken off all her clothes except her bra and her panties and, after looking more closely at the dress, realised the bra would have to go too. Beth was feeling totally at home in Mary Hillier's house.

When she had finally struggled and squirmed her way into the dress, stretching her arms and her neck, shaking out her heavy, light brown hair, she delayed turning to look at herself in the mirror. She had been so relieved that, after years of dyeing it blond and forcing it to be straight and long, now that it was her real original hair again it fell once more in natural waves upon her shoulders. She drank in the expressions on the faces of Mary Hillier and the four young women as they stared at her as if in awe. Well, she thought, I must look pretty good in this dress, but that good? She turned to face the mirror.

It was a glorious dress and she felt beautiful in it. Really beautiful. But something in the looks of the girls, staring at her, awakened just an instant or two of disquiet. They had stopped chattering.

'Does everyone get to wear a dress like this?' asked Beth. 'I think it is just the most beautiful thing I ever wore.'

'The boys certainly don't,' laughed Sue nervously.

'A few will wear the kilt,' added Bella.

'No, no, Beth. You are wearing the Queen of the May's coronation dress,' said Mary Hillier. 'But everyone makes themselves something pretty nice for the coronation. That was what the girls were working on when you arrived.'

'Only Deirdre made this?' asked Beth, as she took off the dress. 'Congratulations, honey. You should be designing for some big fashion house.'

'To be honest, everyone got in on the act,' said Deirdre. 'I just put a spell on it to make it lovelier.'

The other girls all giggled and Mary Hillier looked severe.

'One year,' said Chloe, 'the Queen was so big in the bust and bum department that all the seams had to be let out at the last minute.'

'And several gussets put in,' added Bella.

'Allowing you to try on the dress was exceptional, Beth,' said Mary. 'Please don't tell anyone. But Sir Lachlan and Lady Morrison rather hope that you'll consent to be nominated for election as our May Queen this year. I know they want to ask you themselves.'

Beth was amazed. Her first instinct was to refuse. But she knew that there were many native peoples for whom refusal of a request like this one would be a signal for the hosts to take great offence. This was reputed to be the case with the families of Mexican immigrant help back in Texas. Beth had heard of cases where people, asked to one of their weddings, had refused to eat some delicacy that looked real yucky but which had been specially saved for them. It was immediately clear that the hosts had been deeply offended.

Without those accents and weird customs you could almost imagine some of these Scots as mainstream Americans. More to the point, the Queen's dress was just the most beautiful costume she had ever had an opportunity to wear. Nor was it in any way, shape or form overtly sexy. All the clothes made for her performances stateside were designed to accentuate her breasts, show off her navel, sit tight over her ass, show her inner thighs almost all the way up to her tush. A girl singer went on stage these days like some twenty-first century Delilah, only without the veils. This Queen of the May dress was super feminine. Sure, it plumped up her tits but that look was, like, historic. Otherwise it was just beautiful. A fairy queen's dress. If she decided to play along with this election for Queen of their festival they'd be that much happier to listen to her and Steve talk to them about the Lord. Beth had decided.

'Why, when I think about it,' she said at last, swirling the skirt, with its cascade of little silver leaves and golden flowers, to and fro, in front of the mirror, 'I think I am just going to have to say "yes," I am real grateful for the honour. But you mentioned an election, Mary?'

'If Sir Lachlan and Lady Morrison nominate you... take it from me, you'll be elected,' said Mary, smiling.

'Snakes alive! What am I doing?' Beth suddenly exclaimed. 'You guys must want to try on this wonderful dress too'

Putting on a robe she was handed by Mary Hillier, Beth did not see the look of horror that flickered briefly over the girls' faces.

'Only the Queen ever wears that dress,' said Mary Hillier pleasantly but firmly.

Before she went to bed, Beth read carefully through the concordant section of her Redeemers' Bible to check out nuclear and to see if there was anywhere the Lord took a position on it. There was no record of its being mentioned anywhere, not even in Revelations, where you might have expected to find it, nor in the chapter where the Cities of the Plains had all those problems. It was almost eleven when she asked Mary Hillier if she could call Delia.

'Of course,' said her surprised hostess. 'But don't you think it's a bit late?'

'I know,' said Beth. 'And I feel bad about that. But it is something I promised to do.'

Delia came on the line clearly thinking that this unexpected call signalled some sort of crisis at Mary Hillier's, that the so-far remarkably amenable young Beth had thrown what she called 'a wobbly'.

'My dear Beth, what can I do for you?' she asked, when Mary handed the phone over to her young charge.

'I thought you would like to know that I have checked out nuclear and it's OK. There are no what Terry, my teacher, calls 'contra-indications' in the Good Book that I could find. I heard you say something about not being able to take the suspense of not knowing and wanted to like tell you it's OK just as soon as I could. Not to worry. Good night. Sleep well.'

'Thank you for calling,' said Delia with what sounded to Beth like a choke in her voice. Relief, no doubt. Beth was glad she'd made that call.

The Devil Makes a Call

MAIN STREET IN Tressock that night was misty, almost to the point of fog. Outside the Police Station, where the lights shone hazily through the drawn blinds, the figure of Jack standing close to one of the windows, as if he hoped to hear something from within, seemed as insubstantial as a wraith. After a few minutes, Nevermore fluttered down and joined him, settling on his shoulder. Then Jack made his way to the pub, entering by the back door which led to the very basic, breezy and smelly men's toilet, and disappeared inside.

From the front of the building, the Grove Inn had a much more beckoning air. A dense creeper covered half the grey stone building, having had to be trimmed away from the windows. But a honey-coloured light shone from these, making the whole place seem like a welcoming lantern from the dank gloom outside. Music and high-pitched chatter filtered out into the night.

Inside the inn, Steve was holding court, standing at the bar. So many people wanted to speak to him, shake his hand, buy him another Coke. Nothing like this had ever happened to him. It was like he was suddenly famous. But he knew that simply wasn't so. He was just the guy who had accompanied Beth Boothby into town. He was just a cowboy. Of course to be a cowboy at all was rare enough these days, but these folks couldn't know that. He told jokes he wouldn't have dared repeat back home, they were so old. But these guys laughed like he'd suddenly turned into Steve Martin. He kept off the war. No one seemed to want to talk about that anyways. There were a lot who were interested in his quarter horses back home. It seemed everyone here rode horseback and had some kind of mount.

The little band had packed up, but a plump little lady he'd seen at the bar, swallowing some kind of red wine like she really needed it bad, was now seated at the piano and had started to play and to sing. She had one of those rich voices you heard sometimes, fuelled by wine, mellowed by tobacco, that could deliver a song so it kind of flowed out of her mouth like molasses.

> 'I tempted him with apples, all golden in the light
> He laid me in the orchard, till the day turned into night
> And since he plucked my cherry, all red and juicy ripe
> To savour all the fruits of me is his delight.'

Steve decided that a folk song sung like a torch song was something he'd have liked to hear Beth try, particularly with those words. It made him almost laugh out loud to think of it. But instead he yawned and, making his excuses, made his way towards the stairs and bed. Oddly, everyone in the crowded bar seemed to notice that he was leaving, going to bed. Something like silence fell. A chorus of 'Good night, Steve,' 'Sleep well, Steve,' followed him. The woman at the piano watched him all the time with her big brown eyes. As he climbed the stairs, he looked down for an instant at her cleavage. Big breasts. Like fruits indeed. But the Lord recalled him with an image of Beth's pert, much littler, probably much firmer tits. He felt the silver ring on his finger and walked determinedly on.

In his room he could still hear the song. Peter, the innkeeper, knocked on the door to ask if he had everything he needed. He had. They exchanged cheery good nights. The room had a big four-poster bed and a feather mattress. Steve's grandmother had one of those, he remembered from visiting her as a child. You could jump into it and sink so deep no one could see you or find you. He hauled off his shirt and shucked off his jeans, just kept on his T-shirt and his under shorts and sat down to haul off his precious boots. Beth had bought him those at Neiman Marcus in Dallas and he knew they cost her an arm and a leg because they were made of at least three different kinds of leather. Calf, gator and – he couldn't remember the name of the other.

He took his grey suit, the one they'd bought for him to go door-to-door, out from his case and went to hang it in the big mahogany closet. He opened the door and almost fell back – as something winged and black flew right out of the closet at him, flapping wildly, cawing. The raven. Jack was next. Right behind the bird. He was making a hideous face, leaping right out at Steve, shouting as he came:

'I am Beelzebub, Prince of Darkness,
Lord of the Flies, Devil Incarnate.
I will make you drunk on black wine.
I'll bend you to my implacable will.
Till your miserable soul is all mine.'

Jack's hands grabbed at Steve's chin. It was a gesture not so much sexual as proprietorial, like the slave owner's grasping for his human property. Or so Steve, his mind reeling, the shock only now giving way to a powerful rush of adrenalin, felt as he drew back his right fist and drove it with all his might straight into Jack's face. He was sure he was smiting the Devil.

Jack was catapulted back into the closet, where he collapsed amidst a shower of metal clothes hangers. The crash resonated all through the inn. His nose was pouring blood and one of his eyes was starting to close. He seemed also to have cut his lip. Steve looked at him with anguish. What had he done? Devil or no Devil, violence was never the way. And this guy was borderline crazy. Downstairs they'd like told him this. Warned him even. Crazy but harmless.

'Forgive me Lord, please forgive me,' he prayed. 'I just didn't know what I was doing. Like I couldn't have stopped myself doing it. Are you OK, Jack? Gee I'm really, really sorry. I didn't mean to...'

But by now Peter McNeil was by Steve's side with Danny and Carl close behind. One of them got a wet towel from the bathroom and applied it to Jack's face, while Peter was examining Steve's hand, which had been cut, probably by Jack's teeth.

'Steve,' Peter was saying. 'I am – we all are – terribly sorry. Of course you hit him. Anyone would. He loves jumping out of cupboards and surprising people. It's his favourite sport.'

'He kept saying he was the Devil,' Steve almost moaned. 'He kept on saying it. Oh Lord I can see it now. He was tempting me to hit him. And I failed the test, Lord. Please, please forgive me. I punched him good. I really ain't worthy of this mission Lord. I just hate to think what Beth will think of me when she hears of this.'

Danny and Carl started to get Jack to his feet when suddenly his previously pliable body went quite rigid. He stared around at them, knowing that he now had their attention, but it was to Steve, or rather his hat, that he now spoke – in his sepulchral tone:

'Her fate with thine was intertwined,
So spake it in his inner mind
Each orbed on each a baleful star
Each proved the other's blight and bar
Each unto each were best, most far
Yea each to each was worse than foe:
Thou a scared dullard, gibbering low
AND SHE AN AVALANCHE OF WOE!'

'Stop that, Jack. Stop it!' shouted Peter McNeil. 'Take him to my flat and clean him up, please Danny. Put him under the cold shower if he goes on like that. I'll be there in a minute. Soon as I've seen that poor Steve is OK.'

Danny and Carl did as they were asked, half-carrying Jack who, having delivered his jeremiad, went quietly enough, contenting himself with laughing until he gave himself loud hiccups that could be heard all over the inn.

'Are you OK, Steve?' Peter's deep concern was certainly real.

Steve felt far from OK. But he very much wanted to be alone so that he could sort out his emotions, so he could try and figure what this terrible and totally unexpected incident meant.

'He's just crazy, right?' he asked, hoping for some guidance from Peter.

'He is quite a different kind of human being from you or me, Steve. Something happened to his brain, probably when he was a baby. All sorts of possible emotions and abilities were wiped out. But that left others that have developed beyond those of any normal, every-day person. His memory is extraordinary…'

'And he tries to tell the future?' Steve was anxious to know. Was Beth supposed to be his avalanche of woe? Was this the Oracle thing speaking? What could this – crazy guy really know?

'He knows nothing, Steve. He gets his kicks persuading people he knows. He can't relate to others normally. So at least by playing the oracle he feels he is having an effect on others. Don't let him have any kind of effect on you. What he said was pure gibberish. Put it out of your mind.'

Steve decided that he must be alone to think it through so he reassured Peter that he was OK, and to quote what the waiters in the hotel had kept saying every time he or Beth asked for something, he echoed, 'No problem at all, Peter.'

Woe was not a word Steve had ever used. But his grandmother, she of the four-poster feather bed, was an Irish woman, born in a place called Mayo, who used to give Steve's grandad a real hard time whenever he bet most of his pay packet on some catastrophe of a horse. She told little Steve that his grandad only bet on three-legged horses. The only four-legged one he'd ever backed won big time and from then on in he was hooked.

'Woe, woe,' she would say to the old cowboy. 'You bring nothing but woe on us all.'

So the prophecy of an avalanche of woe was not something to look forward to if you were at all superstitious. However, Steve decided, after some prayer and a long conversation on the telephone with Beth, that he was not superstitious, that those who trusted in the Lord regarded all that oracle stuff as pagan bullshit. To liberate the people of Tressock from such superstitions was part of their Redeemer mission. Looked at like that, everything seemed cool again to Steve and he slept the deep sleep of a man who is secure in the belief that he is still captain of his own fate.

The Rehearsal

HE'D BEEN AFRAID that he would dream of Jack leaping out of closets at him. But, in so far as Steve could remember, as he was awakened next morning, his dream had been of the voluptuous lady at the piano who seemed to have been sharing his bed with a variety of juicy fruits scattered about her ample person. He knew that he felt guilty about allowing her to wallow beside him in this way, particularly as Lachlan Morrison himself seemed to be recalling him to consciousness.

'Steve! Steve! Wake up! Wake up!' Lachlan was shouting.

As he leapt from the bed, in the mistaken belief that Lachlan was in or about to be in the room, he heard the unmistakable neigh of a horse. He rushed to open the window. The first thing that met his eyes was Lolly sitting on a fine grey horse with a rather impatient looking Prince on a leading rein. Right next to them, sitting in an antique car (he was later to hear from Lolly that it was a 1936 Bull Nosed Bentley) was Lachlan dressed for the office.

'Good morning, Steve,' he shouted. 'You'll remember Lolly? We thought you might like to be introduced to the countryside around here so we brought Prince for you to ride. Lolly'll show you the sights. Alright with you?'

'Alright!' Steve shouted down. 'That is – just great! Thank you, sir. I'll be right down.'

A man or a woman who loves horses can love other men and women, that goes without saying. But the bond there can be between a human being and a horse, for those who truly understand these beautiful animals and love them, is unlike any other. Sheep dogs, gun dogs, hunting dogs, even lap dogs come close in their relationships with humans. But a person who is completely comfortable on the back of a horse, for whom the act of riding is as if the person and the animal were fused into one almost indivisible creature, moves, however briefly, in another dimension. To have achieved this fusion is wonderful in itself. For that wonder to last means it has become addictive. Steve had been an addict since only a few years after he had learned to walk.

Hauling on his clothes, splashing water on his unshaven face, Steve gave not a thought to Beth or the Lord that morning. After several long days of dealing with people he was once more going to be in his element. As he almost ran out of the inn, with no thought of coffee or breakfast, he took one look at that black beauty and thought – what a horse! And then there was Lolly.

As the rest of Tressock awoke; as Lachlan changed gears noisily and the Bentley roared and grumbled its way out of town; as the distant hooter at Nuada signalled the change of shifts at the power station; as Steve and Lolly rode across the bridge over the Sulis and headed for the hills beyond; as all this activity stirred, Mary Hillier's household was already bustling with busy girls working hard on their May Day dresses.

Beth came down into the eat-in kitchen wearing a Japanese cotton kimono, the kind you can buy for two dollars in Hawaii, her hair still wrapped in a towel after her shower. She had just completed a long and complex prayer. She was beginning to believe that she would one day, like the Rev. Pat Robertson, be able to have a dialogue with the Lord. Right now, satisfied that the Lord was approving of the course of action she and Steve were taking, she was ready for coffee and hoping for eggs.

'Good morning, Beth,' said Mary. 'There's tea over there. Or coffee if you don't mind instant.'

Beth didn't care for British tea. Iced tea back home was OK, but it was an odd thing about these people, she thought, that they ate or drank everything at the wrong temperature. Instant coffee at least gave you a shot of much needed caffeine, even if it tasted blah. Beer was warm, she'd heard. The OJ Mary poured her was tepid. To her relief she was handed a carton of fresh eggs and told to cook them any way she liked. Beth couldn't cook much, at home. Vashti did all that. But eggs were Beth's speciality. She made a big fluffy omelette and was flattered that the girls, and even Mary, all wanted to have a taste.

'Can I call Steve again at the inn, Mary?' she asked. They'd spoken the night before about the guy he'd hit, with good reason she thought, although she didn't say that. She wanted to tell him about the May Queen dress and to plan the day.

'Why certainly. You know where the phone is,' said Mary, who was putting finishing touches to the Queen of the May dress.

'He might not be there right now, Beth,' said Bella. 'I hear Sir Lachlan has leant him Prince to go riding with Lolly this morning.'

Beth felt irritated at this news, almost angry. What made it worse was that she knew it was irrational to not want Steve riding around on horses together with that Lolly. She forced herself to just shrug and give them all the smile.

'It's all part of their plan, Beth,' Mary was saying. 'Sir Lachlan and Lady Morrison's plan. They're hoping that Steve can be persuaded to be the Laddie this year so that he can be the one to crown you Queen of the May.'

Steve knew all about English saddles, had seen them used in Texas, but had never had an opportunity to do more than just sit in one to see what it felt like. Used to his legs stretched long in the stirrups, having them shortened so that his knees bent and the toes of his precious boots turned up was going to be a novelty. But Lolly, who helped him get the length just right, seemed to think that he would have no trouble getting used to it. Nor did he. The delicacy of Prince's mouth was another thing. The horse's response to the slightest pressure on the bit made Steve soon lighten the use of his hands on the reins.

As they rode out of town, across the bridge over the Sulis River, splashing through the water meadows that bordered it, through yellow carpets of marsh marigolds, slowly moving onto higher dryer grazing land, Steve realized what he hadn't really considered before, that these horses, his magnificent gelding Prince, and Lolly's feisty little grey mare Pompadour, were bred for hunting, for jumping over everything from stone walls to five-bar gates – led by hounds in full cry – in pursuit of deer or fox.

He had his pony jump things as a kid, but cattle didn't jump so there was little call for cowboys to do so. So he let Lolly take the lead at the first dry-stone wall that barred their way. He watched her lean into the jump as she gave Pompadour her head. It seemed effortless and indeed it wasn't very high. Prince followed with a vigour that took Steve by surprise. His backside left the saddle and he lost one of the stirrups for a moment, but the horse had cleared the wall as if he was jumping a much higher obstacle and Steve had entirely recovered himself before Lolly turned to look at her pupil.

Next it was a long gallop side by side uphill towards some woods. She watched him jump a deep ditch, letting the eager Prince lead the way. Steve felt much more in command this time; he was beginning to feel at one with the horse.

Riding was second nature to him. They talked horses. He learned that his saddle was 'straight cut', in other words without much padding. Old-fashioned these days, but designed for hunting. He told her about his quarter horses back home. She confided that Pompadour had been, 'a great head tosser, if you'll forgive the expression. But we disciplined her with a Martingale.' Steve looked at Lolly, after she'd said this. Looked at her straight. She was laughing. A wonderful bawdy, chuckling laugh. Her whole face lit up with her amusement, particularly her eyes. Steve had noticed that laughter was never far away for her.

'A head tosser?' Steve knew perfectly well what she meant, but he liked the sudden sexual tension she had introduced between them. She certainly was one extraordinarily sexy woman.

'Oh you know what I mean, Steve!' she tossed her head, and flicking her reins so Pompadour's bit tightened suddenly, the mare tossed her head too.

'Guess so,' he acknowledged, laughing. 'So where are we going?'

'Lachlan thought you might like to see the route the Laddie takes when we do the Border Riding. By the way, England is only five miles away just over those hills.'

They had gained altitude and could see the little town of Tressock clustered close to where the river Sulis meandered through the water meadows to curl round the castle like a silvery crook in the spring sunshine. Behind the castle, pale purple and green hills stretched under grey clouds blowing in from the chilly North Sea. Beyond that lay the land of the ancient enemy. To Steve this view was but a pretty picture that belonged in a movie, yet not so pretty that it seriously distracted him from the discovery of Lolly.

'Who is the Laddie?' he asked.

'Och, you've never heard tell of the Laddie?' Lolly seemed as surprised as if he'd never heard of Pete Sampras or Muhammad Ali. 'He's always the brightest and best. The handsomest, the goodliest, the kindest... perhaps the best rider. I have known him to be the best lover...'

'No, I mean what is his name?' asked Steve. 'Does he live in Tressock?'

'Didn't Lachlan tell you? Lots of Border towns have them; Selkirk, Hawick, Kelso and others, but ours is a bit different. The Laddie is elected, chosen each year. Like the May Queen. She's the real star of course, but it's the Laddie that crowns her and it is he who spends the day and the night by her side. Suppose she was your friend, Beth? Wouldn't you want to be her Laddie?'

'Beth? May Queen? What the hell is that?' Steve thought the whole idea was so weird he could hardly take it in. He just knew that he really didn't want to think about Beth right now that he'd met Lolly. She had actually said that this Laddie guy – she'd known him to be the best lover. Sounded like she put out big time.

'Is this like the prom at high school? Most popular gal goes with most popular guy?' he asked, because it sure sounded like it.

'Well, a bit different from that. May Day is the spring feast round here. As important to us as your Christmas is to you. But you got the general idea. Look, if they were riding after the Laddie today, you could see it all from up there. C'mon, I'll show you.'

Lolly had pointed to a higher eminence across some upland pastures divided, in some places, by hedges and littered, here and there, with boulders. She turned her horse and spurred it into a gallop as if to challenge Steve to ride just as hard up to their objective.

Perhaps Lolly already knew that he would, this morning, follow her almost anywhere. She gave not a glance backward as Steve really put Prince to the test. They cleared several clusters of rocks, passed some Aberdeen Angus cattle who peered at them lazily, the horses stretching themselves to a pounding speed between jumps. Then, almost hidden in a declivity in the pasture, came a hawthorne hedge. Steve, hugely exhilarated by this chase, had taken his hat off and held it flapping in the wind when the hedge was suddenly upon him. Prince didn't wait for any signal from his rider. He simply soared up and over. But the other side of the hedge was a drainage ditch, quite wide and deep. Prince almost stumbled, stretching to avoid it. The stumble was sufficiently severe to catapult Steve out of his saddle and into a somersaulting landing in a pile of cow pats.

Lolly had just reached the summit of the hill, a hundred yards beyond where Steve had fallen. She turned Pompadour just in time to see Prince nuzzling the recumbent figure of Steve, who was lying flat on his back. Appalled at what had happened, she rode back down the hill as fast as the mare could carry her. But just as she arrived level with Prince and slipped out of her saddle, she found Steve talking to the horse, and starting to stand up while trying to wipe some of the cow dung off himself with tufts of grass and handfuls of dock leaves.

'Sorry to leave you sudden like that, partner,' he was saying. 'But I didn't figure you were goin' to do that. Leastways, not in quite that way.'

Before Lolly had time to speak, he was back up in Prince's saddle and stretching what was certainly a rather sore back. Then they trotted the horses up to the summit of what Lolly called the Laird's Hill and she described the ritual ride of the Laddie to him, all the while wondering whether she had his full attention on what she was saying. Because, while he seemed to be listening, and asked the more or less appropriate questions, he was feeling an urge to touch her, to stop her mouth describing any more of this insane local ritual – with a long lingering kiss.

'We give the Laddie three minutes, start from outside the Grove Inn over there, opposite the church,' she was saying.

'Who's we?' asked Steve.

'Anyone with a mount, a horse, a pony; a carthorse would do if that is all you can find,' she said, 'I reckon you'd see a racing ostrich if one was around.'

'Kids?' asked Steve.

'We don't really have any kids. But if we did, sure. D'you see that island in the river Sulis over there – where the steam is rising from the pool? That's known as the King's Island. The Laddie has to get there without our catching him and then he's won.'

'Betcha I can get there before you!'

Steve was aching to race her. Anything to quench his mounting desire. Lolly looked genuinely hesitant.

'Are you scared for Prince?' he asked her. 'I promise I'll take good care of him. He and I made a deal. If he's goin' to dump me again it'll be in that nice soft old river. Then he can have a swim too.'

Lolly suddenly nodded her head and spurred Pompadour down the hill towards the Sulis. She gave a little shout of laughter as she did this and Steve, trying to gather Prince for the start, knew that the joke was on him for thinking she'd play fair.

But then she knew that he had much the more powerful horse. Quite apart from being at least two hands taller than the grey mare, Prince's bloodlines stemmed from champion steeplechasers. Without her stolen lead it would have been a most uneven contest. Even so, Steve showed that he was a quick learner. He revelled in the jumps he and Prince were able to achieve and he found the horse's speed on the flat, as they approached the river, to rival that of any horse he'd ridden back in Texas. Best of all, he won. Plunging Prince into the steaming river and emerging onto the little island, he turned to see Lolly just approaching the further bank.

At the Sacred Pool

THE ISLAND CONSISTED of a lush field of long grass, its banks lined with bull rushes and several willow trees weeping into the fast moving, vapouring Sulis. In its centre was some collapsed masonry, part of what might once have been a temple. It rather resembled a crude throne. Both Lolly and Steve dismounted, tethering their horses loosely to a bush and a willow respectively, allowing them to graze.

'So you won, Steve,' she called through the mist. 'You'd make a good Laddie.'

'I won?' laughed Steve. 'Prince won! Isn't Sulis, like, the name of some kind of goddess?'

'How d'you know that?'

'I already met up with Sulis,' said Steve, 'on the front of Lachlan's Rolls. I didn't realise goddesses could be that cute.'

'I'm glad you approved of her. I posed for that little statue. It was a great honour... I like to come here and swim, especially when the air is cold like this morning – besides this is a sacred spring.'

Steve now had the uncanny feeling that he was dreaming, that nothing he was seeing or hearing was quite real. As an average young man, even one committed to the Silver Ring Thing, he managed to desire several women every week. A waitress here, a girl in the Seven Eleven store there, a cheerleader seen at a football game. But even though he might visit them in his waking imagination or in his dreams, he never hoped for them to materialise, to throw off their clothes and beckon him on. Why? Because he knew it was just lust. And although this was, he admitted, a convoluted way of looking at it, the Lord never rewarded lust.

But here was Lolly taking off her shirt and riding britches, her bra and her panties, as naturally and unhurriedly as anyone who had no other motive but that they were getting ready to plunge in for a swim. She looked ethereally beautiful in the mist, like one of those nymphs you'd see in very old Coca-Cola ads. This was not 'come and get it' nudity like you saw at the Big Bamboo club in Fort Worth, where the girls writhed down a slithery steel pole from the ceiling to bumps and grinds music. Notatall! This – hell, she, Lolly was beautiful and if she was doing this for anybody – well, he was that anybody.

Still he must cling to reality. He was here on a mission with Beth. They were Redeemers come to save people like Lolly.

'I think you're kidding us with all this Goddess shit,' he forced himself to say. He feared the spell he thought she was casting upon him. The cruder his denunciation the safer he'd feel from its effect. He went on: 'I guess you think Beth and me, we're a couple of retards. You're just kidding me – right? It's just a hot spring, Yeah, I think I can smell the sulphur – right?'

But Lolly had started to part the reeds and walk into the river.

'You believe a certain virgin had a baby don't you?' Lolly paused, splashing her body with the warm water, before she went on:

'You probably believe that your God made the world and everything in it in seven days; that your Jesus fed five thousand people on those few little loaves and fishes – why can't you believe, as I do, that this water has a holy power?'

'I believe everything that is in the Bible, Lolly. That's Holy Writ. But, I am sorry, this is just hot water.'

'People don't just bathe in it, Steve. They drink it. Some people say drinking it makes them horny as hell. Others say simply that it makes wishes come true.'

Lolly had now plunged into the river and risen to the surface, breasting the ripples of the lightly turbulent water, gleaming with its salinity.

'C'mon in Steve! It'll make you feel literally out of this world. Are you thinking about Beth? I can let you into a secret. Lachlan wants her to be the May Queen. How would you like to be the Laddie?'

Beth was definitely on Steve's mind. Beth who wasn't there and need never know. He found himself getting out of his clothes as if impelled to do so. As if it was simply the thing to do. Like rubbing noses with the Inuit or smashing your glasses into the fireplace after toasts if you were – who did that – he'd seen it in a vodka commercial – a Russian? And this, in Steve's current case, without the benefit of alcohol.

'If they'd let me ride Prince – hey, I'd be their Laddie in a New York minute.'

He was developing a million goose bumps and it made him shiver.

'Lolly! Are we insane? This isn't Texas. It is cooooold.'

'Not in here it isn't,' she said.

Steve stared at her for a full minute, as if enchanted. Then he plunged in, surfacing a few feet away from her. He stared again, but this time it was no longer a disbelieving stare but a devouring one. She opened her arms to him and they came together.

His embrace was both passionate and urgent. The tiny scintilla of doubt that this was real never entirely left his mind, but she found ways to channel his passion and calm his frantic urgency.

'No hurry, Steve,' she whispered. 'The Goddess is with us. She'll make it last and last so you'll always remember it – till your dying day.'

Enclosing him in her arms, her hair floating around his face, she seemed to engulf him so that they drifted in the misty water like languorous flotsam.

A Tressock fisherman, a retired clockmaker, was walking along the path on the far side from where Steve now lay, with Lolly kneeling beside him, both of them still naked, still steaming, although the day itself was warming as the sun shone fitfully from a mackerel sky. They were hazy figures, seen across the steamy water. He blessed them as he blessed everyone who had shared in the Goddess's bounty. He hoped she would now give him a trout or two in the cooler water just up stream.

Steve, his head comfortably cradled on a tussock, saw Lolly's smiling face and wild, wind-blown hair so close to his that he thought 'now is the moment to remember every mole and freckle, every pore, every golden mote in her hazel eyes, the gap in her strong white teeth. What a face! What a woman! What a place!'

'You were right,' he said. 'I did think it might go on for ever. I guess I hoped it would.'

He had the odd feeling that Lolly too was committing his face to memory, as one might a map.

'I always hope for something I know even the Goddess Sulis cannot give me – a child,' she said. 'And yet I cannot help hoping. If it ever happens – I know it will have been here.'

'My God, a child! Did you say "always"?' Steve had absorbed so many shocks in such a short time that this 'always' seemed to introduce a reality he had not even considered before. How dumb was that, cowboy? He looked hard at Lolly, wishing it not to be so.

'Oh yes, Steve,' she said, her smiling eyes still smiling. 'I am what the Goddess wants me to be. All things to all men.'

The old clockmaker had settled at a point on the river bank where he had noticed another fisherman, a great grey-blue heron, often worked the river. It was a nice quiet place. Peaceful. But that peace was suddenly shattered by shouts from the direction of the loving couple. The man was rampaging about the place as he hurriedly dressed. The woman remained naked, calmly watching him and laughing a wonderful chuckling laugh. Lolly of course. It had to be Lolly.

'All things to all men! Yeah, we got a word for that back in Texas.

And it aint purty,' the young man had raised his voice.

The clockmaker shook his head. *All things to all men* – a student of Scottish literature, it made him think of Robert Louis Stevenson: 'You will find some of these expressions rise on you like a remorse. They are merely literary and decorative...' But the clockmaker was not a cynic. He had known Lolly since her girlhood. She had become much more than the sum of her lovely parts. He was just congratulating himself for this happy thought when there was a tug at his line. It was a splendid pike and now his poor wife was condemned to making *quenelles de brochet*, a delicious dish but an awesome one to prepare on account of the numerous bones. Happily, the fisherman's wife was French, a cousin of Daisy up at the castle. She would welcome the challenge, he thought fondly.

Meanwhile, Steve and Lolly rode back to Tressock, each silently thinking their own private thoughts. As they entered the town, she put her hand out towards him and, after a moment's hesitation, he rested the reins in the crook of his arm and took her hand and squeezed it. They smiled at each other, two tired people at the end of an unusual journey.

It was when he gently retrieved his hand that he remembered his silver ring. It was gone.

Nuada Keeps its Secret

IN THE ECONOMY of Scotland nuclear power is a contentious commodity, as it is in many other nations, big and small. The French have managed to rely heavily upon it and, so far, no disaster has befallen them. In the United States, with its many earthquake zones and its prevailing fear of terror, nuclear has not fared well. The lands of the old Soviet Union have had their disasters and are likely to have more. How Nuada came to be built, using private and public finance, is a complex story in itself, much of it concerned with the fluctuating market in other competitive forms of fuel. That it survived, it owes to past governments not wishing to put all their power-generating eggs in one basket, and to the fact that a hostile Green movement and an ambivalent press had so far found no glaring fault with it.

The presiding genius of Nuada was Sir Lachlan – it was built on his land; lobbied for by him at the local and United Kingdom ministerial levels. He had been unique among the chairmen of atomic plants in Britain in that he had displayed an evangelising zeal for the technology. No one had come nearer to describing the power of the atom as a kind of revelation of the god-head than this Borders laird. Even a much publicised accident at the plant a few years ago had been brilliantly handled with a PR operation personally directed by Lachlan.

As Steve was experiencing several different kinds of bliss with Lolly in the Sulis pool, the Nuada plant hummed with its usual activity. White-coated scientists monitored and measured and noted carefully on their networked hand computers. Engineers in hard hats roamed amongst the giant turbines, inspecting and testing. Bureaucrats and clerks, secretaries and analysts, anchored for the most part to their desktops, communicated with each other and the outside world by telephone, fax, e-mail and even the Royal Mail. Somewhere, few of these people could have told you exactly where, electricity was leaving Nuada for the national grid.

In the huge panelled chairman's suite that morning, a shirt-sleeved Lachlan was manning an overhead projector, clicking from bar chart to graph to carefully retouched photograph to optimistic conclusions written in several eye-catching colours, all part of his PowerPoint presentation. Sitting beside him at the board room table was the portly figure of Murdoch Craigie, area secretary of the Transport and Universal Workers Union, an official who had been born and bred in Tressock. Although his speeches at regional Trades Union congresses were noted for being savagely against the exploiting classes, treacherous landowners and other vermin, he had always known that, in an emergency such as this, his place was at Sir Lachlan's side, ready to repel boarders, as he put it.

The emergency sat on the other side of the board room table in the shape of two journalists from different publications, who seemed to think that there was a cover up going on at Nuada of a story that could close the power station if exploited in the right way. In addition to a telephone book-sized report that had been placed before each of them, two drams of Nuada Directors' eight year old malt whisky had been poured and the decanter unstoppered in case of need. Both their glasses were ready to be refilled.

'What you have before you,' said Lachlan, 'is the report on the work we have done, since the accident, to make the environment completely secure. You will naturally want to study this at your leisure – but I have asked you here to rebut some absolutely unfounded reports in the press… yes, Mr Tarrant?'

Magnus Tarrant, a rumpled journalist with a purple drinker's face had raised a chewed pencil in the air to attract Lachlan's attention.

'I think you may be referring to my story in last week's *Echo*,' he said. 'Thank you for the pretty pictures we just saw. The word is still that you haven't even begun to solve the nuclear pollution problem – people in Tressock are still not able to drink the tap water. Can you deny that?'

'Completely,' Lachlan was calm and precise in his answer. 'You're twice as likely to die of urban pollution in Glasgow or Edinburgh as we are here. The accident was regrettable – due to human error – and it took place ten long years ago.'

'My question, Sir Lachlan, was: Are the people of Tressock drinking the water out of their taps again?'

'Let me answer that for you, Sir Lachlan,' rumbled Murdoch. 'I speak as the Convenor of the TUWU here. Most people who work here are our members and live in Tressock. They clean their teeth in water. They wash their bairns' bottoms in it. They DRINK beer and whisky. But everyone drinks water too. Although I have to say that, like you, Magnus, I am no addicted to it.'

Meanwhile, Lachlan had used the overhead projector to put a large-scale map of the Tressock area on to the screen. The River Sulis could be seen running from west to east across the map. The topography was clearly marked. The river split and then rejoined itself, forming King's Island. It then wound through fields and woods till it reached Tressock, passing under a bridge on the main street, and then on, through more fields and woods, till it reached the Nuada Nuclear Power Plant. Beyond that, it joined the River Tweed for a short journey before it reached its mouth on the North Sea.

'The Sulis, life blood of our valley,' Lachlan's hand traced the progress of the river. 'As you can see our plant is downstream from Tressock.'

'He's telling you that water tends to run downhill,' interjected Murdoch. 'Sorry but these technicalities tend to get missed in the press.'

Magnus Tarrant, who was in the act of pouring himself some more of the Directors' malt, glared malevolently at Murdoch.

'The river helps in our cooling process at Nuada,' continued Lachlan. 'It was of course polluted by the accident, but only for twenty-four hours. We cleaned up the Sulis years ago.'

Lachlan looked around as if almost expecting applause, so sweetly reasonable had his explanation been. But his other journalist guest, one Patricia Gow, now leaned forward. In demeanour she was as calm and direct as Magnus had been combative. Her face, slightly raddled now, had once been beautiful, and she spoke in an attractive, persuasive voice.

'Well I quite understand you protesting my piece in the *Ecologist*; naught for your comfort there,' she said. 'However, will you not agree that nuclear power stations have had their day? Too expensive to build? Too costly to run? Too dangerous to live nearby?'

This lit an evangelical gleam in Lachlan's eyes.

'Patricia,' he said. 'The greatest power station in our galaxy, the Sun, is dangerous. It can create deserts, melt ice caps, give you cancer. We've lived with it since, according to Darwin, our ancestors crawled out of the primeval slime. It also brings life to almost everything on which it shines. Respect and understanding of these forces of nature is the key to controlling them. Nuclear is just one of them, but it is in so many ways key.'

'Can I quote you on your slimy ancestors?' asked Magnus.

'Our slimy ancestors,' corrected Lachlan with a smile.

Everyone joined in the laughter. The adversarial tension of the meeting had been broken. Lachlan and Murdoch knew they now lived to fight another day, but that such stories rarely went completely away.

A little later, Lachlan drove Murdoch and himself back to Tressock in his bull-nosed Bentley. They were in a festive mood.

'That Patricia said we're the best double act since Laurel and Hardy,' laughed Murdoch. 'After the accident, the press went on about the danger of a nuclear catastrophe. The lowlands laid waste. A no-go area. Now, suddenly, they start worrying about the water. Funny they never do their homework. A river is a river – but the water table is another thing. One flows. The other is static.'

'Journalists, thank heaven, have the attention span of wet hens,' said Lachlan. 'And that's when they're sober. Sick babies they might notice. Even deformed babies. But virtually no babies – no comment. So far... Hullo?'

Lachlan's mobile phone had rung. It was Delia to say that she was sitting in their bedroom by the window, where she had a clear view of the stables. Orlando, the policeman, was walking towards the stables where Lolly was grooming Prince and talking to Anthea.

'That Orlando worries me,' Delia said. 'He's been seen questioning Jack. He's on his way to the tack room. Lolly will cope, I know. But I wish you'd get back as soon as possible.'

'Nothing wrong with his going to see Lolly,' said Lachlan. 'She's giving him the treatment.'

'I remember when she gave me the treatment,' said Murdoch, smiling at the memory. 'I walked like a duck for a week.'

Lolly is Questioned

THE STABLE BLOCK at Tressock Castle was a long, two-storey, red-brick building close to the estate's great gates and at the town end of the Willies Walk. Lolly's quite sizeable apartment was on the upper floor, along with some studio flats for the other stable hands. Apart from Lachlan and Delia's own horses, a number of steeplechase brood mares were stabled there along with their foals.

When Orlando completed the short walk from the Police Station to the stable block he could see Lolly chatting to another girl at the far end of the paddock. Horses peered at him from their stables as he passed. He had a friend, a fellow cadet at Police College, who'd opted for the mounted unit of the Glasgow force when she graduated. Orlando had been curious about what the attraction to these, for him, almost prehistoric beasts was. His friend, a very plain girl called Hannah, had described them as a species you really had to know, so that you understood their psychology, to love them. 'But,' she added, 'I fell in love with them at first, because I thought – they're just so beautiful. Then I wanted to understand them. So I learnt about their psychology and now I love them even more.'

Orlando thought about his new and undoubted love for Lolly – however much she should disclaim and discourage it, he knew it was real. If she loved horses as she obviously did, then he must try and do so too. And, yes, they are beautiful, he decided. Lucky that she wasn't fixated on warthogs. But now he was getting close enough to her that she would soon notice his approach.

Lolly was grooming Prince while chatting to her friend Anthea, who was rubbing down the grey mare.

'So what's he like, the cowboy?' Anthea was asking.

'Anthea, he is really lovely. I'm terribly afraid I'm going to break my habits of a lifetime. I mean, lovely in a different way to...' there was a slight catch in Lolly's voice, which Anthea didn't miss.

'Orlando Orgassissimo?' she asked with a laugh, having teased Lolly about what she had heard. 'Not just another good stud?'

Lolly shook her head vehemently. But at that moment they noticed Orlando, who was already only a few yards away from them. Both women were on the verge of bursting into giggles. Lolly managed to control herself but Anthea was less successful and wheeled the grey mare round so she could hide behind her, while pretending to continue her grooming.

'Hello, Lolly!' said Orlando, wishing he could kiss her, but conscious of his uniform. 'I'm sorry if I'm interrupting something.'

'Not at all! We were just discussing our new stallion. What can I do for you? Is this a duty call?'

'It is. Lolly, you know this place so well. Has there ever been any sign of a cult around here? You know, a religious cult.'

Lolly was leading Prince into his stall, which was reached through the double doors that led from the tack room. Orlando realised that here the horses came first, and an apologetic smile from Lolly told him that he must wait till she had settled Prince in his stall. But then she came and kissed him lightly on the cheek.

'Did you sleep in this morning?' Lolly was affectionately solicitous. 'I called you to wake you, as you asked, but there was no answer. But in response to your question: religious cult? Well the Christian Kirk used to function when I was a little girl. Not any more of course.'

'No, a non-Christian cult. Witchcraft? Paganism? Anything like that?'

'Well ye-es there is.' she spoke quietly, almost in a whisper. 'But it is very, very secret and out of respect for the dead...'

She paused for so long that Orlando wondered if she had decided to end her revelation there.

'The dead?' Orlando cued her gently, willing her to continue.

'The person who was at the heart of it has died. Sad really, but perhaps all for the best.'

At this point, Anthea, having at last controlled her giggling and stabled the grey mare, came into the tack room in order to fetch a blanket for the animal. Orlando therefore lowered his voice. He felt he had made a breakthrough already. No point in pressuring her. They had a date tomorrow. Then it would all come out. Of that he was now positive.

'You can tell me tomorrow – I'm cooking us steaks,' he said, smiling. 'I don't know about you, but I think I'm going to need the protein.'

She smiled back. 'You Italians are so romantic,' she said.

After he had gone, Anthea returned to find her friend sitting on a bale of hay, looking rather gloomily out at the sky. A storm was brewing.

'It always rains right up to May Day and starts again right after,' said Anthea. 'Isn't that what people used to call a miracle? What's his name? The cowboy?'

'Steve.' Lolly sounded slightly panicked. 'Anthea, I can't get him out of my mind. Do you think there's something wrong with me?'

'Not necessarily,' said Anthea, rather wistfully. 'I feel like that about Carl and he doesn't know I'm alive. But variety has always been the spice of life for you. Perhaps Sulis has taken matters into her own hands. Steve bathed with you in the pool, you said. What will you do if you are pregnant?'

'Well I'll know it wasn't Orlando. He's very careful, bless him.'

To Anthea's and indeed to her own astonishment, Lolly's eyes started to fill with tears.

'Steve. It did cross my mind. Oh Sulis, could you have done that for me?'

Anthea looked closely at her friend.

'You don't do love, do you?' she asked. 'I mean as far as I know you never have. So what's going on? I've always thought of you as being as close to the Goddess as it's possible for a mere human female to be. Capricious, ruthless, a sort of sexual pioneer forging paths for the rest of us to try and follow.'

This drew a bitter little laugh from Lolly.

'What paths? You've always said you want four perfect, absolutely normal children and Carl for a husband – if Sulis would allow it. If not – a beautiful stallion would make a very good substitute.'

'True. But I am always hopelessly in love with just one man. You're never in love. Or are you?'

'Oh, Anthea. It may just be some kind of virus. It could not have come at a worse time. But all I can think of is Steve, Steve, Steve and I've got to spend tomorrow evening with Orlando.'

'From what I heard, there could be worse fates. Sulis will help you. She always has. I suppose I'm glad to hear you are a little more mortal than I thought you were.'

Lolly put out her tongue at her friend and went up to her flat to change.

Goldie

AMONG THE MANY *duties of an officer who wishes to gain the sympathy and support of the civilian population is helping pet animals in distress. While the Royal Society for the Prevention of Cruelty to Animals can always be called, an officer gains merit from personally performing simple acts of succour or rescue.*

Admittedly, this excellent advice from the Police College handbook is seldom followed. But in rare cases, where a zealous officer is anxious to make a good impression, it is possible to see a constable risking both dignity and severe injury by climbing a tree to rescue a cat. Such was the scene later that day in Tressock, where Orlando was balanced precariously on the branch of a sycamore tree, situated (as he was to put in his report) on the corner of Wallace Street and Dunblane Avenue. The feline in question was a marmalade orange colour, and, according to the tag on her collar, answered to the name of Goldie.

At the foot of the tree, several elderly female citizens of Tressock, led by Mrs Menzies, variously shouted advice, encouragement, and occasional criticism at both Orlando and Goldie, as the attempted rescue progressed. Eventually, a severely scratched Orlando managed to grab Goldie by the scruff of her neck and negotiating his descent with only one spare hand, arrived on terra firma to the applause of the ladies.

He immediately held out the cat to his audience, assuming one of them would claim her. To his considerable annoyance, none of them were prepared to admit ownership of Goldie. Even Mrs Menzies, who had alerted him to the cat's plight, denied having any idea who the owner might be.

'Tom always took any strays back to the Police Station,' she informed him.

'And if they weren't claimed within a week he very often stuffed them,' shrilled a blue-rinsed lady with a very high voice.

'He did not!' shouted Mrs Menzies. 'Don't you listen to her. Our Tom loved pet animals. He only stuffed wild ones. That's part of the taxidermist's hypocritic oath. Like a doctor's, that is.'

'You're right there; anything wild and regardless of gender,' said Blue Rinse. 'Particularly young owls, from what I've heard.'

The other women looked at Blue Rinse, plainly appalled at this allegation, and started a chorus of protest. Orlando, seeing no point in getting involved in this increasingly acrimonious conversation, made his way to the Police Station with Goldie now clinging to him as if they were long lost friends. But young owls? That was the sort of remark that made Orlando wonder whether inbreeding had made these people loopier than city folk.

Jack's pet raven, Nevermore, sat perched in the belfry of the Tressock church watching out for his patron. Fifty or sixty other ravens chattered and fussed and preened themselves and sometimes each other all over the belfry and the old clock's workings. Apart from a few slats of wood, covered with slates, it was open to the air. The time for the evening feed was close, but there was as yet no sign of Jack. Sometimes he emerged from the inn and sometimes from his home up the road towards the bridge. You could never be quite sure. Between feed times all the ravens made trips to the town dump, where they competed with the seagulls for the bonanza of scraps which arrived each day.

Today, Nevermore had watched an unusual occurrence, the movement of almost everyone in the town to the inn, where groups of them gazed out of the window. Jack didn't seem to be amongst them. Many others had crowded into the side streets behind the inn. Jack wasn't among these either. The great clock below the ravens was very soon going to strike the hour.

Then, all alone, carrying a well-known, extremely dangerous and unpleasant cat, came the man with the shiny badge on his helmet and shiny silver buttons on his clothes. At this point, another man, still not Jack, came out of the inn to talk to the man carrying the loathsome cat. They talked for a minute or two. Then the shiny buttoned man went on his way and disappeared from view while the other man went back to the inn. Almost immediately after that, everybody left the bar by a side door and, joined by all the people in the side streets, made their way by a back gate into the Tressock Castle grounds, and headed for the big house.

Nevermore could now hear the machinery of the clock winding itself up to strike the hour and there, coming down the street from the bridge, was Jack with his baker's basket on his arm.

'Bong,' came the first strike. The ravens seemed to rise from their various perches as one. But Nevermore was ahead of them. Thirty seconds later he was perched on Jack's shoulder, the equivalent of the best table in the restaurant, and chose the choicest little mouse on the menu. 'Bong... Bong... Bong... Bong...'

Orlando had never fancied himself as a photographer, but he was damned if he was going to take the cat to the photo studio when he had a perfectly good digital camera. The cat, on the other hand, had decided to imitate a restless, pacing tiger. Orlando had still got no picture suitable for sending to the *Borders Argus'* 'Lost and Found' column when the phone rang.

It was DS Campbell. Judging by his tone, he was still unsure whether DC Furioso was taking his quest seriously, or whether he was simply settling into country living with his own Police Station, a cleaning lady, and a DC's salary in a PC's job.

'Just to let you know that a message came through from the very top today,' said Campbell. 'Info about these missing persons I mentioned, Lucy Mae and Tad, from their mum, through the American Consul General in Edinburgh, to the Secretary of State. Now it has come straight down to us. Those two young Yank adults that went missing last year. Some evidence has turned up. One of them sent a postcard to a college mate of theirs. It turns out the postmark was Tressock. They sent another from Glasgow a week earlier mentioning a couple of 'kind Scottish people' who'd given them some sort of invite. I'll fax you the copies. It sounded as if they planned to hang around the Borders. So no more dozy country living, laddie. We want some hard graft now, Orlando. Someone must have noticed those Yanks. And let's not have you going to sleep on finding out more about that cult either. OK, laddie?'

'Hardly any sleeping going on in this Police Station right now,' said Orlando, easily managing a note of sincerity. 'Even at night,' he added.

DS Campbell ended the call with a grunt.

The Preach-In

THE GRAND SALOON of Tressock Castle was a Georgian addition to the south side of the building and commemorated a period when Scottish castles were no longer expected to be used for war, but rather for entertaining. Its huge French windows opened on to an ample lawn fringed with pollarded plane trees. Upon the lawn an enormous marquee had been erected.

The Tressock town band, a fiddler, a piper, a drummer, a xylophonist and a guitar player rehearsed with a pianist inside the Grand Saloon, where a large dais had been erected to accommodate them. Several people sang snatches of song to be considered for the May Day concert later in the celebrations. Some of these songs celebrated fire, earthly symbol of the sun, purifier after the dead hand of winter had gone and nature's renewal was to be welcomed by all. Beltane was this feast's ancient name, not forgotten in Tressock, but almost taboo since May Day had taken its place.

Fruit wood fires had been lit in iron trays set between the saloon and the entrances to the marquee. Here the customary suckling pigs would be roasted on the same spits on which long-dead Morrisons had roasted witches and their cats for the edification of their Christian tenants and neighbours, happy in the knowledge that their howling death cries were those of devils vanishing for ever from these once Godly precincts. Lachlan related these tid-bits of historical information to Steve and Beth, who had met in the marquee to rehearse for their Redeemers' presentation.

'That is just the most terrible story,' said Beth. 'I guess they weren't real Christian, those ancestors of yours.'

'Could they have been, like, Roman Catholic?' asked Steve.

'They could very easily have been. But they were protestant Christians just like you. Some things they read in the Bible told them that it was the right thing to do. You've met Jack, Steve. In my seventeenth century ancestors' day they might have thought him possessed of a devil. A burning offence.'

Steve was impressed by this thought. 'Yeah,' he said thoughtfully. 'Like in *The Exorcist*?'

At this point, Lachlan was called away to be consulted by Delia on the food.

'You do realise that was a test?' asked Beth excitedly, as soon as Lachlan had gone.

'Yeah?' Steve didn't quite see how. 'Those cats hadn't done anybody any harm.'

'And the witches could have been denounced by anyone. Old Miss Padewski, our biology teacher, remember her?'

'Sure. The homeliest lady I ever saw. Hey, get real Beth. She wasn't a witch?'

'Course she wasn't. Just a lonely old lady who lived by herself with her cat and spent her days teaching us to dissect animals. Every now and then she'd grab some kid who was, like, tormenting her by the ear – and twist. People said she was a witch. Someone said she cast spells around about Halloween and made this really obnoxious kid sick. His parents went to the cops. Of course nothing came of it.'

'So?' Steve felt he had lost the plot somewhere.

'None of that is Christian, Steve. Not up-to-date American Christian. Lachlan wanted to see if he could sow some doubt in us. Because, years ago, these people here were ignorant and, like, superstitious. We're completely different from that. We know that the Bible we've read is the Good Book. No way could we get dumb stuff like that about witches from it, right?'

'Or cats,' agreed Steve. 'Although there is a bit about swine. They had devils in them, didn't they?'

An exasperated Beth eventually got Steve back on track. The songs she was going to sing. What she wanted him to do, and when. A list of answers to questions they might get asked. She was to do the preaching and introduce each new phase of their 'preach-in,' as she called it. They were timing it all to take roughly forty-five minutes and both Lachlan and Delia had agreed that was just fine. Then they went into the Grand Saloon and started to rehearse with the musicians.

At the end of April, relatively high up in the Northern Hemisphere, where Scotland finds itself, the evenings are already lengthening a good deal, summer solstice but six weeks away. The good people of Tressock, crowding into the Grand Saloon, sniffing the already cooking suckling pigs outside, knew that they had a long summer evening ahead of them and anticipated it with relish.

First, as advertised by word of mouth to every household, was to be a 'preach-in' with religious songs to be sung by Beth Boothby, the well-known young American singer who would, with her partner Steve, a genuine cowboy from Texas, talk about the virtues of the old religion. Afterwards, there was to be the election of the Queen of the May and the Tressock Laddie. This would be followed by the traditional feast and dancing till midnight. A gentle reminder from the castle: smoking tobacco was strictly prohibited. High quality hash would be served, as on all previous May Days, in Lady Morrison's special recipe brownies.

Standing about or seated in rows upon benches, once belonging to the church, the crowd chattered away, circulating, greeting old friends and feeling thoroughly prepared to relax and be entertained. Buses had been driving up the Willies Walk and depositing people from the Nuada Nuclear Power Station so that all the familiar faces from the bar at the inn were there. In a way what seemed curious to Beth, peeking at the audience through a gap in the curtains behind the dais, was how much this crowd resembled her idea of pilgrims. Currently their pilgrimage was about celebrating May Day. She had looked it up on the internet. Pilgrims made a journey to reverence or worship something or someone dear to their religious belief. Everyone had been quite frank with Beth. Their May Day celebrations were not just holidays but holy days. For them, May Day had nothing to do with the workers of the world uniting, which sounded to Beth vaguely Christian – until, to her slightly shocked surprise, the net went on to say it was Communist or Socialist. The people of Tressock she'd met were rather shy about speaking of it. But Beth gathered it was really a celebration of spring. The world born again, Bella, the chattiest of Mary Hillier's girls, had said. Mary Hillier had added smilingly that this was probably clearer to people living in their climate than it would be in Texas.

Meanwhile the rising excitement in the crowd was palpable. The band had collected their instruments and set themselves up, ready to play. Beth felt she had got to know a couple of them already at rehearsal, something she always tried to do. There was Podge, the drummer, a very cute guy, a tad portly, but with a pixie's face and a roguish eye, and on bass guitar there was Laurie, a beanpole topped with a red-dyed mohawk. He'd called her Baithe and talked in an accent so thick she'd had to guess when to say yes or no. People wore a lot more jewellery here than back in Texas, much of it silver. The band, all locals seemingly, were real quick at catching on to what she wanted. Quite like professional musicians. She found it real surprising since Tressock was what, back home, they'd call hicksville, not that Beth would ever dream of saying that out loud. Although the castle, what little she'd seen of it so far, was awesome, straight out of a Disney cartoon. Beth closed the curtain. The gig was about to begin. Lachlan and Delia passed her, giving encouraging smiles, on their way to the stage. Steve, who had seemed real nervous, sweating a lot and wondering whether to wear his hat, was now at her side.

'We gotta talk, Beth,' he said. 'After this.'

'Sure Steve, I feel like we've been cut off from each other. But after this May Day thing it'll be OK. We can have some quality time together. Go see some sights.'

'That's not quite...' began Steve.

'Ssh!' interrupted Beth. 'Lachlan is going to speak.'

Murdoch, the only person present who, by virtue of his Trade Union experience, had some capacity to analyse Lachlan's undoubted success as the leader of this small community, enjoyed this annual event because it usually showed the Laird at the top of his form. His Tressock audience was greeting his arrival on the dais with prolonged applause. In spite of his wealth and his hereditary standing there was a sense of community that clung to this lowland tribe and he sometimes seemed to lead them by divine right. For better or worse, he had proved himself a strong and imaginative leader. Behind his back they might some of them imitate his anglicised accent or joke about his colossal self confidence. But these jokes were sympathetic. They knew that he had risked much for them and been clever enough to see that when the coal mines were closing all over western Europe and soon to close near Tressock, alternative energy was the answer. National prestige demanded more than just oil, now that coal was to go. Scottish oil was important but it was finite. One foreseeable day it would run out. Nuclear could never do that.

Other Scottish grandees like him had preserved great estates. Lachlan certainly preserved his. But he was far more entrepreneurial than most of them. Taking his tenants and employees and neighbours all into his confidence, he had created an industry that some people believed doomed and which he ran on a co-operative basis. His employees were nominally his partners. He fought with the Edinburgh and London bureaucracies when they opposed him and he usually won. He mocked the ecologists who opposed nuclear, defending it as if it was part of his religion, which, as Murdoch well knew, in a sense it was. If he had been born an American he might have run something like Tammany Hall in New York, a great political patronage empire. But his ambition was both smaller and larger. He was content to have the small following that crowded this room and whose attention he held effortlessly for every word he said. He had needed to prove he could lead them wherever his imagination drove him... for their sake as much as his. Like a Roman emperor of old, he gave them bread and he gave them circuses too.

Others saw Lachlan slightly differently. They welcomed that he used their ancient traditions to suggest a renewed vigour in their lives. For him the music and mythology of Scotland's past were an inspiration for her future, at least in the microcosm of the country where his leadership held sway. He reminded Beth of Kenny at her Cowboys for Christ church. He often spoke like an evangelist.

'Ladies and Gentlemen,' began Lachlan, prosaically enough, 'this evening I have great pleasure in introducing two guests from America, Beth Boothby and Steve Thomson...'

This was Beth and Steve's cue to walk out onto the stage, where they took two seats next to Delia. For almost a minute there was silence as the audience stared at and registered the persons of Steve and Beth. Then there was thunderous applause. Beth stood, and then Steve, rather hesitantly, got up, and they both acknowledged the applause, in her case with a cheery wave, in his case by doffing his hat and waving it. They then sat. But neither could entirely disguise their surprise. After all, they had so far neither preached nor sung.

'Beth and Steve have come here specially to tell you about their God,' continued Lachlan. 'He was a God we knew very well in the past. We still have his church, although every Sunday, the day when once our ancestors all worshipped the Sun, that church is empty, abandoned, except by our dear ravens. I have had the honour and pleasure to make music with Beth. For me the great heritage for which we all have to be forever grateful to the Christians is a musical one. And one of the great rewards for being here this evening is that you will hear her beautiful voice. I have promised them both that you will give what they have to say a good hearing.'

Lachlan then turned to his guests and, like a host on a talk show, beckoned for them to rise and come forward.

'I give you Beth Boothby and Steve Thomson!'

For Donald Dee, the pianist, this was the cue to start playing 'Power in the Blood', with the rest of the band taking up the tune after the first few bars. As Beth bounded forward, her whole body in performance mode, she filled the saloon and stunned the amazed audience with her enormous, glorious sound:

'Would you be free from the burden of sin?
There's power in the blood, power in the blood;
Would you o'er evil a victory win?
There's wonderful power in the blood.'

They had rehearsed Steve coming in with the chorus at this point even though he really couldn't sing, but he managed to say the words quite tunefully in a rich baritone:

'There is power, power, wonder working power
In the blood of the Lamb;
There is power, power, wonder working power
In the precious blood of the Lamb.'

The audience were thrilled, as well they might be, at the unique sound they were hearing. Their excitement was infectious and soon they had all risen, at Steve's signal, to join with him in the chorus.

Within a couple of minutes, Beth had her audience, including Lachlan, roaring the song with her, and had even Delia joining in rather self-consciously. When Beth had finished and acknowledged their applause, she motioned everyone to sit and, using a device she had seen Judy Garland use in her great old movie, *A Star is Born*, she sat on the edge of the dais, one leg tucked under herself, denoting her total comfort with herself, her message, and, above all, her audience.

'We have come a long way, folks, to remind you about Jesus,' she said. 'I just know you've already heard of him. Like you've heard of Braveheart or Mr Bell, the great Scottish gentleman who invented the telephone. It's just that many of you have forgotten that Jesus was braver than Rob Roy, he gave his life for all of us, not just the people of his time, but the people of all time. You may have forgotten that he was a great innovator and inventor. He was the greatest of all because he invented a new kind of love. What kind of love was that friends? Can any of you remember?'

A few people close to Beth in the front row had leant forward to touch her dress or the shoe on the foot that was not tucked beneath her. All were watching her intently in complete silence. Delia, who had now placed herself in the front row, was the first to try and answer.

'It is love of everyone but yourself,' she said. 'Really hard wouldn't you say, Beth?'

'Delia that is a good answer, and such a good, good question... I see Steve would like to answer you... Steve?'

Steve had been hanging back self effacingly, watching the audience, trying to figure out what was so unusual about them. He had, after all, never before in his life faced an audience. Perhaps they were all more like this than he ever imagined.

Now he suddenly stepped forward to Beth's side. This caused, he noticed, a further, disconcerting stir in the audience; a murmuring, sibilant sound, like the low buzz of an excited swarm of bees.

'No ma'am,' he said, looking straight at Delia. 'If you can love other people like Jesus loves us, you don't need to love yourself, you're like some great big...' Steve searched desperately for the right word. He knew what it was, but it just wouldn't come to him. But Lachlan finished his sentence for him.

'...Like a beacon,' he said.

'Right!' intervened Beth, the experienced showperson taking control once more. 'Friends, I'd like to ask Steve to pass amongst you. He'll be handing out some thoughts about Jesus,' she waved some pamphlets in the air, 'which we hope you'll read real closely. And there's a few pretty hymns for us all to sing together. Please friends – the words are important. If you try and believe what you are singing you will open your hearts to Jesus.'

Laden with pamphlets, Steve had now stepped down from the dais and tried to proceed with the distribution of them, but to his further surprise many wanted to shake his hand and nearly all looked into his face in an especially cordial way.

'And while Steve's doing that I'm gonna sing you another song – one that comes right from my heart.'

Beth spent a moment speaking to Donald Dee at the piano and to the other musicians. Then she picked up a guitar and faced the audience. The vast majority watched her expectantly, except where Steve was making his progress. There, the dozen or so people closest to him seemed in a turmoil of excitement. From the stage, it looked somewhat like a whirlpool moving through a calmer body of water. Beth's enormous voice was once more filling the Grand Saloon but this time she was belting it out, stamping her feet and playing and rocking her guitar like a metronome.

'Would you be free from your burden of sin?
There's power in the blood, power in the blood
Would you o'er evil a victory win?
There's power in the blood of the lamb.'

As Steve passed through the crowd, Mary Hillier, Bella, Deirdre, Danny, Carl and Peter, the innkeeper, everyone in a little town denuded of people, except Lolly, Jack and, of course, Orlando, was there to take his pamphlets. They seemed to try for a few instants to share the space through which he moved and, if possible, to touch him. In a way that really impressed and bewildered Steve, his very presence seemed precious to them.

But was he as astounded as another Scot might have been? No, these people, for all their white skins and similar looks to the Caucasian majority inhabiting Texas, were profoundly foreign. Had they all wanted to rub noses or ritually kiss him he would have been surprised, yes, but astounded – no. Neither Terry nor any of the Redeemers' other mentors had made the mistake of suggesting that these folks were normal, like Americans. If they had been they would probably have found their own way back to Jesus, and not needed the Redeemers to come help them. But Steve, smiling and laughing and accepting their curious adulation with the 'aw shucks' charm that was natural to him, nevertheless felt a little uneasy.

While the sound of the 'Power in the Blood' hymn floated out of the open windows of the Grand Saloon and could probably have been heard half a mile away, out on the terrace, where the little pigs revolved and sizzled on their state-of-the-art electronic spits, Jack could be seen loitering.

He had picked up one of the carving knives from the serving table nearby, when Lolly arrived looking flushed and slightly dishevelled. She seemed surprised to see Jack.

'Hullo Jack, what are you doing?' she asked, although his intention to cut himself a nice morsel of pork and crackling seemed plain enough.

'Hungry, Lolly,' he said in that monosyllabic way he spoke when verse had somehow deserted him.

'Not murder most foul,' he added, brandishing the knife and giving an eerie high pitched laugh. Lolly laughed in unison. She and Jack were often allies. But one thing did worry her and that was the black, flapping, strutting presence of Nevermore nearby.

'Go on, cut yourself a piece,' she said. 'You're as entitled as anyone else. But for heaven's sake don't feed Nevermore or we'll have the whole flock down here.'

Jack had cut himself a modest sliver of pork and was chewing on it, the fat running down his chin. He shooed Nevermore away with a threatening slice of the knife in the air.

Lolly peeped through one of the windows at the crowd inside. 'There's someone I want to see, Jack,' she said, 'but I don't want him to see me wanting to see him, if you catch my drift.'

'You're in love with a wonderful guy?' hazarded Jack.

'No I'm not!' said Lolly.

'Yes you are!'

'No I'm not!'

'Yes you are! Yes you are! Yes you are!' Jack was laughing.

Lolly scowled at Jack, but it was a thoughtful scowl. Then she gave him a kiss on his cheek and disappeared in the direction of the Willies Walk and Tressock town. Jack gathered up Nevermore and made for home murmuring to himself in a pleased voice:

'Say I'm weary, say I'm sad
Say that health and wealth have missed me
Say I'm growing old, but add
Lolly kissed me…'

The Elections

INSIDE THE GRAND Saloon Lachlan was addressing the crowd.

'The day after tomorrow we will be crowning our Queen of the May. Can anyone here imagine a more perfect Queen than Beth, with the gift of that incomparable voice?'

The band played a noisy flourish and there was a unanimous shout of approval from the audience.

'Do you accept, Beth?' asked Lachlan.

Beth was clearly very moved. Her eyes were misty as she made her reply.

'I am deeply honoured,' she said. 'Sure I accept! Lachlan has explained to us how the next two days are, like, very special holidays for you. As soon as they are over, Steve and I hope you will come and talk to us about Jesus, like, we'll be waiting and hoping...'

'...and praying that you'll come,' added Steve.

'And now let us sing one of our old songs to Steve and Beth,' invited Lachlan. He had only to sing the first line in his deep bass tones for the whole audience and the band to join in with gusto:

'Will you go, Laddie, go
To the braes o' Balquiddher
We'll crown the lass your Queen
We'll feast the night together...'

They sang it boisterously as one sings a national anthem.

As the song ended, Lachlan put his hand on Steve's shoulder, leading him forward. Steve, who had accepted what was now to be announced, out of a sense of adventure more than duty to the Redeemers' cause, nevertheless felt deeply hesitant without fully understanding why.

'And here to crown our Queen – is your Laddie!'

Uproar in the Grand Saloon followed. Up on the dais, Steve stood bemused, smiling slightly as Beth tucked her arm through his. Well used to being the subject of public adulation and playing instinctively to the crowd, she kissed him on the cheek. Some of the audience gave a little gasp of pleasure at this.

After the election of the Queen and the nomination of the Laddie, the crowd milled around in the marquee feasting off the food on the trestle tables. The fare on offer was traditional Scottish cooking. There were haggis and blood puddings to go with more prosaic steak and kidney pies, made with suet not pastry, game pies and several different kinds of pasty; there was fresh wild salmon and smoked fish too. Mountains of hot, freshly baked rolls in baskets sat beside the many puddings, jellies, syllabubs and custards. The dishes with Delia's hash brownies were emptied within a few minutes. Wine and whisky and beer were all available and there were plenty of takers for all three. Moving backwards and forwards to the spits to cut themselves slices of pork, people in the crowd all agreed that Sir Lachlan and Lady Morrison had secured them an outstanding Laddie and a May Queen who, with her great musical talent, was superior to anyone offered up in recent years.

While this was going on, Mary Hillier led Steve and Beth off to a hunting lodge in the deer park, reached by a stone bridge, called the Bridge of Sighs by the Morrisons, although it scarcely resembled the original in Venice. It had been arranged that the two of them should have a short time to themselves before Steve rode off with Lachlan to be prepared for the Laddie's ride the next day, while Beth would be collected by Delia to come and relax as a guest in the castle overnight.

As Mary Hillier led them across the bridge, she chattered like the excited little bird she rather resembled. They could already see the hunting lodge, an oddly gothic looking little building with mullioned windows, situated where the once extensive deer park now bordered ploughed fields.

'Like I said,' Mary was sounding slightly schoolmarmish. 'This was a hunting lodge once. But our government has started to ban all that. Fishing will be next, they say. Too painful for the poor wee fish!'

'So how do you think it went, Mary?' asked Beth.

'D'you think they bought it?' added Steve, before Mary could answer.

'Bought it? Oh, don't worry your heads about that! They loved you, my lambs, couldn't you tell? They – well – we all thought you just perfect.'

Mary Hillier had reached the front door of the hunting lodge and opened it for them. But she simply ushered them in, not following herself.

'This is all set up for you to have a wee while together, without anyone disturbing you. They've left a flagon of punch – oh, it's not alcoholic – we know you might not want anything like that – and plenty to eat if you're hungry. Sir Lachlan and Lady Morrison will be by to collect you well before dark.'

With which Mary Hillier was gone, closing the door behind her. Beth and Steve both gave a sigh of relief. In their different ways, they both thought of the Tressockites as potential subjects for their evangelism. It was difficult to completely relax in their presence.

But there the similarity between their moods ended. Beth was floating on a post-performance high. And yet she had only to look at Steve to see that he was deeply troubled. He had started to sip the punch and, testing it and finding it undrinkable, went to the refrigerator in the little wet bar off the great panelled room. Taking two Cokes out, he popped their tops, giving one to Beth.

'We'd best pour that punch down the drain. It sure is yucky. Lord knows what's in it. But lets not hurt their feelings.' Steve poured the punch into the basin of the little bar, flushing it away with water from the tap.

Beth had learnt not to be too direct with Steve. But now she could not resist challenging him. His mood seemed hard to explain given what they had both just experienced.

'You got a problem, Steve? Don't you think it went well? I mean it seemed to me it was, like, a triumph beyond our wildest dreams. How many prospective souls were there? I mean that was a big number of people.'

'Guess so,' said Steve. 'Still, somethin' about it seemed kind of weird to me. They loved you because you're a star. You look like a star and of course you sing like a star. But I'm not a star. Yet they treated me like one. Isn't *that* weird? I mean there's somethin' goin' on and I just can't figure it out.'

'What is there to figure out?' asked Beth. 'Mary says they love us. They want me to be Queen of the May and you their Laddie – which means riding the horse you love…'

In spite of Beth's persuasive tone, Steve seemed increasingly doubtful.

'Beth, I have a confession to make. I'm not worthy to be no Redeemer. I'm a sinner, Beth. You don't want to know. But I am a sinner. Big time.'

He was standing, staring moodily into the fire. Beth put her hand on his shoulder. She was astonished and upset by what he had said, but, more than that, puzzled.

'Is this about us? About what happened in that hotel in Glasgow? When we suddenly thought about our silver rings…'

She was staring at his ringless hand.

'Steve!' she shouted. 'Where is it? Your ring?'

'I lost it, Beth.' He made it a simple statement of fact.

Beth was now in shock, utterly distracted by Steve's lack of his silver ring.

'I'm not the guy for you Beth,' Steve was saying. 'Can you be a believer AND a sinner? I guess you can. 'Cause that's me. Tomorrow I'll be their Laddie and after that, hopefully, we'll gather a whole wagon load of souls for Jesus. Then I'll go right back to Texas, where I belong. And I hope you'll come too, honey. Because something about this isn't right. I mean who are we to try and change these people? I know Jesus wants us to do it. But I still ask myself the question.'

A little later, Lachlan rode over the Bridge of Sighs on Prince. He was leading a fine bay horse all saddled up for Steve. As he neared the hunting lodge he slowed Prince to a standstill and listened. The voices of his guests were being raised in – it sounded like anger – but perhaps anguish. Either way, it was a disturbing development. He had rather hoped that, buoyed by the success of their preach-in, they would fall into each other's arms and do whatever Silver Ring Thing lovers did with each other. A torrent of chaste kisses perhaps? He would have liked to have thought she had even gone so far as to have yielded up her cherry to Steve in wild celebration. Perhaps that is sheer sentimentality on my part, reflected Lachlan.

Someone was knocking at the door. Steve, hugely relieved at the interruption, hurried to open it. Beth followed him, hissing in his ear. 'You do still love me, Steve?'

'I do, honey. We go back a long ways. No, I really do. Don't you worry about that!'

Steve had now opened the door and there stood a smiling Lachlan, looking at them slightly anxiously.

'Everything alright with you two?' he asked lightly.

'Oh sure,' said Beth, summoning up the smile with some difficulty.

'Yeah, sure thing,' added Steve, who had just seen the handsome bay next to Prince. 'Who is that?'

'His name is Killiecrankie. Called for a famous battle that we won.'

'Against the British?'

'We Scots are British too, Steve. Against the English.'

'Where is Delia?' asked Beth, brightly enough, but slightly irritated by this totally irrelevant conversation.

'She'll be here shortly to pick you up, Beth. Mary Hillier is bringing your things,' said Lachlan.

'So, see you later,' said Beth to Steve, covering the anger and disappointment she felt with a cold nonchalance.

But this was slightly lost on Steve, who was already looking closely at Killiecrankie. He patted the horse's neck and then turned to lengthen the stirrups somewhat.

'Yeah, see you later, honey,' he replied. 'Take care.'

'Yeah, you too,' she responded rather mechanically, watching for a moment as they both mounted their horses. Then she shut the door and rushed to bury her head, sobbing, into one of the cushions on the sofa. She was still there, still trying to staunch her tears when Delia arrived.

Beth Goes to the Ball

WHEN DELIA CAME to call for her, Beth was feeling real mad with Steve. Wild thoughts flew around in her poor anguished mind. So Steve couldn't handle the Silver Ring Thing. He thought that chastity, abstinence, at any rate for men, was dumb. Not human, he'd said. As if, thought Beth, we should all have the morals of the apes. That was probably another of Mr Charles Darwin's hellish theories.

Delia had arrived with Mary Hillier, who had brought Beth's clothes.

'You've been crying, my lamb, haven't you?'

'Does it matter?' asked Beth. 'I think I'll go straight to bed, if you don't mind.'

'You'll do nothing of the kind, Beth!' said Delia quite firmly. 'If that Steve's been unkind, put him out of your mind. Just for a while. Till you're good and ready to forgive him. For quite a high price. Never forgive a man for little. We've arranged a party for you fit for a Queen of the May. Some of our best-looking young men will be there. Nearly all good dancers.'

They were going through her suitcase, the one suitcase allowed by the Redeemers. It was full of sensible missionary's clothes. An expensive but plain little black dress for the rare social occasion someone born again, wearing a Silver Ring Thing and preaching door-to-door might expect to attend was, Beth knew, the best she had to offer.

'Have you got absolutely nothing to wear to this party, Beth?' Delia's voice was pitying rather than censorious.

'Nothing in here that's "drop dead gorgeous",' said Mary Hillier as kindly as she could, but speaking to Delia.

'A good thing that we brought some clothes along with us,' said Delia. 'In case you were caught short.'

Mary Hillier had disappeared out to the Range Rover, in which they had arrived, and came back with a large garment bag. Out came some gloriously chic clothes by the likes of Stella McCartney, McQueen, Versace and others. A clutch of extravagant shoes, silk and lace underwear, and costume jewellery to match had been brought along too.

'You're really putting on this party for the May Queen? I mean, that is like my role for tonight?' Beth asked.

Even as Delia and Mary Hillier were reassuring Beth that she had described her role exactly, she was suddenly revelling at the very idea of walking into a room in one of these outfits. Not just Queen of the May, but Beth Boothby, star once again – and seeing the effect of it in every woman's and every man's eyes. To be that terrible cliché 'drop dead gorgeous' just for this one night. To sing some old appropriate hit like 'I'm the tops! I'm the Coliseum! I'm a waltz by Strauss...' No, that wasn't quite right, but the band would know it and she would get it right on the night. And to hell with Steve! Plenty of time to bring him back into the fold, she told herself. Bringing him back to her might have to be a priority over bringing him back to Jesus, but she would wrestle with that later. 'Tomorrow,' as another southern belle had famously said, 'is another day.'

'This is your night,' said Delia. 'You'll never have another like it.'

And they went to work to make her prophecy come true. When three women, belonging to roughly three generations, from three vastly different backgrounds, set out to prepare one of their number to make a fashion statement, to look attractive, even sexy, but not vulgarly so; to inspire respectful lust in men, and envy, mixed with admiration, in women, the result could very easily have been disastrous.

In fact, under Delia's inspired leadership, they ended up with just the right effect. Beth's youth, as reflected in every detail of her face and hair, as Delia had noted at the cathedral, meant that any make-up was superfluous. The Versace halter-necked dress they chose clung so tightly to her body that on anyone with a less perfect figure than hers it would have advertised their imperfections for all to remark. And yet it seemed irreproachably modest and ladylike. Until she turned her back. There the dress was cut right down to almost the base of her spine, revealing as beautiful a naked back as any woman could dream of having.

Beame, dressed in a kilt of dubious authenticity, looked nevertheless imposing and convincingly butler-like as he greeted Delia, Mary and Beth in the front hall. Music and the rhythmic sound of shoe-leather on a well-sprung floor told Beth that the dancing had begun.

Delia saw that she was suitably impressed with the slightly tattered grandeur of this space. Beth had indeed read some history, mainly about the American civil war, the background to *Gone with the Wind*. She asked with genuine interest about the battle flags, hung high above her head, and learned that they had belonged to long dead lowland regiments, bedecked with the far-flung battle honours of those men of Tressock who had fought at Cawnpore and Seringapatam; at Quebec and New Orleans; at Ypres and Gallipoli. Interspersed amid all this history of valour in far off places were the beautifully preserved, stuffed heads of crocodiles and rhinos, tigers and leopards, but mostly deer with magnificent antlers.

'The flags used to hang in the church,' explained Delia, 'and Beame here stuffed all those stags' heads, didn't you Beame? He was a professional taxidermist before he came to work for us.'

'Yeah? Interesting!' said Beth politely, disguising her distaste. 'So what do you..? How do you..?'

On her many starry singing tours around America she had, every now and then, had some R and R organised by women's groups anxious to point out local colour and history. In Berlin, Florida, which proclaimed itself, on a big sign as you drove into town, *Iron Lawn Flamingo Capital of the World*, she had to spend two hours watching the whole process of making the birds, from casting, through painting a lurid pink, to putting out to grass. Then, as now, she had managed to look genuinely intrigued and delighted throughout. Queen Elizabeth of Great Britain couldn't have done it better. It was a gift from the Lord and when Beth added the smile her hosts were invariably enchanted by her. Now she was fixing Beame with the look which said: I'm really anxious to know the answer.

'Everyone works different, miss,' said Beame, highly gratified at her interest. 'Some people start with grinding out the bones. But I always commence with the organs. The brain, for instance, comes straight out of the eye sockets...'

Beame had just caught Delia's thunderous look.

'...anyway it's just a hobby now, miss.'

He said this hastily before opening the big double doors to the Grand Saloon. To Beth's relief, their entrance was not immediately noticed, so that she had time to take in the scene. The band, which consisted of pipers as well as the more conventional instruments of a dance band, gathered close to the piano they had used that morning. They were dancing in eights, four men and four women, criss-crossing in intricate patterns. Every now and then a woman and a man would break ranks and move forward to dance with each other and then return to the eightsome. The women were dressed in party dresses with plaid sashes, often held by a silver brooch at the shoulder. Some of the men had dressed in tuxedos, but discarded the jackets for dancing. Others wore the kilt, but they too had open-necked dress shirts.

'We have clubs that do this back home,' Beth told Delia. 'Only the girls wearing kilts. I guess the guys think it would look too gay. But, hey, these guys look good in their kilts. Is it true they don't wear anything underneath?'

'I think it depends which way they swing, Beth,' Delia replied. 'Of course you could check it out if you want to make Steve jealous. Want to try? To dance, I mean.'

Delia led Beth off to a corner of the room, where she started to teach her the basic steps. The band had seen them and continued to play, only changing to another tune. A group of mostly young men gathered to watch them. Delia suddenly stopped.

'The Queen of the May would like to dance,' announced Delia loudly.

This announcement took Beth rather by surprise, although she was longing to dance the eightsome. But now a dozen young men had moved forward, laughingly jostling each other for the honour to dance with her. She was clearly expected to make a choice. It made her suddenly very self-conscious, a rare feeling for her. What had made her decide to wear this sexy dress? Just Steve's behaviour? She was here on a mission for Jesus. She felt a moment of remorse and wanted somehow to make amends with the Lord, who must be disappointed at her behaviour. Looking at the men, trying to think what the Lord would want her to do, she remembered a visiting preacher once saying to her class at high school, quoting some famous dude: 'there's a special place in heaven for the man who winks at a homely girl.'

The young men were a good-looking group for the most part, paler than Texans and shorter, and most of them slimmer. None of them anywhere near as attractive, in her eyes, as Steve, with his sun squinty eyes and his wonderful smile. She had noticed a particularly nerdy looking young man who had hung back when the others came forward, shorter than the rest, skinny and with slightly poppy eyes behind Coke bottle lenses.

She strode forward into the crowd and put her hand out to take his.

'What's your name?' she asked.

'Cameron,' he replied. 'Cameron Crawford.'

'I'm Beth. I'm just a beginner. But would you dance with me?'

'You are no just Beth, you're the Queen. It's an honour – I mean, why me? Oh heck, I'm not that good at dancing myself,' he said, astonishment mixed with pleasure. 'So that'll make two of us.'

With which he led her onto the floor, followed by Bella, Chloe and Deirdre, and Danny, Carl and Dawcus. The rest of the hundred or so people in the Grand Saloon watched their first dance, but Delia soon signalled for everyone to join in again. The Scottish dancing soon became more intricate, more energetic, more hectic. Beth was propelled into ever wilder movement as Cameron, Danny, Carl and Dawcus took it in turns to improvise steps with her, while the girls clapped.

Two hours later, she had danced, apart from the Scottish eightsomes, everything from an old fashioned waltz through to that good old American export, the line dance, and even some rather dated disco while the band were getting their share of the champagne. Beth now felt a wave of exhaustion such as she had not experienced since her last major gig. By now the crowd had thinned to about two dozen people. Soon, she thought, I can reasonably say I'm going to bed.

Meanwhile, Delia introduced her to Donald Dee, who was playing the piano. People offered her more champagne, but she waved it aside and gave them the smile.

'I'm just so sorry that Steve cannot be with us,' she confided to Donald Dee. 'That guy just loves to dance.'

'As Laddie, he'll need his rest tonight,' said Donald Dee. 'He has an Olympic-sized task tomorrow. We have a special song for the Laddie. Would you like to hear it?'

'Oh please. For a singer it is such a pleasure just to sit and listen sometimes.'

Delia had just entered with Beame, who was carrying a huge tray with a giant silver coffee pot and cups and saucers. Donald Dee had started to sing. He had a light tenor voice and the soft Scottish lowland accent that perfectly suited the lyric of the song he was singing:

'He will have a horse of the gods' own breed
He will have hounds that can outrun the wind
A hundred chiefs shall follow him in war
A hundred maidens sing him to his sleep
A crown of sovereignty his brow shall wear
And by his side a magic blade shall hang·
And he shall be Lord of all the land of youth
And Lord of Niam the Head of Gold.'

'That's real pretty,' said Beth to Donald Dee. 'You must teach it to me sometime. Right now, this little old Queen needs her bed. It's been a wonderful evening and all. So where's Delia and Lachlan?' Beth had risen and was looking around for Delia, when she found her and Beame, carrying his coffee tray, at her elbow. Lachlan, too, now re-appeared. He looked rather magnificent, she thought, with what Delia had told her was his dress kilt and the foam of white lace at his throat, right down to some kind of bowie knife in his hose. She'd danced with him earlier and he had performed with a rhythmic elegance which was nevertheless a bit stiff – as if the lessons of the boyhood dancing class came back to him well enough, but were still a bit of a chore. For the rest of the evening she glimpsed him occasionally talking on his phone.

'Delia, d'you mind if I go to bed now?' asked Beth. 'It has been a long day and, for some reason – I think everybody's response – I feel rather emotional. And thank you so much, you and Lachlan, for what you did for us today.'

'Some coffee, miss?' asked Beame.

'No coffee for me, thanks.'

'Would you prefer decaf, tea, hot milk?' asked Delia.

'Hot milk! Could I? You do spoil me, Delia.'

'Take some hot milk up to the guest room, will you, Beame?'

'Good night, dear Queen,' said Lachlan.

Then, as if by some telepathic consensus between the remaining guests, they all seemed to be conscious of her impending departure. They had drifted into a semi-circle by the piano and now they echoed Lachlan's words.

'Good night, dear Queen,' they chorused.

'Good night everybody,' she replied, with a departing wave, and followed Delia up to the guest room that had been prepared for her.

Orlando Takes Up the Challenge

ORLANDO HAD DECIDED that, in his ongoing relationship with Lolly, if it was to be both non-platonic and unsentimental there was no reason why it couldn't be stylish and romantic – like in a movie. If this feeling he had for Lolly was not love he couldn't imagine what love could be like. Maybe her bravado about not being able to love anybody would change if he kept his cool, if he played the games she liked to play. Unlike her, he had no degree in history but the time they had already spent together had served to fire his imagination. He felt, too, that he now needed to take the initiative.

Lolly, when she arrived at the Police Station that evening, was mildly surprised to find Orlando dressed in a black Ralph Lauren shirt and slacks with a gold chain and several medallions around his neck, nestling in the profuse curly hair on his chest (pieces of jewellery inherited from his grandfather and worn, so far, only when on a date with Morag).

The steaks were already cooking on the tiny stove that lived in a small closet-sized kitchenette inside the bed-sitting room. He had left the Police Station door open while he started to cook.

'Hi Lolly!' he shouted, seeing her arrive through the bed-sitting room's open door. 'Shut that door after you please and come and tell me how you like your steak done. There's some Asti Spumante in the fridge, already opened, with some nice cold glasses. Get pouring and we can eat in about five minutes.'

'The steak – rare please...' Lolly said, taking in the Italian costume with a sense of mild relief. He was ready to play. She herself was wearing a red crepe scarf around her neck, a loose white blouse, a leather mini skirt, riding boots and nothing much underneath. Helping her take off the boots would be a useful starting point.

'The new, improved, macho Italian Orlando, I presume,' she said, coming up close behind him and caressing him for just long enough to put him slightly off his cooking. Then she poured the wine and they started their somewhat spartan dinner. Each was sizing the other up; two friendly antagonists anticipating the pleasures of a new game. At least that was how Orlando was starting to see it, hoping it would all lead to something much more.

'Here's looking at you, schatz!' he toasted, trying for Italian.

'Schatz? That's Italian?'

'Wrong language. Sorry! That's German for doll face. It's a line from *The Eagle Has Landed*, Ingrid Pitt and Richard Burton. At least I think so. Anyway, quite irrelevant. Listen... pizza, pesto, cappuccino, macaroni, carbonara, tutti frutti. You've now heard nearly all my Italian. Let's talk Scottish shall we?'

'Then you'll know what Rabbie Burns, our national poet, said?' Lolly, having drained her glass, playfully beckoned him by raising a boot in his direction.

'A cock is a cock for all that?' suggested Orlando, rising to tug at the boot, causing a canyon of lovely legs to open before him.

'He very easily could have said just that,' agreed Lolly.

Lolly's boots and clothes lay where Orlando, still in macho Italian mode, had flung them, at the webbed feet of a stuffed snow goose. But she still wore her red crepe scarf. In the first breathless moments that followed she had again challenged him to outdo Caesar Borgia. However, while aiming at all times for historical authenticity, she felt it was unnecessary to imagine the horsemen outside the window, because the current Pope was unlikely to be as intrigued and titivated as his Borgia predecessor. Too transported by Lolly's first moves to think straight, Orlando rashly accepted the challenge.

Now, several hours later, with the score at four, Lolly allowed him a little rest. She had played the convent-bred princess to perfection, praying to St Theresa of Avila and crossing herself repeatedly, a stage direction suggested by Orlando himself from a scene in Visconti's *The Leopard,* with him playing Burt Lancaster's role. (His knowledge of films scarcely matched her well of historical trivia, but it came in useful.) He had been Napoleon consummating his marriage to the Archduchess Maria Louisa, his new Empress, in the Imperial coach minutes after she crossed the French frontier. Lolly was not wholly successful, he thought, in conveying a young princess so innocent that even tom cats had been kept from her presence.

Mary, Queen of Scots, ravished by Bothwell, the monarch torn between surprise and pleasure, was very successful. The Roman Empress Messalina dishonouring her husband Claudius Caesar by playing the whore with a barbarian mulateer found Orlando lagging. She tried switching to Thomas Mann's *Felix Krull* but he hadn't read it. By now he was getting so pissed off with the game that he finally gave a superb impression of a barbarian giving a Roman matron a good deal more than she'd bargained for (or even a rather pleased Lolly had expected). It wasn't that Lolly, the instigator and fantasist of all this, had found her imagination running dry but, being as careful with men as with the horses in her care, she knew when they must be rested and watered if they were to stay the course.

'Does everyone with a Bachelor of Arts degree in History get up to all this?' asked Orlando between deep gulps from a bottle of Kelso spring water. He had been seeking a moment when he could wean her off the subject of sex to discuss the cult and he had waited this long because he didn't wish to alarm her by making her think it was pre-eminently important to his police work in Tressock.

'Don't suppose so,' she said. 'But you rather like it, don't you? I can tell that, because you're so good at it. Plain shagging – well, anyone can do that.'

'Put like that...' Orlando spoke gently, a smile on his lips. 'Your answer could just as easily have been: Isn't a girl entitled to a hobby? Speaking of hobbies, is that what this cult here was?'

'For some, I suppose,' she said. 'Just as choral singing and church flower arranging was in the old Christian kirk. But now, as then, for some it is probably a sustaining faith.'

'Is – not was?'

'For some. In Soviet Russia, for instance, although atheism was a state-ordained belief for seven or eight decades, Christians couldn't be prevented from having private unspoken faith. When communism was overthrown they came out of the woodwork. People have shared certain ancient beliefs for thousands of years. Some people. Not very many of them in Scotland. Mostly in private.'

'You said you would tell me who is involved in this – you called it "a very secret" cult?'

Lolly was silent for a whole long minute, looking around at the stuffed birds and then at Orlando, who was waiting patiently, trying to concentrate on being, and therefore looking, relaxed.

'Poor old Tom. I think he would like to have mutated into a bird. I certainly hope he has. He deflowered them you know, before he stuffed them.'

The potential enormity of this revelation took Orlando completely by surprise. Who had been deflowered before being stuffed? She surely couldn't mean the birds themselves. But she could equally surely not mean that Tom Makepiece had raped young virgins of Tressock before stuffing them. All in the name of some cult? The notion was so preposterous that this led him to blurt out a single word of disbelief:

'What?'

'Deflowering is taking their virginity from somebody – in this case, young owls.'

Orlando felt the kind of a relief that comes when extremely bad news is delivered, but the recipient has been expecting utter catastrophe.

'I know what deflowered means, Lolly. But you can't be telling me that our Tom, the late Police Constable Makepiece, my predecessor here, an officer with a long service award for excellent police work – that he deflowered those poor innocent birds here in this very room. Is that what you're saying? You have to be kidding me!'

'I am not! I personally never saw him do it, Orlando, but that is what they say. Apparently, in the days before the Atomic Power Station, taxidermy was the local cottage industry. A lot of people still do it – stuff animals I mean – for shooting parties. Of these, only old Tom deflowered young owls. He evidently saw it as a kind of regeneration – put lead in his pencil – a more eco-friendly form of Viagra.'

She was looking him straight in the eyes as she said this. He was waiting for her to break up and howl with laughter at the sheer absurdity of what she was relating. But she stared at him almost beseechingly, as if daring him to disbelieve her.

'Eco-friendly. What about the poor owls? You have to be joking, Lolly. I cannot take this seriously.'

'I never joke about sex, Orlando. Speaking of which – that was only number four. C'mon, let's do it!' She was hauling him to his feet and leading him into the bathroom. The back of her body interrupted his thoughts, his strong doubts that what she had been saying could be anything other than a smoke screen. Later, later he would ask a lot more questions. But what, just for the moment, did they matter, these doubts, when Lolly's body, seen from any angle, was beckoning? The back of her head, topped by gorgon-like coils of hair, damp still from her exertions as Messalina; at the base of her beautiful back two dimples moved like apostrophes atop her freckled butt, the rugger buggers' song come true; her endlessly long legs, almost racing him to the shower; her feet, dancing with excitement as if they were entering the first set of a tennis game.

Generals sometimes survey the detritus of a battle they have won with mixed feelings. This is when they realise that it remains to win the war. In just such a mood, Lolly surveyed the ravaged bed on which Goldie, the marmalade coloured stray cat, now competed with an utterly exhausted Orlando for space. The cat, which she hadn't noticed earlier in the proceedings, had marred their last act by sinking her claws into Orlando's lower back at a moment when Lolly's finger nails were poised to do something similar to his shoulder blades. Orlando was so convulsed with multiple sensations of pleasure and pain that he collapsed on the startled feline, hardly aware of what had occurred. Goldie emerged, screeching and hissing, but clung to the bed even as Lolly tried to remove her.

Lolly carried the protesting Goldie across the room to a cupboard, shutting her in. She then slowly mounted the bed again, kneeling astride Orlando but giving him a little more time to recover. The moment would soon come to use the red crepe scarf she had still not removed from her neck.

Lolly, watching the undeniably beautiful face of her lover, thought how Mediterranean his features were, in spite of his protestation of Scottishness. Her fellow countrymen could be beautiful too, those with Irish or Scandinavian blood in their veins, or the Pictish dark ones with their blue eyes. Lolly knew them, in all their variety, almost as well as she knew horses. But Steve was from a different mould. He had excited in her a tenderness, a passionate gentleness almost foreign to her nature and quite different from the exuberant lust she lavished on Orlando.

Her inspiration, where men were concerned, dated back to a school visit to New York City when she was fourteen. Her class had disembarked from the bus at the United Nations building and was led into the huge atrium where visitors are received. Other school tours were in progress. While they awaited their turn, Lolly noticed an Italian convent school group next to them, being shepherded by a nun. She saw that they were all staring at a bronze statue near the entrance. Her own group followed the gaze of the Italian girls and her teacher, a Scottish woman of the Miss Brodie type, said simply:

'The god Jupiter; Zeus to the Greeks.'

In both groups the statue excited giggles and whispered comments. The father of the gods was depicted as a beautiful man, not old but in his prime. Lolly had thought that this slim hipped, perfectly proportioned man, exuding pride in his manhood, must have been the ancients' ideal. Unlike the Christian depiction of their God as a venerable, heavily bearded man sitting on a cloud, this paternal deity was clearly a lover. His beautiful erect member curved like a scimitar as he strode through heaven and earth – an inspiration to men and a promise to women.

It was as Lolly was thinking this that she heard the Italian nun speaking loudly to her flock: 'Non è bello,' she said authoritatively, referring to the statue.

But one of her charges clearly disagreed.

'...ma è molto simpatico!' the pretty blonde added.

The Scots didn't have to be linguists to catch the Italian schoolgirl's drift. A murmur of agreement came from both groups. For Lolly, the great god's image was now always to be with her in every sexual encounter she had with a man. He was the ultimate lover she sought and the one she never quite attained.

Orlando's eyes opened once more, his breathing now normal, his member looking less than scimitar-like but trying to make a comeback. He was once more amongst those present and was trying to remember where he had left off his questioning about the cult.

'You're a hero Orlando,' Lolly was saying. 'If we go on like this you'll make seven easily.'

She had untied the red crepe scarf from around her neck and held it out before her in a rather ritualistic way that made him slightly nervous. He couldn't know that she was imitating the pose of a figurine of the white goddess at Knossos. Religion for Lolly was simply the way she chose to live. The liturgy of her paganism was something she tended to make up as she went along.

'For our next encounter you can leave most of the action to me,' she said, noting his anxious consideration of the crepe scarf. 'And you're going to love it. Nothing you have ever experienced before, between the sheets or anywhere else for that matter, was anything quite like it...'

'Do the names of two young Americans, Lucy Mae and Tad, mean anything to you?'

It was a shock tactic, straight out of the book, and it worked.

'What?'

An officer who has caught his interviewee off balance, must press home his advantage at once, the police manual had said.

'Tad and Lucy Mae, two Americans who are thought to have gone missing hereabouts, a year ago?'

Lolly stared down at him, a deep frown puckering her face.

'There were some Americans,' she said thoughtfully. 'Tourists, I think. They came to goggle at the Willies Walk. Stayed at the Grove. One couple said they were off to Istanbul afterwards. But I can't remember any names.'

Progress, thought Orlando, of a kind. Peter at the Grove would know more. His own superiors could contact the police at Istanbul. The consulate there too. Of course, it didn't say much about the cult in Tressock. If there had ever been one outside the room he was lying in right now. Awkward for the Borders Police if that turned out to be the case. Where was she going to put that crepe scarf? Well, he could give a good guess...

'As I was saying. You're going to love this, Orlando. And I know what you may be thinking: Not the old crepe handkerchief trick! Nothing so new or wonderful about that. I hope you're not doubting Lolly's originality?'

Relying on past form, any doubt in this regard seemed pointless. So he was laughing and shaking his head vigorously when an unexpected diversion occurred. Goldie had mysteriously reappeared, mewing, from the cupboard and been almost instantaneously hit, with surprising accuracy, by one of Lolly's shoes – hurled from the bedside. The cat ran, howling and spitting, back into the cupboard.

'Bloody cats!' Lolly shouted. 'Mutated souls of wicked people, mostly spiteful women, was old Tom's theory.'

Orlando knew that what she had just said might be very significant. But Lolly, not to be distracted any further, was choreographing the new, the wonderful thing she had promised. Like every act of love she designed, the preliminary use of so many different parts of her body as agents of pleasure drove any other thought from his mind. He surrendered himself to her will completely, becoming just a part of her erotic fantasy.

On the street, outside the Police Station's windows, indeed only about thirty feet from where Lolly and Orlando were making love, Jack stood listening. He had been there for some time. Now he was interrupted by one of the very few people who was likely to share some vicarious pleasure from the little drama going on in Orlando's bed-sitting room. Returning home from the Grove, Anthea was walking the fairly short distance back to her rooms above the stables.

'Orlando Orgassissimo?' she asked a grinning Jack.

He gave what he knew was a Harpo Marx affirmative, nodding his head extravagantly.

Before she could ask more, they were interrupted by a great roar of masculine pain from inside the bed-sitting room. Anthea immediately moved to put her ear to the window. A low howling followed, sounding like the agony of a wounded beast. She turned to Jack.

'He's quite seriously hurt. She's calling for an ambulance,' she said. 'What do you think she can have done to him?'

As the terrible groans and moans continued, Jack's face took on a knowing look. When he spoke, it was confidentially to Anthea, imparting information that might be foreign to her:

'When the early Jesuit fathers preached to Hurons and Choctaws

They prayed to be delivered from the vengeance of the squaws
Twas the women, not the warriors, turned those stark enthusiasts
pale
For the female of the species is more deadly than the male.'

Just then the blind behind the window went up. Lolly was about to
put Goldie out into the street. But before she had opened the window
and dumped the expostulating cat, both Anthea and Jack had fled in
opposite directions.

Steve and Lachlan

WHILE BETH WAS still enjoying her triumph at the Ball, Lachlan and Steve reached the summit of the Laird's Hill, with the sun setting, reflected in the distant Sulis River. The fields below them were already completely shadowed but the two riders and their horses were sharply silhouetted against the sunset.

'By this time tomorrow, Steve, it will all be over,' said Lachlan. 'What you have got to remember is not to let them trap you before you get to the river. Keep your eyes open. Keep watching, 180 degrees, 360 degrees if you can, because they can come at you from anywhere. Beware of anyone who tries to persuade you to follow them. An old trick that. Thanks to Prince – oh yes, you'll be riding Prince – you can always outride anyone. On the island you will find a pile of stones in the shape of a chair, a kind of throne. Sit there. Savour your victory. Wait for us to come for you.'

Steve nodded his understanding of these instructions. But then he seemed hesitant to say what was on his mind. Lachlan examined the young cowboy's face. He clearly had a question he was half afraid to ask.

'Yes, Steve? What is it?' asked Lachlan quietly.

'Well, I guess it's like this, sir. Does it matter to you that I like think you guys are out of your minds with this Laddie game?'

'Does it matter to you that you think that?' replied Lachlan.

'Hell no!' laughed Steve. 'For me it'll be just one great ride all the way and I sure intend to win. But you guys seem to take it real serious. But it's just a game, isn't it?'

'It is a game alright, Steve,' reassured Lachlan. 'Important to us. Like your Super Bowl or World Series are to you.'

Steve seemed suddenly relieved. The Border Riding, weird though it still seemed to be, now had a context he could understand. He gave a little sigh of comprehension.

'I got it,' he said. 'That's cool, sir.'

'If it is cool with you Steve, it is cool with me too,' said Sir Lachlan.

The sun had by now dipped behind purple hills, leaving crimson streaks in the underside of some rain clouds approaching from the west. Lachlan turned Prince's head towards the lights of Tressock, which were just now coming on. Did Steve worry about Beth as he trotted in Lachlan's wake? No, he thought about the ride that tomorrow would bring. Still, Beth was there in the back of his mind. Later, he'd write her a note. But he'd want to be sure he got the hunting saddle he'd used when with Lolly that morning, not the much fancier, stiffer ones both Prince and his horse were carrying right now. It started to rain and he pulled level with Lachlan, who agreed immediately with his suggestion about the saddle and said he'd tell Lolly. The two men spurred their horses to a canter and discussed saddles the rest of the way to the inn.

When they reached the Grove, the cowboy slipped from his saddle and gave his reins to Lachlan, who said a cheery 'good night' and trotted off with the two horses towards the castle's stables.

Standing opposite the inn, sheltering from the rain at the bus stop, a boy aged approximately ten had been watching for Steve's return. Now he ran across the road to intercept him, shouting:

'Hey, Laddie. Can I have your autograph?'

Steve was startled but he stopped and smiled at the boy, the first kid he had seen. His hat was behaving rather like a chute, sending a steady stream of water ahead of him as he bent down to talk to the boy.

'Sure thing, kid,' he said. 'But why don't we go inside in the dry?'

'I'm no' allowed,' said the boy, clutching his autograph book inside his anorak to keep it dry.

'OK,' said Steve. 'I'll take the book inside and sign it. You wait here. I'll be back in a minute. What's your name?'

'Angus. Thank you, Laddie.'

With which, Steve disappeared inside for what seemed to Angus quite a long time. However, as it turned out, the wait was well worth it, for Steve reappeared with the autograph book wrapped in a piece of newspaper. He also had a five pound note in his hand.

'Angus, I've signed your book. Now I got something real important I'd like for you to do for me. OK?'

'Important. Is it secret?' asked Angus anxiously.

'No, not secret. Just real important. Big time important. I want you to give this note to a lady called Beth.'

'The singing lady?' The awesome responsibility of this mission for Angus was evident in his voice.

'Right, the singing lady. You try and give it to her in person. You say it is from me, Steve, the Laddie.'

'Sure thing, Laddie,' said Angus, staring at the five pound note.

'Yeah,' added Steve, as if he had forgotten. 'This is for you. Don't spend it all at once. D'you know something? You're the only kid I've met since we got here. Are they all away at school someplace?'

'There are very few kids here since the accident,' said Angus. 'I was born just after it happened. But you'll see a few my age or a bit older tomorrow. So where are your shooters, Laddie?'

'I left my shooters behind in Texas, Angus. Those dumb airlines don't like you to carry them onto a plane. So what was this accident?'

'Ancient history, my dad says. I wish you had your shooters, Laddie.'

'Angus, that message is real urgent,' said Steve, who was just beginning to wonder whether Beth spent as long talking to each of her many fans as this, when Angus took off, running down Main Street towards the castle gates.

Before going to bed Steve had a drink at the bar. There were less than a dozen people there, but the attractive middle-aged woman was playing the piano, singing a ballad he'd heard before somewhere since he'd been in Tressock.

'Delightful is the land beyond your dreams,
Fairer than your eyes have ever seen
There all the year the fruit is on the tree
Nor pain nor sickness knows the dweller there
Death and decay come near you never more…'

The song made him think of Beth. He would like to have had her hear it. The new type of music she was planning to sing when she returned to America might include songs like this. He felt guilt about Beth, like an ache. He had never dreamed that sex could be as wonderful as it had been with Lolly. But Beth was still his buddy, his friend of so many years – and yes, of course he still loved her. But Lolly was, he felt sure of this, unique. Probably never to be repeated. She was like some wonderful wild horse. Never meant to be tamed. He opened the window. Somewhere in the distance there was the rhythmic sound of dance music.

He was happy to feel that the note he had sent to Beth would restore peace between them, at least for a while. His conscience clearer, well a little bit clearer, he got into bed.

But before he was quite asleep the sound of an ambulance's whining siren disturbed him. Its lights briefly flickered on his ceiling and then it was gone. Steve slept.

God and Magog

BETH KNELT BY her bed. She was used to the routine of living a regular life while on the road and this prayer was as much part of it as cleaning her teeth and spraying her throat against any infection.

'Dear Lord,' she said. 'I gotta get this in the right order. Thank you, as always, for my wonderful voice and for making me so – well, OK looking. I am real sorry about wearing that provocative dress tonight. That was certainly the sin of pride. Thank you for making that wonderful prayer meeting such a success. And dear, dear Lord – Steve. I do so want him back. I know that you help those that help themselves and I guess I didn't use the womanly wiles you gave all us females any too wisely where Steve is concerned. But, dear God, please rekindle in Steve's heart the love he used to have for me. Amen.'

As she finished her prayer and was about to get into bed, there came a knock on the door and she heard the gravelly voice of Mr Beame outside.

'Beame, miss, with your hot milk. And there is a note that came for you, miss.'

Beth let him in and he crossed to one of the bedside tables and placed there a silver tray with a large crystal wine glass of milk upon it. Just as he did so, they both heard a cat mew. Looking around, they saw a big black tom cat, clearly focusing on the milk. Beame stooped to try and pick it up, but it easily evaded him.

'He's been following the milk, miss,' he said. 'Come here, Magog.'

'Oh no, leave him,' said Beth, sleepily. 'I like cats.'

'Very good, miss. If you're sure?'

'Quite sure. Thanks. Good night.'

Beth closed the door on the departing Beame. Quickly, she seized the note, read it; read it again, kissed it and smiled happily to herself. She briefly cooed at Magog, who rubbed himself against her leg, confident that this strategy usually worked with humans. As soon as she had got into bed he used another well-tried tactic. He redoubled his beguiling purr.

'That's not for you, Magog. Anyway, it's too hot. I'll give you a little when it's cooled.'

Sensing delay in her voice and possibly refusal, he waited until she was plumping up her pillows and then leapt on to the side table. It was a serious misjudgement, because a twelve-pound cat, delicate feline though he normally was, can nevertheless skid a small silver tray clean off a side table, carrying the glass of milk upon it crashing onto the floor.

A startled Beth looked down at the mess of broken glass, its stem intact, but part of its rim shattered, and the puddle of fast-cooling milk on the castle's stone floor. She gave a weary shrug. Magog, the clear cause of the mishap, was nowhere to be seen. She was, she decided, too tired to do anything about it now, so she turned on her side and, almost immediately, fell asleep.

Magog, aware, from similar experiences in the past, that this was a good time to hide, had taken refuge under the bed. A little later, he emerged and started to lap up the spilt milk.

The Eleventh Hour

THERE HAVE BEEN many May Day's Eves at Tressock in recent centuries when the sun has hidden itself behind a uniform grey sky, without much rain, just damp and cold. Some might think, some still do, that the absence of sun, when so much has been done to celebrate and propitiate it, makes for an especially bad omen.

On the particular May Day's Eve morning when Steve and Beth were present in Tressock waiting to play their starring parts in the local ceremonies, the sun rose, unveiled by cloud or mist, over the North Sea and Scotland's south east coast. Gather your omens where you may; Lachlan and Delia were cheerfully optimistic, and Steve took the view that God was in His heaven and he was going to have one heck of a ride on that wonderful horse, so all was right with the world. His desire to high-tail it back to Texas had not been entirely forgotten, but put on hold.

Just as he emerged from the shower a knock came on the door. It was Peter, the innkeeper, carrying a smart blue hunting jacket, britches, boots and a peaked black riding hat.

'Your uniform, Laddie,' announced Peter. 'Hope it fits. We took the liberty of checking out your suit in the cupboard for size. So it should.'

Steve had to admit that he really liked the costume. Just for once he'd look like a real old European dude. Except for one thing:

'Looks great, Peter,' he said. 'But I just gotta wear my own hat. It's, like, my lucky charm. Is that OK?'

'Anything the Laddie asks, the Laddie gets,' said Peter. 'So I'm sure it'll be OK.'

Steve who, fresh from the shower, was wrapped only in a bath towel, tucked in round his waist, now tried on the jacket and went to look at himself in the mirror.

'Looks good,' he said to Peter. 'Can someone photograph me when I get dressed? My pa, he'll sure be impressed as hell to see me in this outfit.'

Peter hesitated. Then he smiled.

'Actually we don't usually take photographs before the riding,' he said. 'But I'd be happy to take one for you afterwards.'

While people were riding into Tressock from outlying farms on ponies and cart horses, hunters and eventers, piebalds, greys, bays and browns, to join their friends and relations in the little town, up in the castle's west tower guest room Beth still slept undisturbed.

She did not even stir when her hostess opened the door a crack and peered in. Delia was dressed in well-cut beige jodhpurs, a smart black hacking jacket and carried an ivory-handled riding crop. It was at once clear that even if Beth was deeply asleep, the cat that lay on the floor beside the bed was dead. She entered the room and turned Magog over with her crop to make quite sure. Stone dead. By the look of the glass debris next to the bed he had certainly drunk the milk. Delia hurried from the room, quietly closing the door behind her.

In the dining room of Tressock Castle the Morrison family's routine for a May Day morning was much as it was for any other. On the heavy Victorian serving table more than half a dozen silver chafing dishes simmered over tiny methylated spirit lamps: porridge, devilled kidneys (a favourite of the master of the house), sausages, bacon, kedgeree, kippers, eggs scrambled, eggs poached, salted and unsalted butter, and two different thicknesses of cream.

Lachlan was already well advanced with his meal and reading the *Financial Times* when Delia entered the room. Seeing that Beame hovered with the coffee pot, ready to refill Lachlan's enormous cup, she went to help herself to the kedgeree, which was her usual choice for breakfast if the day promised to be strenuous. She did not want Beame to sense in any way that she was panicked by what had occurred upstairs.

'Lolly called to say that she has hospitalised the policeman. She thinks he will be away for a few days.' Lachlan spoke from behind his newspaper.

'Well, I'm afraid we have not been so successful with Beth. Magog is dead, having drunk the milk. What will only drug a woman will apparently kill a cat. Not entirely your fault, Beame. Beth had somehow dropped the glass. The cat which, of course, should not have been there, obviously drank the milk.'

'Oh damn,' said Lachlan, putting his paper aside. 'Well, Beame you'd better go and deal with her after breakfast. Give her a shot of the usual. You know what to do?'

Beame was being charged with what might turn out to be a very delicate task. A realist, Beame knew that delicacy was not his strong point.

'Beg pardon, sir,' he therefore said. 'What if she's awake?'

'Then put her to sleep. Good god, man, how long have we been doing this?' It was Lachlan's nature to be a planner; he expected others to see to the details.

Beame took these instructions in silence. He poured Delia's coffee and added hot milk to it, measured just as she always preferred.

'Pity about Magog. A nice cat. We'll miss him,' said Delia.

'The mice won't,' said Lachlan. 'He was a good mouser. Beame, you'd better get Miss Beth ready for tomorrow before there are any more mishaps. Daisy will help you.'

'Daisy always frets a bit, sir,' confided Beame. 'She doesn't really like helping me. She'd rather be following the riders. "Gruesome" was a word she used. Ah well, the weaker sex, you might say. Although – not, of course, you, ma'am.'

Delia's cold stare confirmed this. Then she and Lachlan got on with their breakfast and as Beame went about his unwelcome task she raised her voice slightly and leaned across the table to attract Lachlan's attention:

'Mary Hillier asked me a very odd question yesterday. She said: "Does Sir Lachlan believe in the old religion? Oh I know he loves the rituals of it. But does he really believe the sacrifices we make will do any good?"'

'And what did you say?' asked Lachlan.

'"Of course he does," I said. "How can you possibly doubt it?".'

'The right answer surely?'

'Is it?'

'If I am a Rabbi, Jehova is my God. If I am a Mullah, Allah the merciful is He. If a Christian, Jesus is my Lord. Millions of people worldwide worship the sun. Here in Tressock I believe the old religion of the Celts fits our needs at this time. Isn't that all you can ask of a religion?'

'You haven't answered my... Mary's question.'

'Oh, I think I have,' said Lachlan, returning to his breakfast.

The Hunt

THE CROWD OUTSIDE the inn was so big that it spread right down the street in both directions. But of course it was not just the people who took up all that space. Almost everybody had some kind of horse. Immediately outside the front door of the inn was a roped-off area where Lachlan, Delia, Murdoch and other senior members of the Tressock community were gathered. All three, like almost everyone else, were already mounted. Donald Dee, Carl and Paul were close by, eagerly discussing tactics for the coming ride. No one doubted that this Laddie was going to be a real challenge. Circulating among the crowd were several young women carrying trays of Stirrup Cup. Their horses, by special dispensation, were tethered at the back of the inn, where Lolly was in charge. No one ever wanted to miss the 'off', although inevitably it tended always to be a bit ragged, the beautiful hunters of some getting away a lot faster than the shire horses and ponies of others.

Inside the inn, in the main bar, Steve sat drinking coffee with Peter.

'I'm glad to see the sun god has decided to shine on you guys today,' joked Steve.

Peter just smiled at this, because both were now listening to a speech Lachlan was making to the crowd outside. With the windows open to the spring sunshine, they could hear him clearly enough.

'In just a few moments, my friends,' he was saying, 'I will introduce you, those of you who have not already met him, to your Laddie. This year we are exceptionally lucky to have elected a man who is both handsome and an excellent horseman. He is a really good man, worthy to be your Laddie...'

Steve heard a commotion at the back of the bar. Some double doors, used in summer as an entrance to the patio and garden at the rear, were being opened. Through these, a rather skittish Prince was led into the bar by Lolly. Other horses were being held by Anthea and another groom outside on the patio.

Prince seemed uncomfortable in the bar and Lolly did her best to calm him as Steve came to greet her with a kiss on the cheek. She seemed to be controlling herself carefully as she gave him a quick peck of a kiss back.

'Good to see you, Lolly. Are you coming with me, Lassie?' He asked this with an attempt at a Scottish accent.

Lolly opened her mouth to answer, but oddly no words came. After a few seconds she managed to say: 'Wish I could. No, Paul and Carl are escorting you out of the village. Then when the church bell starts tolling...'

A curious gulping sound came from her, interrupting her sentence, which Steve didn't notice because he was in the act of mounting Prince. Peter McNeil, spotting Lolly's hesitation and guessing it was caused by an emotion which he would never normally have expected of her, quickly, loudly said: 'Lolly!'

'You were saying,' said Steve, now mounted, checking his stirrup lengths, '...when the church bells ring. Hey, I thought you didn't use the church anymore.'

'Just for this,' said Lolly, relieved to have found her voice again. 'We use the church bells just for this. So when they toll...'

'Toll? Isn't tolling for a funeral?'

'No, in this part of Scotland we use toll and ring interchangeably,' said Peter.

'I was going to say,' added Lolly, 'that when they toll – ring – whatever – dig your heels into Prince's flanks and ride like hell – because, after that, the whole town is after you, Laddie.'

Lolly squeezed Steve's thigh, the involuntary farewell gesture of a lover, and hurried out to where her horse awaited her on the patio. Anthea thought she saw tears in her eyes.

'They are waiting to greet you, Laddie,' said Peter McNeil, opening the front door of the inn. Steve nodded and rode Prince out into the sunshine and the hubbub outside. His appearance was greeted with a wild cheer that seemed to go on for several long minutes. Trying to make itself heard above the din was the voice of Lachlan:

'People of Tressock! Here is your Laddie! All hail the Laddie!'

There was a further roar from the crowd.

Paul and Carl had wheeled their horses around so they now flanked Steve on either side. A fiddle and an accordion and a kettle drum, all played by mounted musicians, were attempting 'The Ride of the Valkyries', which Steve only knew as the *Apocalypse Now* theme. Lachlan leaned forward and shouted to Steve:

'These lads will now escort you out of the village. The bells will ring and then you will be on your own. Remember what I told you yesterday. They can come at you from any direction. Now turn and wave to the crowd.'

Lachlan waited while Steve waved. Then he said: 'Go! Go! Go!'

The crowd parted for Steve, Paul and Carl, as they made for the bridge. Paul and Carl could only join in the hunt when the bells had finished ringing and the rest of the field had joined them.

The bells began their toll, Steve dug his heels into Prince's flanks, and he took off, accompanied by a great roar from the assembled crowd.

He made for the Laird's Hill. His plan, such as it was, consisted of seeking cover as soon as possible in a place where he could watch his pursuers and see what routes they were taking. He had the advantage of riding a black horse. He figured that with this bright spring light, and the deep shade among the pine trees which lined one side of the Laird's Hill, he could enter the wood lower down and then ride up amongst the pines till he had reached a vantage point close to the top of the hill. If he had Prince stand well back from any patches of sunlight on the fringe of the wood, he would be able to see and not be seen.

This manoeuvre worked well enough. He saw the Tressock Pack (as he thought of them – although there were of course no dogs, only humans on horses, with a few straggling on foot behind) split into three groups. One, in which he was pretty sure he could see Lachlan and Delia, was heading alongside the Sulis River. Another, led by Carl and Paul, was coming straight up towards the Laird's Hill. A third, in which he thought he could identify Lolly and her friend Anthea, seemed to be riding right around the Laird's Hill, putting themselves behind him.

Steve decided to break cover now. It was hard to ride at any speed in the wood. He would make straight for the peak of the Laird's Hill, another vantage point. From there he should be able to see the King's Island and who, if anyone, had a chance of getting there first. Prince was jumping obstacles with ease and seemed hardly affected by the steepness of the climb. Steve felt glad he had accepted this challenge. In a short life spent almost entirely on or around horses, he had never had so much fun as this, never come near to riding an animal of the superb quality of Prince.

Steve had been right in identifying Lachlan and Delia in the group riding along the banks of the Sulis. Bella and Danny were just ahead, with dozens of others stretched out behind. These groups had some of the best horses and they surged over fences, hedges and walls like a continuous wave.

'Aren't you glad we went through with it, Delia?' asked Lachlan, remembering her attack of nerves when they were heading for Glasgow Cathedral.

'Very glad,' she agreed. 'You were right. Once it gets this far, I absolutely love it. But picking them up is the hard part. I always rather dread that. Dangerous, too.'

'Wouldn't be any fun if it was risk free,' said Lachlan. 'I see he's making for the peak now. A good move. Who's that coming at him just across from the pine woods?'

It was too far for Lachlan or Delia to see. Their quarry had disappeared over the brow of the hill.

Beame and Beth

BEAME, WHO HAD been busy readying all his taxidermist paraphernalia for the preparation of the Queen of the May, was climbing the winding stone staircase to her room. Still kilted – it was part of his butler's uniform – he was a threatening figure to view from the rear as he mounted the stairs. His hairy piano legs protruded from a kilt that left the mottled backs of his huge thighs on view, while in his right hand he held a large veterinarian's syringe, like a gunslinger at the ready.

Nevertheless, like many corpulent men, he was remarkably light on his feet. His entry into Beth's room was virtually noiseless. The lovely girl lay flat on her back, her arm folded over her brow, her breathing irregular, showing that she was near to awakening. In his concentration on reaching Beth, Beame somehow forgot the cat. He had just calculated that one more long step would bring him to Beth's side, when his foot hit the dead Magog and he staggered forward, only saving himself from falling by reaching out with his free hand to the side of the bed.

Beth woke from a dream about Steve. They were back in Texas at the Cowboys for Christ church and Steve had decided to be 'born again' which meant being ritually immersed in the big zinc cattle trough kept in the front of the auditorium during a service. Being born again would mean he could resume with the Silver Ring Thing after whatever his lapse had been (Beth had not wanted to know) and a sopping wet Steve, re-emerging from the trough, was able to continue with their mission as if nothing much had happened. But Steve was hyperventilating, staggering against her, as he stepped from the trough. She opened her eyes with a start.

The huge head of Mr Beame, snorting like a hog, was only feet from her face. He seemed to have collapsed by her bed. She smothered a desire to scream. There must be some rational explanation. He was picking something he had dropped up off the floor. It was an ominously large syringe and he picked it up from beside the shattered glass. Magog lay there, clearly a very dead cat. Surely, she thought, this is just a nightmare. Soon I'll be awake. But as he regained his balance, Mr Beame, an unmistakably, hideously real Mr Beame, looked her straight in the face:

'Just lie very still, Miss,' he said, his face screwed into a repellent smile. 'I'm just going to give you a shot and you'll wake all nice and peaceful for your coronation. Looking your best you will after this.'

'No!' she yelled. 'No shots!'

But a great hairy hand had covered her mouth and he was hunting for a vein in her arm. She snatched her arm away and her hand connected with the broken glass beside the bed. Grabbing the stem of the glass she drove its jagged lip upwards hoping somehow to stop him using the syringe. Her hand struck with a desperate speed and force, up under his kilt, not stopping till the jagged glass connected with his soft ganglia.

The sound of his howling, his shrieks of pain, must have penetrated and echoed around the thick stone walls of the castle's guest tower. In an instantaneous reflex, the syringe had fallen from hands that now clutched protectively at his groin.

Beth, barefoot and clad only in her terry towel robe, was running, running, whimpering with fear, for the spiral staircase that led down from the tower to the kitchens. She had a good lead on Beame. After a couple of long minutes' delay, while his agony receded to mere acute pain, he too was running down the stairs, leaving a trail of blood behind.

The sound, as it were of a wounded beast, had reached the kitchen and Daisy, the cook, knowing that Beame had been going up to start 'preparing' the Queen, sensed a real crisis and rushed to the foot of the spiral stair. It was standing there that she was suddenly aware of a human projectile in the shape of Beth hurtling towards her. Daisy spread her arms in a futile attempt to stop her. But Beth was charging, leading with her head like a good all–American girl who has watched her share of football plays. Daisy went down like a ninepin and Beth was through the kitchen and out into the vegetable garden beyond, before Beame reached the foot of the stair.

The kitchen garden had been freshly planted where the young leeks had been harvested, and the soft loam was kind to her bare feet. Not so the gravel path that followed and led out to a wicket gate and some fields bordering some beech woods. Beth was relieved to be running on grass now, moving parallel with the extraordinary row of phallic-shaped trees, which she had not noticed the evening before when arriving with Delia in the car. She made for the woods. There she could hide, she hoped, and think. She looked around as she reached the edge of the wood, but Beame didn't seem to be following her. Indeed, no one was in sight.

The great beech trees in the grounds of Tressock Castle had seen hunts in medieval times, when the town had been no more than a hamlet, in which the hunters, following French horns, were armed with bows and arrows and the dogs had been great shaggy Scottish wolf-hounds and talbots, breeds now as extinct as the feudal lairds that bred them. But a slim, shivering American girl, naked but for a terry towel wrap, would have been the rarest quarry they had ever seen.

Beth crouched amid a bed of tall ferns, resting her aching feet, which were grazed and sore from running on the old crumbling beech nuts that carpeted the floor of the wood. Never had she needed her God so desperately. Never had her faith in Him been so tested. She spoke to Him, a she always did, in the tone of someone who is half afraid that their listener is, if not slightly deaf, then perhaps distracted by His many other legitimate preoccupations. The God who noted every sparrow's fall was very hard for Beth to visualise.

Now her desperation cancelled any lurking disbelief she may have had. God simply had to help her and she prayed to Him in the fervent belief that He would not, could not, fail.

'Dear God,' she prayed aloud. 'Please don't forsake me. I am so afraid. Please give me courage. If I'm in mortal danger, and I know I am – then so is Steve. Please protect us both from all harm, dear Jesus. Amen.'

The sound of her own voice trailed away and the only noise that remained was the rustling of the beech leaves in the canopy above. She started to feel her courage returning. The desperate aloneness of her position was ridiculous. A mad butler had attacked her and a misguided cook had tried to help restrain her from escaping him, but that didn't mean that the whole world had gone crazy. In the town there must certainly be plenty of sane people who would come to her rescue, shelter her, call the police. Her hosts, the Morrisons, would surely be appalled and furiously angry if they knew what had happened to her. The sooner she reached them, the sooner she would be safe and could make sure Steve was safe too. But to make for the castle right now was out of the question. Feeling like a kid playing some weird hide and seek game, she moved cautiously among the beeches, always watching out in case someone in that obscene avenue of trees might be Mr Beame or the cook.

No one appeared except for a man in a small red truck with a crown and 'Royal Mail' written on the side of it, heading towards the castle. She knew that Lachlan was a big deal industrialist boss but if this was a royal truck, the driver should be someone she could trust. She had only to wait for him to come back. She waited, intending to run out and signal him as he approached the castle gates. But, disappointingly, having stopped at the castle's front entrance and presumably left his letter, message, whatever, he drove away down a second drive she had not known existed towards some outlying buildings, and on from there. By this time she had made her way half a mile through the woods, and parallel to the Willies Walk, until she reached the castle gates. She peered up the street and saw it to be completely empty, not a person and almost no cars and, eeriest of all, no sounds of human habitation, no noises whatever, except the distant cawing of the ravens in the ruined church belfry.

To Beth's enormous relief she saw that her prayer seemed to have been answered. For only thirty yards away was a cottage with a blue light outside its front door and a sign, clearly readable even from that distance: 'Police Station'.

The Hunt Continues

STEVE SAW LOLLY coming toward him over the Laird's Hill. She was riding on terrain that she knew much better than he, and there were obstacles aplenty on the far, or northern, side of the hill. Still, he could now see his objective shimmering in the steamy atmosphere surrounding the island. The rocky throne was clearly visible through the haze. He realised that he was in danger of being cut off by Lolly. She was shouting at him:

'Steve! Stop! Stop! I've got to talk to you.'

She was wheeling just ahead of him. He had to pull Prince up so sharply that the horse reared up in protest.

'No way! Lolly, I mean to win this game and you're just trying to distract me. Ain't that right?'

'No, Steve. This is a trap. Ride for that silver birch wood down there. There's a track all the way to Probast. You'll be safe there. Just don't go near that damned island.'

The sound of fifty or more horses came thundering from the pine wood. In little more than a minute, they'd be breaking cover just behind Steve. He could see that they were unlikely to beat him to the island with the lead he already had. Yet what to make of Lolly's warning?

'Trap?' he shouted back at her. 'Part of the game, isn't it? Why are you telling me this? Ain't you, like, the decoy?'

Steve laughed out loud at the thought she might have been sent just to distract him. Well she sure as hell had distracted him the day before in that pool. But not today.

The horses he'd heard in the wood were now bursting out into the open. Seeing them, Lolly turned her horse toward the birch wood. She shouted to Steve: 'Follow me! Ride, man, ride! It's your only chance.'

Steve hesitated; calculated that the group coming out of the pine wood behind him would be all round him in no more than a minute or two if he stayed where he was. He ignored what he felt sure was a deliberate trick by Lachlan in sending Lolly to distract him. The Laird had never denied that all this was a game. Obviously one that the Tressock folks took very seriously, but a game all the same. The throne on the island remained the goal. He rode straight at it.

Prince didn't like the steam much when they reached the river bank opposite the island. Looking round, Steve could see that the group coming from the pine wood still had a way to ride before they caught up with him. Lachlan and Delia's group was still half a mile away, following the twisting Sulis River route.

Steve dismounted and led Prince through the stream. Safely on the other side, the horse was content to graze while Steve tried out the odd-shaped throne. It certainly was not comfortable to sit upon, so he stood in front of it in his version of a triumphant pose. He had won. The game was over. After the game, Lachlan had said yesterday evening, came the feast.

The hunters were starting to arrive. The ones who had emerged from the pine woods first, then the contingent that had gone round the back of the Laird's Hill and, finally, Lachlan and Delia with those who had taken the Sulis River route. Steve thought he would wait for Lachlan to open the proceedings to celebrate the Laddie's victory, whatever they might be. Everyone else seemed to be waiting for that, too. For there was a strange lack of chatter amongst those on the other side of the steamy Sulis, just a few muffled voices and the sound of the horses moving around. The only other noise, and it wasn't a pleasant one, was the cawing of the ravens circling overhead.

Nearly the whole crowd was now standing staring at him through the mist. Lachlan and Delia were among the last to dismount. It was as the Laird came forward, leaving Carl to tether his horse, that Steve decided to speak.

'So what took you guys so long? I hope you brought something to eat, because I'm starving.'

There was quite a pause before Lachlan responded. It was as if he was waiting till he had the attention of the whole crowd. He spoke now in the deep sonorous tone that was almost his singing voice.

'Laddie, you are a prince among men. A king. We all salute you.'

To Steve's astonishment the whole assembly joined Lachlan in bowing deeply to him. Steve didn't care for this. He didn't like it at all. It was weird. Worse than weird. Far-out creepy.

'You will give your life,' Lachlan went on, 'so that a new generation of our community will be born blessing your name. Babies will be named after you. Hallowed be your name. And now we will sing the song – hymn, if you like – that you and Beth taught us.'

Religion for Steve was a simple thing. You believed in God and Jesus and a whole lot of stuff in the Bible that you could get by handily without knowing or remembering, as long as you were prepared to tell one of those pestering folks that did the polls that you believed every goddone word. Before coming on this mission he had learnt about the Old Testament from an-easy-to-assimilate strip cartoon book. He'd learnt the list of the prophets by heart. Ezekiel was his favourite. Combative as hell was old Zeke. Right now Lachlan was talking religion and none of it made sense. But it didn't have to make sense to Steve, because this was their religion, not his.

They were indeed starting to sing that hymn that Beth had sung for them and for which he, Steve, had handed out the words with the other pamphlets. The sound of the whole mass of them singing the hymn was pretty impressive. He wished Beth was there to hear them sing:

'Would you be free from your burden of sin?
There's power in the blood
There's power in the blood
Would you o'er evil a victory win?
There's power in the blood of the lamb.'

He'd tied Prince's reins loosely around an old tree stump. Now, suddenly, the horse was dragging at it with his ears flat back on the side of his head like he was real scared of something. Steve went to reassure him. He had a natural sense of how to comfort animals, particularly horses. He'd talk to them real quiet and stroke their noses. They just loved that, some of them. The hymn went on and it was getting nearer. The whole lot of them were coming to join him on the island. For some reason this terrified poor old Prince. Maybe it was all those pesky black birds, cawing and swooping. Well, you couldn't love all animals the same and those birds were real creepy and dirty. They seemed to get more excited as the folks came walking, wading, sloshing through the river towards him. Maybe because they were expecting some more of those pinkies Jack had been feeding them. But he couldn't see Jack. There were most of the other familiar faces: Lachlan, Delia, Carl, Donald Dee, Danny, Paul, Dawcus, Anthea, the gal from the stables, but no Lolly. Of course she could still be playin' the dumb game. That made him smile. Some of those little old girls were up to their busts in that steamy water, but they looked like they didn't even notice.

He had tried not to think back to the magical time with Lolly in that water because it was sinful, but now it came back to him, as he waited for all those folks to join him. The wonder of it, it was like the real, heavenly, everlasting bliss they talked about in church... how else could you describe it? No need to describe it. He could still almost feel it...

Their faces were getting close now. He had never seen expressions like that before except, yes, once – in an old photo his grandaddy had of a lynching. It was the flash of memory that showed him that picture again that at last told him the truth. Steve had time to give one great shout, one terrible cry of disbelief, as they fell upon him. He tried to fight them off. Using his fists, kicking and wrenching himself away from them. But they were already tearing his clothes off him, dozens of hands, hundreds of hands, clutching, ripping, stripping...

'NOoooooooooooooooooo!' he roared, with the last breath left to him.

On the flank of the Laird's Hill, Lolly heard his terrible cry and watched until it was all over and the human maggots had devoured everything but what was left for the ravens. She had never felt such anguish in her life, such gut-rending pain. Watching was the punishment she felt she had to inflict upon herself, because, although Lolly didn't believe in good and evil, she had a keen sense of what offended the gods. She knew that her gods were as good at punishment as the god of the Jews, the Christians and the Muslims. Was it because her gods loved Steve, as she did, that they were offended by what was happening? Was that why she alone seemed to know of their displeasure?

As a joyous pagan, Lolly herself had feasted on those kings-for-a-day, the Laddies, in the past, but devouring the man she loved was a gift she could not have brought herself to give the gods. She dried her eyes and rode aimlessly to and fro, while down by the Sulis the satiated citizens of Tressock prepared for the feast that must follow the rite. Their May Day's Eve Saturnalia would soon take place, and continue until May Day dawned. In the past, no May Day's Eve would have been complete without Lolly to urge everyone on to duplicate her endlessly imaginative excesses. But the Goddess, who had always inspired her, seemed to have deserted her now. She felt as dry and as cold and as withered as a once rich, juicy fruit that has barely survived a harsh winter and clings still to its tree or vine.

Certainly Lachlan was content that his priestly duty had been well discharged. As was the custom, at the height of the devouring he held up his bloody hands to heaven and shouted in his enormous voice:

'Oh blessed Sun!'

This was the cue for all but the frantically excited ravens to raise their faces heavenward.

'Oh blessed Sun,' Lachlan repeated. 'Our ancestors feared that one terrible winter day you would set in the western sky, leaving us in perpetual night. Yet you shine on us still. Oh glorious sun, accept our sacrifice and make us fruitful once again. We pray that soon we may hear the laughter of children in our midst once more.'

Beame and Daisy

DAISY AND BEAME had known each other well for over twenty years and yet they had never been intimate. To use one of the police forces' favourite euphemisms: intimacy had never taken place between them. Although in days gone by the two of them would have been the twin peaks of authority below stairs, as they used to say, ruling over a small army of kitchen staff and footmen between them, by the beginning of the twenty-first century the running of Tressock Castle had been streamlined. Dozens of necessary tasks or duties had been given to part-timers or completely outsourced. Their relationship now was a little like that of two veterans who, having seen their staffs decimated, were loyally carrying on the battle to serve the Morrisons by other means.

In the wake of the Queen's escape, they worked as the team they had always been. The Morrisons would hopefully never know of the disaster. The Queen, they fervently hoped, would make for the totally empty town and not know what to do. Beame meanwhile must be patched up as fast as possible. Daisy, wife of lusty Hector MacTavish, Tressock's grave digger and a caber thrower of note, was not a woman to blush or gag at the sight of Beame's mutilated paraphernalia. She at once assembled the time honoured specifics for wounds of this sort; a pack of ice to numb the pain and treat the swelling, raw kitchen salt and alum to staunch the bleeding, brandy and iodine as a disinfectant. A groaning, protesting but nevertheless obedient Beame lay on the kitchen table, his kilt lifted up to his chin, while she ministered with deft hands and soothing words. But Beame urged her on with frantic pleas for speed.

'Hurry! Hurry!' he shouted. 'She'll be making for the village...'

The alum had just been applied and he roared with pain. Then:

'That American bitch! Can you believe the Laird coulda chosen a woman that wicked as Queen?'

'Be still man, will you, you big baby you. She nearly severed one of your googerlies. They say one does just fine. Not that that will comfort anyone here in Tressock right now. This may sting a little...'

Daisy had just applied the iodine as liberally as she might have poured tarragon vinegar into a salad bowl. Beame howled like a dog.

'She'll be making for a phone, Daisy,' he croaked when he got his breath back. 'She'll need money. She's got no money. Where'll she go?'

'They always leave Jack in the village. I don't know why,' said

Daisy. 'Mrs Morrison says she's afraid it would send him "right over the edge," whatever that means. He may have seen her.'

Beame was now struggling to stand up. Wincing with pain, he took a few exploratory steps. His face set into a look of intense concentration. His mind was struggling to overcome the matter of his personal pain. He thought at once of taking the Rolls. To drive it for his own purposes would anger Sir Lachlan, if he knew. But Beame was certain that the Laird would be angrier still if he let the Queen get away. He was on his way to the garages when Daisy called after him:

'Mr Beame! You'll no forget she's the Queen. You'll respect that, man. Promise?'

'Oh aye!' he called back. 'She'll be in mint condition for her coronation, I promise you that.'

Beth left the Police Station almost in despair. A notice in the window said that the station was closed and that in any emergency a collect telephone call could be made to the number 999. A glance up and down Main Street showed no public phone boxes. The mobile phone, she'd heard, had all but put the public phones out of business in Europe. So she just had to find some citizen who would let her use a phone. She spent ten minutes running from house to house, and trying even the inn, only to find them all empty of people.

She once again stood still and tried to think her way through what had happened, what was happening around her. Apart from the ravens, which had taken off to fly over the castle on some collective mission, the town of Tressock seemed to have been abandoned. Why? Various explanations occurred to her. Some kind of plague? Maybe something nuclear, since the plant was nearby?

Just as she was thinking this, she heard a human sound, faint at first but, as she walked towards it, loud enough to make out a lyric. It was a couple of male voices singing some old part song about a hippopotamus, accompanied on just a piano, no band, no group. Sounded early sixties, maybe even fifties. It had the unmistakable tone of old vinyl, 78 or maybe 33 rpm? She was amazed that such thoughts were going through her head at this time of total crisis. But the lyric was catchy. It almost made her smile.

A window was open in a Victorian semi-detached house. Lace curtains stirred in the breeze and somewhere inside an old, old gramophone was being played. Beth stopped to listen outside the house. Why did she hesitate, she wondered? Because, desperately though she needed help, she could no longer be sure who was really a friend. The matter was decided for her, however, because suddenly the door opened and there stood the guy she'd seen with the black bird. Only now there was no bird to be seen, which was a relief because Beth was a little frightened of birds, up close at any rate.

'Hi!' she said, trying to sound vaguely normal. 'You're the guy who feeds the birds, right?'

Jack was smiling at her and started taking off his Harris tweed jacket. She gave him the best smile she could manage back, considering her teeth were chattering and her whole being felt suffused with damp cold as she shivered under the skimpy terry towel robe, her sore, bare feet a mottled reddish blue. He handed her the jacket. It was a gesture for which she felt deeply grateful. It also seemed a good omen that, weird though he was, he might be helpful with her other problems. He responded – oh dear Lord, why couldn't he be normal? – in sort of nonsense talk – it could have been verse:

'Am an attendant lord, one that will do,
To swell a progress, start a scene or two
Advise the prince; no doubt, an easy tool,
Deferential, glad to be of use...'

Beth interrupted him as politely as she could. But a car was definitely coming from the direction of the castle. There was just no time left.

'I'm so sorry,' she said. 'I just have no idea what you're saying. I just gotta get to a phone. That crazy butler attacked me with a syringe. How can I reach the cops – the police? You do have police?'

Jack seemed to turn anxious at the word police, but he continued from where he had been interrupted:

'Politic, cautious and meticulous
Full of high sentence, but a bit obtuse:
At times indeed, almost ridiculous
– almost, at times, the Fool.'

The car was visible now at the very end of the road. Beth could bear this non-dialogue no longer. She pushed past a visibly disconcerted Jack, into the living room of his house.

'I am sorry,' she said, as she pushed past. 'But I guess you speak – well, different from what I'm used to. You've gotta have a phone?'

She mimed the use of a telephone for him. Jack fell silent. But she spied it at once, a bakelite rotary phone, coloured green and looking quite as antique as everything else in the room, as if each object had been acquired in a Salvation Army bring and buy sale.

While Beth struggled with the rotary dialling, the first she'd ever seen outside a movie, Jack stood motionless beside his gramophone, watching the front door. The Flanders and Swan vinyl had finished the 'Mud, Mud, Glorious Mud' song and started another number on the same album: 'The Cannibal Song'

A few lines in, the song was forcefully terminated, with maximum aggression, by Beame, who had entered the house like a human tornado. Beth had just dialled 999, been asked to press button A, which didn't seem to exist, and turned to appeal to Jack for help, when she saw Mr Beame, and felt herself seized and thrown over his shoulder.

'So what is this shite song you've been playing, you miserable little prick?' she heard him saying to Jack. Whereupon, she could see him smashing the gramophone with a few hard kicks. Having stamped on the remains, he carried her out of the house. From the moment he touched her she screamed with all the power of her awesome lungs, trained over years to create a huge volume of sound, and this lasted until the car doors slammed outside, the motor revved, and Beame sped away.

Jack remained motionless, staring at the wreckage of his gramophone for a full minute. It is hard to visualise how despair and anger, or joy, registered in Jack's brain. Possibly they were simply negative and positive thoughts. If that was so, an exceedingly negative thought now seized him and he went to the phone.

He looked at the rotary telephone for a moment, like a swimmer contemplating a dive, singing a song to himself, as if to keep his courage up, in a distracted voice:

'I put a nickel in the telephone
To dial my baby's number
Got a buzz, buzz, buzz, busy line…'

Ceasing suddenly to sing this old ditty, he took a deep breath and dialled o for operator. When a voice saying: 'Operator! How can I help you?' came on he managed to croak more than say: 'Police! Help! Police.' The operator immediately put him through to the Constabulary HQ in Kelso. He somehow repeated the message and something about his strange voice made the Woman Police Constable, who received the call, take it seriously. 'Stay right where you are, sir,' she said, checking his number on her computer. 'We'll be there. Your address is 67 Main Street, Tressock, right?' There was a long pause, then she heard: 'Right.'

Having taken this step, which he knew meant enormous danger for himself, Jack wondered what he would say to the police. How would he put it? It would not do to simply point to his smashed property, write the guilty party's name on a piece of paper and intone:

> 'My purpose all sublime
> Is to make the punishment fit the crime
> *The punishment fit the crime.*'

The Queens' Eyes

THE KITCHENS AT Tressock Castle were huge. Once part of the dungeons, they still seemed a somewhat sinister place, as if the hooks that hung from the ceiling might once have had a more gruesome load than the hams that now hung from them. A quantity of recently dead creatures did indeed suspend in festoons from other hooks; rabbits, hares, pigeons, haunches of venison, pigs' trotters and calves' tongues.

The great cast-iron cooking ranges, radiating dry heat, were fed these days by Nuada's electricity, where once a gang of little maids and kitchen boys toiled round the clock feeding them with coke and anthracite.

Right now, an array of saucepans single, saucepans double, pans actually dedicated to making sauces, fish kettles, stew pots and frying pans, steamed, bubbled, and sizzled while Daisy, calm and totally in command of her great task of preparing the May Day feast, darted back and forth from her preparing table with chopped ingredients, condiments, spices, cream, butter, olive oil and the eviscerations of fruit and household bats (less pungent than garlic, flavourful and excellent for the liver), a secret ingredient learnt at her late mother's side when she was being taught to ignore every stricture and almost every recipe contained in Mrs Beeton's famous cookery book.

The Lady Morrison of the day, Sir Lachlan's mother, fondly believed that Claudette, Daisy's French mother, was a reliable disciple of Mrs B., the guide and friend of every British housewife. How to fire a footman? Mrs B. had the formula. What to feed a wet nurse? Mrs B.'s advice on this, as on everything else, was as infallible for British females as pronouncements by the Pope in Rome for Catholics. Claudette, however, had considered Mrs Beeton a barbarian and the late Lady Morrison another. She had acted accordingly. Her daughter now did the same. In this way, although Delia might censure her for her 'little weakness for alcohol,' as she saw it, Daisy always took comfort in the fact that she, at least, knew and controlled what the Morrisons were eating – and if that opera buff, Sir Lachlan, had known that *Die Fledermaus* was on the menu he would have been very surprised.

Every now and then Daisy would leave the range and go and play her somewhat reluctant part in the preparation of the Queen for her coronation. Upon a wheeled steel and guttered trestle (the kind to be seen in the morgues of forensic scientists) Beth was laid out. Daisy removed Beth's terry towel robe from her limp, senseless, but still-breathing form, leaving her lying on her stomach. Taking a pastry bowl, she poured some olive oil into it and, using a basting brush, stated to paint Beth's back. She peered curiously at the big band-aid on Beth's bottom. An odd place for a wound like that. Perhaps that Steve wasn't as saintly as he seemed...

Beame, meanwhile, was carefully assembling the tools of his taxidermist's trade, which he placed at the end of the trestle, at Beth's feet. Amongst other things were a large bottle of formaldehyde, assorted knives and small surgeon's saws, a bowl containing swabs and an ominous looking pump contraption, as well as quite a lot of Polyfilla.

It was at the moment when Daisy felt that enough of an already stressful day had passed without her having had a little drink, and she was just getting the port decanter out of the butler's cupboard, that Mary Hillier's car could be heard pulling up outside the tradesman's entrance. Daisy put the stopper back in the decanter and hid it behind a soup tureen as her guest entered her kitchen.

Mary was carrying the Queen's May Day dress, on a hanger, very carefully in front of her. The puffed sleeves were stuffed with tissue paper. Separate bags carried shoes and tights, and the crowning garland Beth would wear.

'Good morning Daisy! Morning Mr Beame! Lovely day for it, isn't it?'

'Mary, that is as bonny a Coronation dress as you've ever made. Oh, Mr Beame!' cried Daisy, speaking quite sincerely, 'Will you just look at that dress – isn't that gorgeous?'

'Och aye,' agreed Beame, glancing up at it. 'Beautiful. Not that she deserves it!'

'Mr Beame!' chorused Daisy and Mary Hillier, both deeply shocked at this sacrilege.

'Forget I said that!' said Beame, looking genuinely contrite.

'Help yourself to some tea, Mary. That pot's fresh,' said Daisy, indicating a large brown teapot and some kitchen mugs. 'Poor Mr Beame and I have had a spot of bother with the Queen this morning, but as you can see it's alright now.'

Mary Hillier had gone to hang the clothes on the customary hooks where every year they waited for Mr Beame's work to be completed.

Now, looking at Beth for the first time since she'd arrived, Mary Hillier examined her closely.

'Beth really inspired everybody this year,' she said. 'Such a very lovely girl, and that beautiful voice – what a gift for the gods that is!

I've always wanted to ask, why the oil? It's not as if you're going to cook her.'

Beame gave her one of his gaunt smiles.

'No, certainly not,' he said 'It just makes the skin more flexible. It peels better. I could use the analogy of a peach...'

Beame was about to launch into a little lecture on his craft, which Daisy had heard many times before. Enough to make her cut him short.

'That's quite enough, Mr Beame. We don't want to hear the gory details, do we Mary?'

But at that very instant, Mary Hillier, who had been staring curiously at Beth, wondering if she had really loved Steve and thinking, if she had, what a perfect ending this was for both of them, suddenly exclaimed: 'Oh no! It looks just as if she's breathing!'

'Oh yes,' said Daisy. 'She's just sedated. Mr Beame likes a Queen to be absolutely fresh when he starts to work on her.'

While Mary was digesting this arresting revelation and deciding she had learnt all, and perhaps more, than she really wanted to know, Mr Beame was hunting frantically through the kitchen drawers.

'What on earth are you looking for, Mr Beame?' asked Daisy.

He had at last found a box in one of the cupboards and from it taken a single glass eye. 'Just one of these eyes, and not at all the right colour!' he said accusingly to Daisy. 'Where's my bowl of eyes? It was over there on the dresser, I could swear.'

Daisy was about to deliver an indignant rebuttal when she suddenly remembered what had actually happened to the Queens' eyes.

'That Dougie!' she exclaimed. 'Dear gods, he forgot to give them back. He was trying to match an eye for poor Glencora, who had that awful car accident and was half blinded. It was over a month ago. He promised faithfully to return them at once – and I mean at once.'

'Are you mad, woman?' shouted Beame. 'You lent the Queens' eyes, which are absolutely sacred and irreplaceable, to the idiot Douglas McCree?'

Daisy has gone over to Beth and, with Mary Hillier peering over her shoulder, raised one of the Queen's eyelids.

'As I thought,' said Daisy. 'Hazel green, a wonderful colour. Mr Beame, I am so, so sorry. What can we do?'

'Go get them. Douglas's shop. We'll have to break in if necessary. Is your car outside, Mary?'

Mary nodded and they started to leave. But Daisy protested:

'You can't be leaving the Queen in my kitchen.'

'You're right. We'll put her in the Queen's own room,' said Beame to Daisy. 'You do the doors.'

Beame hurried down the passage with Beth unconscious on the trestle. Mary followed with the dress. Daisy opened the doors for the trolley. They left Beth in a huge curtained room, bathed in pink light, locking the door behind them.

The Optician's Shop

BREAKING INTO DOUGLAS McCree's opticians was easy enough. The shop had a glass door in a wood frame. While the glass was presumably triplex, there was not, as far as either Mary Hillier or Beame knew, anyone else except Jack in the village to hear them. Jack's house was three blocks away on the other side of Main Street and anyway, as Beame put it:

'He'll be too frightened, that loopy little turd, to breathe a word just now. I broke his gramophone. One more peep out of him, I'll break his bird.'

Mary Hillier didn't doubt he meant it. She gave a shudder and followed him through the doorway he had just shattered with his boots. Once inside, she tried to be as systematic as possible in searching for the eyes, opening drawers, cupboards and closets, looking in boxes and closing and shutting as she went.

Beame, on the other hand, emptied every drawer and box he opened either on to the floor or a table, replacing nothing. But it was he who found the Queens' eyes first. They had been on a high shelf that even Beame, with his considerable height, could barely reach. The box toppled, burst open, and showered glass eyes all over the floor.

Beame could not have known that his wanton destruction of Jack's beloved gramophone would lead to such swift retribution. Yet within seconds of his discovery of the Queens' eyes, Scotland's ever vigilant guardians of the peace were upon him. If he had been able to see the report that Sergeant Pringle of the Kelso police dictated to Woman Police Constable Judy Laurie later that evening all would have been clear:

Following a complaint call from a Mr Jack Summers of 159 Main Street, Tressock, I called at his address, accompanied by WPC *Judy Laurie. Complainant had suffered an assault on his property, namely an antique gramophone which had been totally destroyed. Complainant was distressed but could not describe assailant as he appears to be suffering from some infirmity, speaking only in verse. Some problem with an albatross, and stopping one in three, was all we could make out.* WPC *Laurie will be contacting social services to see if they can assist this individual…*

I was just about to remark to WPC *Laurie that the town seemed quite remarkably empty when we noticed a single Ford Escort car outside an optician's shop. The shop's door was completely shattered and two people were inside.*

Just as we left our car, moving fast towards the optician's shop, a large man in a kilt emerged holding, cradled in his hands, what, at first, looked like small eggs, but later were revealed to be glass eyes. The man was a Mr Colin Beame, butler to Sir Lachlan Morrison of Tressock Castle. Because of his obvious fear of dropping or losing the eyes, he was quite easily apprehended.

The woman, who followed him out of the shop, claimed to have seen the break-in, which she alleged was to retrieve some of Mr Beame's own property, and to have attempted to restrain him from making a violent entry. We thought there might turn out to be a connection here with the assault on Mr Jack Summers' property, but saved this line of enquiry for later. Clearly the woman, a Miss Mary Hillier, was a material witness in the case of the china eyes, which both she and Mr Beame claimed were his property and had been somehow purloined by the absent optometrist. We took both Beame and Hillier to Kelso for statements and, in the case of the butler, held him on suspicion of breaking and entering.

WPC Judy confided to Sergeant Pringle that Tressock 'gives me the creeps. Did you notice all those black birds hovering around that Jack Summers when he came to see us off?'

'He probably feeds those birds,' said the sergeant. 'Are you afraid of birds?'

'A bit. But he isn't,' said Judy. 'He was talking to one of them. In verse. How creepy is that?'

'Allegedly stealing three dozen glass eyes comes close, I'd say,' said Sergeant Pringle. 'But the longer I spend on the Borders, the less anything surprises me. Starting long before the Romans came here, they've faced hundreds of invasions. Some have left innovations and improvements behind, others have left little pockets of sheer insanity. But one thing I'll say for them, they don't go in for graffiti. Very discreet they are. Some would say secretive.'

The Sergeant expected to release them on bail. It was fishy, there was no doubt about that. A break-in and burglary in broad daylight for china eyes. He couldn't recall anything like it. Yet the Morrisons of Tressock had wide influence. The Sergeant thought it was an excellent opportunity to play it by the book but, at the same time, to be seen to be flexible.

Waiting for Beame

DAISY HAD COOKED and stored in refrigerators or freezers enormous quantities of food for the May Day feasts. But she had a terrible sense of things having gone wrong. Mr Beame and Mary Hillier should have been back over an hour ago.

She had long ago succumbed to the temptation of the port wine decanter. Two thirds of the bottle that had been poured into it by Mr Beame the previous day had already gone. She had sipped it at first, then regularly imbibed it during the hour of waiting, and now that the telephone call from the police had come she had fairly gulped it down.

'Tressock Hall, here,' she had managed to say quite formally, if a little breathlessly, when the phone rang. The instrument was at the other side of the kitchen and she had steadied herself on several chairs while making the journey.

'Who is this?' she asked. The man had said 'Sergeant Pringle' clearly enough, but she was playing for time. He repeated his name and asked if Sir Lachlan or Lady Morrison was at home.

'Sergeant? Police. Yes. No they're out riding... no, not riding. Driving. I'm just the cook here. I don't know nothing.'

'Yes, he's the butler here. Drives them too. Sometimes,' she replied, in answer to a question about Mr Beame.

'No good coming here. I'm off home. They're – I don't know where. They don't tell me – do they?' To Daisy's even greater alarm, the sergeant, this policeman, had hung up. Said he was coming to Tressock and for Daisy to wait. And then hung up. He was on his way. That was when she took the large gulp of the port that almost emptied the decanter.

Back in her bedroom, Delia had stripped off and taken a hot bath, scrubbed her body with a soft brush and added various oils and unguents reputed to keep the skin well toned, repel wherever possible the sags and wrinkles of oncoming old age. But most of all she bathed to cleanse herself of the experience she loved and loathed, an ambivalence which could never be admitted to Lachlan. It was not, in hunting terms, the quarry gone to earth, the glimpse of terror that facing certain death showed in animal or human that she hated. It was the sight of maddened frenzy in the hunters' faces, lost to all dignity or restraint, and the knowledge that her face too looked just like that before the orgy of tearing, biting and clawing at flesh, the cracking of bones, the sucking of marrow and the slurping of blood. She saw herself in the all too familiar countenances, distorted almost beyond recognition. It appalled her. She felt as she might had she just experienced enormous sexual pleasure with a filthy, drunken monster picked up off the street.

But introspection was a rarity with Delia. Regret was rarer still. Crisp, clean underclothes, a shirt of cool shantung, a suit of good Scottish tweed, some smart Ferragamo shoes and she was ready once more for the play that must go on. And, as if on cue, the front door bell had rung.

Delia peered out of the window; the winking blue lights proclaimed that the car she saw by the front door was the police. She wished Lachlan was there to deal with this, whatever it was. Why, she wondered, wasn't Beame answering the door – or, given that he was occupied with the Queen, why did Daisy not answer it? She walked onto the landing and looked over the stair-rail into the great hall below.

Daisy was there. Sitting, of all things, on one of the huge uncomfortable Jacobean chairs that lined the walls, staring balefully at the door as if trying to will the bell not to ring again. It did ring again. And the length of the ring spoke of some policeman's growing impatience.

'Daisy,' shouted Delia. 'What the hell are you doing?'

'It's the police, my lady. Can you no see the blue lights?'

'So it's the police. Go and answer the door at once. Tell them I'm coming right down.'

Delia went back into her bedroom and anointed her wrists, the cleft between her breasts and the backs of her ears with just a discrete whiff of Arpege scent. Then she went back to the landing and walked unhurriedly down the stairs, seemingly unaware that she was being watched every step of the way by a sergeant of the police.

Pringle stood in the open doorway. Behind him, WPC Laurie sat at the driving wheel of the Panda car. Daisy came, swaying slightly, to see if Mr Beame was in the police car. Delia noticed, on the hall table, Steve's passport, with his suitcase nearby. Peter must have dropped them in before following the hunt.

'Back to the kitchen, Daisy,' said Delia. 'I'll be down in a minute to see how far you've got with the feast… Sergeant, what can we do for you?'

'Is Sir Lachlan here, ma'am?'

'Afraid not. It's the power plant's annual picnic today. I'm Lady

Morrison. Where is Constable Orlando?'

'In hospital,' said the sergeant. 'He had an accident. Nothing serious. It's about Mr Beame, your butler. He was apprehended breaking and entering and, I must add, vandalising the optician's shop in Main Street. He says he was reclaiming his property. A Miss Hillier, who was with him, supports his story but says she discouraged him from breaking the door down. She has signed a statement and gone home.'

'Goodness gracious,' said Delia. 'I am deeply shocked. Beame, of all people. How can I help? What about bail? I'm sure we can arrange that.'

'Very well, Lady Morrison. After that, we'd appreciate it if you'd bring him back here. He gave the castle as his address. I should warn you, though – he can obviously be violent sometimes.'

'Not with me sergeant, I assure you. He has these funny spells sometimes. Occasional hallucinations. But we know how to deal with them. He may have forgotten to take his pills.'

Ten minutes later, Delia was following the Panda back to the Police HQ in Kelso. She was thinking not about bailing Beame; rather her thoughts, jogged by Steve's passport, were on who should be the fortunate couple to take both Steve and Beth's luggage and passports on a free trip to – where? Last year, Tad and Lucy Mae's passports and baggage had gone to Istanbul. The fact that these things had been left at a hotel, while their owners had disappeared, should have been fully reported to the US consulate by the local police, and the next-of-kin back in America informed. One could never be quite sure if that part of the plan had worked. The young Tressock couple they'd sent were highly reliable and had reported no problems. They'd checked into a hotel, leaving their own things in another hotel. They'd handed over the young Americans' passports to the reception for return in the morning, a system followed all over Europe. They'd disturbed the bed in their room and left the Americans' luggage there. Then they'd gone out, ostensibly to dinner, and never returned. Next morning they flew back to Britain using their own passports.

Delia wondered which young Tressock couple would make good look-alikes for Beth and Steve. Young Deirdre had a look of Beth, the colouring was right...

They had arrived at the Kelso Police headquarters. Delia became suddenly the Good Samaritan come to rescue, care for and cherish her slightly demented butler. Formalities followed. She was very good at formalities. Sergeant Pringle, who was dying to get home to watch

Match of the Day, was grateful to her. Beame, who received nothing but loving kindness from her, at least until they got into the Rolls, was grateful too.

Beth in the Queens' Room

THE CAREFULLY CALCULATED drug dose injected into Beth's bottom earlier in the day – a quite sufficient sedative to keep her from waking until the hour Beame's taxidermy procedures commenced – was now wearing off. She lay much as Beame had left her when he hurried off in search of the glass eyes. His arrest had delayed his proceeding by the timetable he usually followed. If she had not been disturbed, she might have remained unconscious for another hour or so.

Daisy, however, was one of those people in whom alcohol begets hyperactivity rather than sleepiness. As the evening wore on, with her cooking all finished for the May Day feast, and Mr Beame still absent and nothing else to do except listen to a pop programme on the radio, she worried that Beth might awake in the Queens' Room and wonder where she was.

Remembering how destructive Beth could be when aroused, she wanted to make sure that all was well. If Daisy had been sober she would have realised that there was very little she could have done if she had found the Queen wide-awake and anxious to escape by any means possible. However, as she was already well into a freshly opened bottle of cherry brandy, nothing inhibited her from going to the Queens' Room, unlocking the door, and swaying over to the gurney that held the trestle on which the unconscious Beth lay.

Daisy peered at the beautiful Queen and noted that she was still breathing regularly, but was otherwise in a satisfactory state of sedation. Her peering, in the dim, pink light of the Queens' Room, caused her to step forward and jog the gurney. Daisy did not notice this as she whispered 'sleep well, my lovely!' and tottered, rather unsteadily, back out of the room, locking the door behind her. However, the wheeled gurney had started to move slowly but steadily towards a gentle collision with one of the walls.

The shock of this slight collision was sharp enough to jerk Beth awake. People who have been sedated usually return to consciousness by stages. If they awake in strange surroundings it takes a little more time for them to find their bearings. If they awake in a huge room bathed in pink light where some twenty elaborately dressed women sit absolutely motionless in rows upon gilded thrones, all staring into space, a normal person will close their eyes again and hope the nightmare will go away and that next time they open their eyes they will be in a normal bedroom, preferably one they recognise. In Beth's case the scene that met her was still the same – same motionless women, same pink light.

Her head ached and she was very conscious that her feet were sore, and she wanted to examine them, but more urgent was her need to go to the toilet. This need was great enough to make it a priority even over finding out where on earth she was. Seeing the door by which Daisy had just left, she tried to open it. But it was a big heavy polished mahogany door and firmly locked. She banged on it as hard as she could with her fists but all she could hear from the far side was the very distant, muffled sound of Franz Ferdinand on a disc or radio. It told her she was somewhere in the twenty-first century, nothing more... Another thing, there was a nasty sweet rancid odour about this place. It baffled her that she was quite naked, although there was some kind of garment that had been draped over her when she slept. But no time to examine that now, her other need was too urgent.

Beth literally raced around the room looking for some way out. Five sets of huge French windows lined one side of the room. All were heavily curtained and locked. In between each was a large Chinese vase containing a potted plant. Since she could find no other exit, she very soon dispossessed one vase of its plant and used it for her own purposes, replacing the plant as tidily as she could.

Now, with this necessary chore complete, she examined her surroundings quite carefully. The motionless, staring women were presumably waxworks. Her priority still lay elsewhere. Apart from about fifty little gilt chairs stacked in one corner there was no furniture except the gurney and trestle on which she had awoken. There were no chests of drawers and no closets. Apart from the garment that had been lying across her, like a blanket, when she awoke, none of her clothes were anywhere to be seen. Accordingly, she went and examined this one available garment. Holding it up to one of the pink lights, which resembled sanctuary lamps in churches, she saw at once that the dress was beautifully made. She remembered having once worn it, but not where... It looked like a costume for Titania, the Fairy Queen, which she had once seen in a production of *A Midsummer Night's Dream* she had witnessed in Central Park when doing a gig in New York. The sight of it started to trigger her memory of what had happened in the last forty-eight hours. The dress was of course that which Mary Hillier had made for her as Queen of the May. This room must be in Tressock Castle.

She was about to put the dress on when she saw the hideous collection of taxidermy instruments. Their intended use was still obscure, until she remembered the stuffed animals in the hall. Memory was now kindling memory. Mr Beame in particular loomed as a monstrous threat. She knew she was still in terrible danger. The locked door might open at any moment and he would be there with his dreaded syringe. There were, she now noticed, next to the taxidermy things, two clothes bags hanging from the end of the gurney. To her great relief, she opened them to find a pair of tights and some horribly ornamental shoes, which were something other than her bare feet to walk on nevertheless.

Dressing hurriedly, she turned her attention to the waxworks. There were actually ten of them in all. The larger number had been an illusion created by an enormous mirror at one end of the room. There was also an empty throne.

Beth knew that finding some way of getting out of this room was desperately urgent, but she couldn't resist a closer examination of the waxwork figures. The one sitting closest to the empty throne had a beautiful high cheek-boned face, but her most notable feature was her hair. It was a deep red colour, glossy and thick and wavy. Beth moved closer to examine the girl's face. It had a waxy look to it, but it was almost too full of natural blemishes – one eye very slightly higher than the other, for instance – to not be based on a real person. Beth touched the hand resting on the arm of the chair. It had a clammy feel to it. But it wasn't wax. There seemed to be a crack where the thumb joined the hand. Beth touched it and a chunk of matter fell away. Below was the bone structure of a woman's thumb. She gave a silent scream.

Moments later, she was searching frantically behind the curtains for some way out. She found that all the windows were locked, but that the locks were of course to guard against intruders from outside. Keys hung from little hooks inside the window embrasures. The window locks were set into the sides of the frames, twelve in all, and they were stiff from lack of use.

Panic and fear that the door behind her might open before she had finished the job gave her extra strength. Within minutes, she had forced a window open and was running, gulping fresh air, across a terrace punctuated with pots of ornamental shrubs. As she ran, weird animal sounds, shrieks and moans, laughter and occasional screams seemed ever nearer. But all she cared about was that she was leaving that dreadful room behind. She was impelled forward. The sound of singing, bawdy songs and folk airs, drifted towards her. Smoke from bonfires eddied in little gusts. Beth ran towards the sound of humanity.

There were quite a lot of people up there on the hill that overlooked

Tressock. The hill loomed over the ornamental trees that fringed the garden. As she started down a path which led to the stables she saw, riding towards her, a woman leading a lame horse. Because they were backlit by the setting sun, which still shone from just above the hill, she did not recognise Lolly until she had drawn level with her.

The woman looked at Beth with a face so drawn and reddened with weeping that it was hard to imagine it had ever been that of the laughing, provocatively sexy female she had so instinctively disliked. Beth was filled with dread by the sight of her. For, astonishingly, she was wearing Steve's hat and riding the black horse they called Prince.

'Where's Steve?' she asked at once.

Lolly looked for a moment as if she was going to ride on without answering. Then she gave an involuntary sob; it sounded almost like a groan.

'It's too late, Beth,' she said. 'I tried to save him. I begged him to follow me. Steve's no more, Beth. Dead. Can you ride? This mare is lame. But come with me to the stables and I'll lend you a mount so you can ride the hell out of here...'

'Dead – Steve?' these were the only words Beth had really heard. Her tone was one of total disbelief. 'That's not possible.'

'You've got to understand, Beth. The Laddie is like a – like a sacrament. We need the blood of the best, sweetest, goodliest, the bravest young man we can find. That is the perfect sacrifice. Steve! Why did it have to be Steve? Because he was the perfect Laddie, Beth. Just as you are the perfect Queen of the May. I could have saved him. I tried. But he thought it was just a silly game.'

'They killed him? Steve? That Lachlan? That Delia? I've gotta hear this from them. I mean I just don't believe this.'

'Don't you?' asked Lolly wearily. 'How did you manage to escape? Did Delia wake you up with a nice cup of tea and send you off sightseeing while they and the whole town killed your fiancé? I don't think so.'

Beth suddenly realised that Lolly was telling the truth; that there was no point, would be no point, in her lying about something as dreadful as this. This woman she hated was telling her the truth, was the only person to do so for days now. Her own experiences confirmed that Steve was dead. How long would she have lived if those terrible instruments had been used on her? But this woman had Steve's hat and that she just could not bear.

'Gimme that hat!' She shouted it at Lolly. 'You stole that!'

'It was all that was left, Beth,' said Lolly. 'You can have it if you like. You probably have more right to it than I do.'

She handed Beth the hat. The young Redeemer snatched it from her hand and walked determinedly towards the bonfires that dotted the hill just ahead of her. Lolly rode after her, dragging her limping mare behind her.

'Don't go up there, Beth!' she cried. 'You must know by now what they are going to do to you. Somehow you escaped from Beame. Run now, while you can, girl! Come with me, I'll help you.'

Beth stopped and turned. Her face wore an almost trance-like expression of shock and grief.

'If Steve is really dead, I am certainly not going to run away. I think the Lord has chosen me for this, Lolly. He saved me from Mr Beame. He'll protect me now.'

'But you're forgetting,' shouted Lolly, as if decibels would somehow penetrate Beth's fixed resolve, her blinkered vision of herself. 'You are the other perfect sacrifice! You just have to be next to die! Because you're the Queen of the May!'

'That is right. I am one Queen of the May no one is ever going to forget.'

May Day's Eve

BECAUSE THE SUN was rimming the top of the hill with an amber light as it set, Beth found herself walking in search of Lachlan and Delia through a shadowed, chilly upland, but one alive with scattered bonfires and people roaring drunk, people dancing, people singing, people rutting, people freed from all civilised restraint by their shared experience on the King's Island. When, together, you have devoured another human being, then any merely sexual enormity is but a bagatelle. When you can tell each other, the morning after, that it was all in honour of the god, an offering bound to bring a great reward for all concerned, then councillor, trade unionist, laird, shop keeper, labourer, housewife and whore can all express mutual satisfaction and look forward to next spring. For May Day comes but once a year.

Beth had seen her quarry far away in the distance, at the very top of the hill, where a huge tree was silhouetted against the setting sun, bleeding through its branches and foliage.

Standing to one side of the tree, supervising a number of people hanging votive offerings, was the tall, unmistakable figure of Lachlan.

Beth hardly looked at the frolicking men and women of Tressock and, at first, they were totally unaware of her. The Coronation normally took place on the terrace outside the Queens' Room on May Day at about noon, before the festival's major and final feast. The great gates of the castle were closed while the embalmed Queen was carried around the building three times, seated upon her throne. She was then crowned with a garland, to great acclaim, by Sir Lachlan, and carried to her last resting place in the Queens' Room. Everyone bowed to her as she passed and applauded and, before the windows of the Queens' Room were closed for another year, the whole community filed past her. Some left requests for favours or cures at her feet. It was assumed that the Queen, in the state of ecstasy, bliss and endless love that she now found herself, would be glad to grant their requests and she certainly had the power to do so. She had been turned into a latter-day saint.

This being the case, it is easy to imagine the shock of a group of three or four men and women, each gratifying him or herself with some sensitive and pleasurable part of one of the others, when one of them hisses: 'Good gods, we're being stared at by the Queen herself. I'm not kidding. It's her. Do you think I don't recognise her?'

But for the most part, those who saw her were awe-struck by her beauty and dignity as she moved on and on, up the hill, closer to Lachlan.

Word was going around now, from camp-fire to camp-fire, that the Queen herself, dressed for her coronation, was amongst them. No Queen had ever appeared before at the Saturnalia. People started to rise to their feet, to disengage from whatever they had been doing, to move up the hill behind her. It became so that it seemed, by the time she was getting quite close to Lachlan, that she was leading a great crowd of murmuring people.

Lachlan had been performing another of his priestly duties, the hanging of the votive offerings upon the 'great tree'. Since each year the great tree was ritually burnt with all its presents, this ceremony moved geographically around Tressock, always on some hill or eminence where the dying sun, if it should be visible, could form part of the spectacle.

The gifts people gave were supposed to be precious or dear to them personally but not necessarily financially valuable. Everything from a once favourite toy, when Tressock still had relatively young children, to a pet canary singing in its cage. Images of limbs and organs, carved from wood, were supposed to invite godly intercession for the cure of rheumatics or even cancers. Of course, Lachlan did not personally hang these objects, but merely supervised, while young men and women with ladders did the work of attaching them decoratively to the branches. Around the base of the tree dry brushwood was piled ready to be lit.

About the time Beth was coming into hailing distance of Lachlan, he was calling for more kerosene to be poured on this kindling. He personally used a hand pump device to spray the lower branches with gasoline so that they would quickly catch fire when he ceremonially lit the tree. Standing to one side was a young man with a flambeau, a sturdy stick tipped with flaming tar. He stood by, waiting to pass this to the Laird when he was ready. A piper, too, was at hand to play the 'Morrisons' Lament' when Lachlan gave the signal – an air the ancient family had brought with them from the island of Lewis, and probably from their Viking home in Norway before that. For these Morrisons were not truly Border people, but transplants from Scotland's Hebridean Islands. A hoary family joke was to wonder whether they were over-staying their welcome. Lachlan turned to the youth holding the flambeau. 'Are you ready, Eric?' he asked, but the youth was staring, slack jawed, at something that was happening behind Lachlan. Eric was a rather slow-witted boy, a nephew of Mary

Hillier's, selected for this honour to please her.

'The Queen, sir. The Queen. It's herself coming right at us.'

Lachlan was irritated at this absurd suggestion, but he turned to see what utter nonsense could be so distracting.

She stood now, no more than fifteen feet away from him, looking like an avenging angel in a Renaissance painting. Her whole body, in its clinging, fairy queen dress, was tinged with the golden light of the dying sun. But more striking by far than that rigid, defiant little body was the expression on her face. Lachlan saw in those terrible accusing eyes a nemesis he could never have imagined. Here was a terrible creature of his making – alive, vengeful and perhaps beyond his control. Behind her, the people of Tressock, his people, watched him as closely as they watched the Queen.

'Where is Steve? Dead? He can't be dead. Is he really dead?' she shrieked at Lachlan, holding up Steve's hat.

He hesitated. No clever, witty answer, no easy lie would work here. For he was not simply answering her. He was answering her in front of his people. How they judged his answer was almost as important as what she did next. She was like a genie who had escaped from a bottle. He had no idea how he would get her back into it. But he must try:

'Steve won, dear Queen,' he said. 'You should be very proud of him. He was the finest Laddie we ever had.'

'Had?' Beth looked around at the crowd, silent, sobered, listening intently. She spotted Donald Dee, Bella and Paul among those standing at the front. 'So, Donald with the wonderful voice – is Steve really dead?'

'Yes, he is, my Queen. And no one will ever find his body. It is all gone. But his spirit, his new self, is in a heaven beyond our imagining – remember the song? He will have a horse of the gods' own breed. He will have hounds that can outrun the wind. Play it, Piper, for our Queen.'

And the piper, who had been wondering when his cue would come, gladly pumped a few times and started to play the 'Laddie' tune. Beth, finding that she could not be heard over the sound of the pipes, moved forward so that she was just a few paces from Lachlan.

'Bullshit!' She spat the expletive furiously in Lachlan's face. 'You cannot seriously believe all this. Jesus says I must forgive you, for you know not what you do. I'm going to try, really I am. But I'm not the law. You just can't seriously believe in all this stuff about the sun being a kind of god. God, my God, created the sun and the moon and the stars all in just four days.'

'Have you seen your God?' asked Lachlan. 'No. But you can see the sun. Would anything grow without the sun? Ask a farmer. Could you live in perpetual night with hundreds of degrees of frost? Not for a nanosecond. Do you believe that on the day that Biblical Israel is once more one country, Jesus will come again..?'

'Of course I believe it. It says so in the Bible.'

'Has anyone thought that through? Jesus is back. What happens next?' Lachlan was playing for time. Where was Delia? 'Yes, what happens if Jesus is back? There he is at Tel Aviv airport. Planes leaving for all over the world. Does he go east to meet the Dalai Lama? Does he schedule a meeting of Christendom at Rome, hosted by the Pope? Has America invited him to visit Ground Zero while offering him the Congressional Medal of Honour and his very own programme on the Fox Network?'

While Beth listened to this horrific description of Jesus – as if he had returned to earth as a kind of travelling salesman for God – she saw with enormous clarity what had been obscured by sheer shock and all the fantasy going on around her. She was face to face with Steve's murderer. However it had happened, he had planned it. Jesus may have been for forgiving. God, the Father, in the Old Testament, was all about 'An eye for an eye and a tooth for a tooth.' Now she saw Lachlan very clearly; this clever sophisticate – Big Bill's typical European. The totally amoral, condescending murderer of her Steve was feet away from her, blaspheming.

What Beth did next came from no plan, but simply a reflex driven by bitter, furious anger and hunger for revenge at any price.

Shouting: 'Blasphemy, you murderer!' she ran straight at Lachlan as hard as she could. When she collided with him, her head lowered so it impacted with his gut, he crumpled, winded and in pain, staggering backwards to fall onto the great pile of kerosene-soaked kindling behind. Standing over him for no more than a second, with Steve vividly in her mind, she dropped Steve's hat and grabbed the burning flambeau from the stunned Eric and thrust it first into Lachlan's face and then into the kindling. The Laird's scream was almost lost in the crackling roar of the fire as it took off up the tree. Lachlan tried to rise but the flames had engulfed him. Almost every part of him was on fire. His hands seemed to claw upwards. But they were now two burning brands.

Anyone who had been anywhere near the tree had now fled and as Beth, the flambeau still in her hand, turned quickly away from the horror of what she had just done, she saw that the villagers had retreated somewhat and were now talking animatedly amongst themselves. They had heard nothing of what had passed between Sir Lachlan and the Queen because of the piper playing the 'Laddie' song. Perhaps they expected something from her. Perhaps she should make a speech. Perhaps they all intended to kill her and deliver her to Beame. But somehow she didn't think so. Deprived of their leader they seemed a little lost. For some reason, the Queen of the May had killed Sir Lachlan. For some reason she had not been ritually killed and stuffed. For some reason she was alive and in a vengeful mood. Beth guessed that these were mysteries to them – and as to why she had not been stuffed, like the other Queens, that was a mystery to her too.

What Beth did not know was that for the people of Tressock she was still in a sense the Goddess that the Queen of the May represented, almost an avatar – her very presence, alive amongst them, was divine.

She decided that if, as seemed the case, they still found her kind of awesome (why otherwise had they not come forward when she killed Lachlan?) the best thing she could do was to play out her role with as much authority as possible.

She waved the flambeau in the air, until the crowd, sensing this was a signal from her to attract their attention, fell completely silent.

'I want all of you to go home. When you get there, pray for Steve. Pray for Lachlan. Pray to my Lord Jesus Christ for forgiveness. I am the living Queen of the May. Now go home. Go! Go!'

There was little hesitation. A muttered conversation between Peter McNeil, Murdoch and Danny, in which they kept staring curiously at her, continued after the vast majority had started back down the hill to Tressock. But they soon followed. She was left alone with the blazing tree, from which branches had started to crack and fall and upon which occasionally an offering, a toy or a clock, would explode in the heat.

Now she prayed to God, her God, thanking Him for her deliverance. So far. And she asked further protection and help, which she just knew she was going to need if she was ever going to see Dallas and Texas again.

'Lord,' she prayed, 'I know I'm not safe yet. I have just killed a man and broken one of your most important commandments. But I believe he was a deeply evil man and he had killed Steve who was as good a man as you could find. I ask for your forgiveness, not only for what I have just done. But, Lord, if I ever make it to a safe place in this country I just want to go straight home. I don't know what these people will do now. But if I am going to die, please take me straight to

Steve so we can be together with You for ever and ever. Amen.'

Now she saw that there was a figure approaching with a bird fluttering on his arm. This could only be the weird guy who talked in riddles. The guy with the rotary telephone.

'Bless your beautiful hide,' he said as if he was pleased to see her alive and intact.

Jack had walked past her far enough to see Sir Lachlan's remains. The Laird lay there like a grotesque charred marionette amid the ashes of the still fiercely burning tree. Nevermore fluttered around the tree cawing hoarsely, then flew back to Jack's shoulder. He strolled towards her, although she held her flambeau defensively pointed at him, and as he came he spoke to her, in his unique way, reassuring words, up to a point:

'Our Gods have little quirks
Their world and all its works
Are subject to
One weird taboo.
They hate the pride of CEOs
Conceited Moguls are their foes.
For pretty girls they'll come disguised
As Bulls or Swans for virgins prized.
And you sweet Beth,
They'll save from Death.
But never think you know their rules.
They love to make us humans fools.'

'So who would worship gods like that?' asked Beth. 'Anyway, who the heck are you?'

'The oracle round here. Or so it would appear,' answered Jack.

'So you knew the future and you let it happen?'

Jack nodded his head sadly.

'That's right,' shouted Beth. 'You knew and you did nothing. Damn you to hell!'

Her bellow of anger frightened Nevermore into flight. The bird cawed anxiously and took off across the hillside for the distant church tower. Jack laughed and went on laughing even after Beth had hurled the firebrand at him. All he did was turn and walk off in the direction of Tressock.

The End Game

BETH STOOD ALL alone alongside the grisly horror at the foot of the blazing tree. She found that she could gaze anywhere except at what remained of her mortal enemy. The series of fantastical events that had occurred since awakening to find Beame by her bed kaleidoscoped in her memory. She could still not grasp that they were real – but the merest glance at the crumbling, charred figure of Lachlan was so real that she could not bear to look longer.

The eminence upon which the tree stood allowed her a view of Tressock below, its street lights just coming on in the gathering dusk. Beth could no longer hear the chattering of the retreating crowd, but the hillside still wore the guttering bonfires around which so recently humans had behaved like beasts, if beasts could ever imitate humans. These people had obeyed her, but for how long? She had not seen Delia in the crowd. She must be down there in the castle. However much the Laird's wife had already been involved in Steve's murder and the plot to kill the Queen of the May, the news that Beth had killed Lachlan would surely make her an implacable enemy. It was only slowly dawning on Beth that there was no one – absolutely no one – she had met or seen in Tressock who was not implicated in the murder of Steve, in her murder too. A lynch mob in Texas, that was something you could understand. People thought a wrong had been done. They took Justice into their own hands. Beth thought that was against God's law. It was plain evil. But this? Was Mary Hillier evil? Was Bella? Were the guys who'd played at the preach-in gig? She'd seen them all there in the crowd.

Looking to the west, where the sun had only just sunk below the hills, the silvery Sulis meandered through meadows in a valley skirted by pine woods. No road was visible. Beth knew that was the direction she must take. She could dimly see a village with tiny pin-pricks of light on top of a hill. There just had to be a telephone there so she could call the police. But Beth had a nagging memory that, back at the nuclear power station, the police she'd seen seemed to answer to Lachlan. She tried to think what she would do if she was in Texas. Suppose she had just killed the Mayor of Osceola in front of hundreds of witnesses, because she had reason to believe he had killed Steve – would the police be the first call she'd make? Hardly. She'd call her lawyer. Terry had mentioned the American consulate in Edinburgh as the place to go if she was in trouble. They'd help her for sure, and they'd have access to a lawyer. But the consulate number Terry had given her was in her room at the castle.

Frightened to hesitate any longer, Beth started to run down the hillside towards the river. The terrain was covered with heather, patches of fern and nettles and, every now and then, a drainage ditch, which she either saw and jumped or else, several times, fell into, grazing her shins. Gorse bushes caught at the gossamer material of her dress, tearing it, and one of the gilded buckle shoes she was wearing lost its heel. Still, she was covering ground fast and was within about a quarter of a mile of the river when a figure loomed up before her. It seemed to be standing on a stile. The head was silhouetted against the shiny surface of the river beyond. It took a few seconds, while her headlong rush brought her closer, for her to see that it was a boy, about ten years old. His face was smiling and he had put out his hands to stop her colliding with the stile.

'I know you,' he said. 'You're the May Queen.'

Struggling to control her shock, Beth blurted out:

'And who are you?'

'I'm Angus. I brought you that note from the Laddie last night,' he said. 'I was supposed to give it you myself, but Mr Beame he said he'd do it.'

Beth was overcome by an immediate feeling of warmth for this boy. He had seen Steve only last night. He had brought her that wonderful note in which Steve said that he still loved her – he still wanted to go back to Texas but, much more importantly, he still loved her.

'I got the note. Thank you so much,' she managed to say.

'The Laddie shoulda brought his shooters,' said Angus. 'What's a cowboy without his shooters?'

'Did you see how he... what happened... to Steve... the Laddie?' What an impossible question to ask the kid, she thought. But she desperately wanted an answer.

'My parents don't allow me outta the house over May Day. "When you're a man," is what they keep saying. It's so unfair. But they been gone to the May Day's Eve picnic and I'm here aren't I? They canna stop me.'

Beth looked back up the hill at the still blazing tree. It was a long way from where they stood, at least a mile she reckoned.

'So what have you seen while they were at the picnic?' she asked, wondering if he could possibly have seen her killing Lachlan.

'I saw crazy Jack comin' back just now. He said...'

'What? What did he say?'

'It's what my dad calls gibberish... Jack said: Horror... upon horror's head! Something like that. Then I saw the tree burning up there. I thought if I go up there, my mum and dad'll see me. So I watched from down here and saw you running this way. Where are you goin'?'

Beth hated telling lies. Even white lies to spare folk's feelings were a problem for her. But now she saw no alternative. To lie successfully to Angus she must discover what he already knew of the truth. But how? Her hesitation seemed to be making Angus nervous. The innocent question asked direct was worth trying.

'I'll tell you where I'm going, but first – why did you think that the Laddie should have had his shooters?'

'To frighten away the hunters. No Laddie has ever had shooters, my dad said. 'Cause I asked him. But no Laddie was ever a real cowboy like Steve. My dad had to admit that if the Laddie had shooters it would make the hunt more exciting.'

'So what happens at the end of the hunt? Do you know?'

'No, that's what the grown-ups call the Tressock Mystery. Mum says: When you're fourteen. When you're no longer a boy. Then you'll know. It's a grown-up game. A bit like charades. So where are you going?'

Beth's plan had been forming as they spoke.

'You see those lights on that hill over there?' She pointed across the valley.

'You mean Kirkallan? It's just a wee village. No very nice people either, in my mum's opinion,' said Angus.

'Well nice or not, I've decided to hide out there. As part of the game, the Queen of the May has to hide till the morning, then they find her and bring her back to Tressock to be crowned. Angus, will you help me find the best way to get there, so that no one from Tressock sees me?'

Beth was relieved that no further lies were needed. Angus seemed delighted to participate in a game from which he had hitherto been excluded. He led the way, whispering warnings about obstacles such as rocks and ditches, until they picked up a sheep's trail which took them straight to the tow-path along the banks of the Sulis. Around a bend in the river they could see a stone bridge. It consisted of five arches, three of which were planted in the fast flowing water.

'There's a road over the bridge where people might see us if we use it to cross to the other side,' said Angus. 'The tow-path goes under the near arch, like. See?'

Beth saw that the tow-path was indeed leading straight under the near side of the bridge. But if they didn't use the bridge to cross, and she could see the risk, they still had to cross the river somewhere in order to climb the hills to Kirkallan.

'Why don't we just swim across right here?' she asked.

'Swim? Here?' Angus seemed to be considering the possibility, but shook his head.

Perhaps he can't swim, thought Beth.

'Leeches,' he said.

'What?'

'Suck your blood,' added Angus. 'If we go quiet under the bridge, my dad's boat is moored a coupla hundred yards further on.'

She had been wrong to doubt him, Beth thought, as they left the comparative light of the midsummer dusk for the dank darkness under the arch. But Angus had stopped just in front of her, so that she bumped into him. He pushed her away from him as he shouted:

'I did it! I did it like you said! The Queen's here. Come and get her.'

The instantaneous terror that gripped Beth made her legs start to give way under her. She thought for no more than an instant of diving into the water and swimming for it, but there were already men in the water wading towards her and other men crowding in along the tow path from both sides of the bridge, amongst them Beame, with Delia at his side. As Beame grabbed her and held her on high, like a trophy, she heard Angus, his child's voice whining with anxiety that he might not get his prize: 'But you promised that next year... That's just not fair...' he was saying to someone, perhaps Delia, perhaps his mum.

But that was in the world Beth knew she had already left. She tried to concentrate now on the world to come, as certain as any human being can be that that she had earned her place in heaven. As she waited for Beame's needle, and the oblivion it would bring, Beth's heaven was already peopled with Steve and her mother and her music, that music she could hear in her inner ear where no other sound would ever penetrate.

Nine Months Later

SIR LACHLAN WOULD have disapproved. His sudden and totally unexpected death in the accident at the Nuada employees' annual picnic had left Lady Morrison with substantial (and unplanned for) inheritance taxes and it was generally accepted that opening the castle to tourists, starting with the Easter holiday, was unavoidable if she was to keep the estate from being sold. It would be open for four weeks and then closed until July when the schools' summer holidays began.

One of the first groups to arrive was a busload of American Ivy League college kids, exchange students from Edinburgh University, majoring in European History, doing the castles and the cathedrals of Britain. Delia had decided to train a pair of docents by leading the tour around the castle herself, starting with the great entrance hall, with its battle flags and its rich collection of dead animals' heads.

She was herself later to recognise that her introduction to each room was too long, her anecdotes perhaps too British to amuse students for whom the portrait of an old red coat general who sent a message to his superior saying 'pecavi,' meaning 'I have (conquered the province of) Sindh,' required too much explanation. In short it was not altogether surprising that two of the students detached themselves from the tour and set about exploring the spiral staircases, looking into rooms conspicuously marked 'private', and finding their way down into the labyrinthine passages that led to the kitchen and the Queens' Room.

It was there that Beame found a giggling co-ed actually trying the handle of the Queens' Room door. Her male companion, although slightly over-awed by Beame's bulk and his ferocious expression, was quick thinking enough to say, 'She's looking for the toilet.'

'Upstairs, Miss,' said Beame pointing back to the spiral stair. 'Down here's private,' he added.

'What about torture chambers?' asked the young man. 'Don't all these real old castles have those?'

'Yeah and, like, dungeons. Got any dungeons?' asked the girl, quite forgetting her need for the toilet.

Whereupon Beame bellowed a great laugh. Not a humorous sound.

'Why, Lassie?' he asked. 'Would you like to be walled up in one for all eternity?'

Perhaps it was more his terrible laugh than what he actually said that frightened them into hurrying up the stair to rejoin the tour.

Inside the Queens' Room the rosy light bathed all the motionless young women in its pinkish glow. Beame had ended up by doing Beth's eyes great justice. They were just the correct colour. Right beside her an empty throne already awaited the new Queen of the May.

If no miracle had saved Beth, it seemed to most of the population of Tressock that over in the Kelso Hospital's Maternity Wing a miracle was indeed under way. Lolly was having a baby. At seven pounds four ounces her little son represented the hopes of a whole town. Lolly did not know that Delia had jokingly suggested he be 'offered' to the sun. Although Sir Lachlan's mantle had descended upon her shoulders, even he would have found that a difficult proposition to sell to the people of Tressock. Delia had anyway promised that there would, as ever, be a new Laddie and a new Queen. Little Steve would live a much cherished life in Tressock. Beame, who had retrieved his father's hat, wanted to give it to him as soon as he learned to ride.

Back in Texas, some anxiety had grown when nothing further was heard from either Beth or Steve. Inquiries by both the Redeemers organisation and the young people's fathers were made through the US State Department. It turned out that they had last been seen checking into a hotel in Copenhagen, Denmark from where they seemed to have completely disappeared, leaving their passports and all their clothes and effects in their room. As the months wore on and there was no further news of them, folks back home searched for some explanation. When the Cowboys for Christ Church learnt that they had apparently shared a bed in the Danish hotel their worst fears were confirmed. Big Bill's prophecy had come to pass. A Godless Europe had somehow consumed two of their beautiful, innocent children. Amidst the universal sadness at the news of these events only Beth's recording company celebrated, doing so with the release of an album of her greatest hits. Their marketing people came up with an inspired title, adding to the romantic mystery of her disappearance with an authentic Scottish flavour. They called it:

WILL YOU NO COME BACK AGAIN?

Post Script

A Report of an Incident at the Cowboys for Christ Church
in Osceola, Texas

BEFORE THE MYSTERY of Beth and Steve's disappearance completely faded from the collective consciousness of their friends and relations in Texas and, indeed, from that of the public at large, a further incident occurred.

It was a story that never made the front pages of the Texas tabloids, but was stuck somewhere near the entertainment sections because it featured singing star Beth Boothby (missing, presumed dead). A typical wire service report on the story went like this:

'It was like a miracle,' Mr Benny Jones told reporters. 'I was all alone in the Cowboys for Christ church off Route 171 at Osceola, on the night of April 30. Suddenly, I heard Beth Boothby's beautiful singing voice coming from where the preacher normally stands at the lectern.' Astonished, Mr Jones checked if the church's sound system was on, and it definitely was not, he claims. Nor could he have mistaken her voice having known her and her family since she was fourteen years old and driven her in his limo whenever she was in the Dallas/Fort Worth area. He absolutely denied that he saw any kind of ghostly apparition, insisting he heard only her voice.

He was quite familiar with the song she was singing – 'I Have a Dream' – an Abba favourite, remembering that it had been a big hit some years earlier and that Beth had liked it.

He can now particularly recall two lines of the song because Boothby repeated them several times. He says that he was struck by the fact that she used the word 'we' again and again and not the word 'I', as in the original song. He believes that by using the 'we', she was including Steve Thomson, her Silver Ring friend, who also disappeared when they were both on a missionary trip to Scotland.

Mr Jones, who works for Buckingham Livery and Hire as a limousine driver, found time on his hands when Beth, a regular customer, went off to Scotland with her friend Steve and the Redeemers, an evangelical group. This resulted in his doing part-time work as a cleaner for the Cowboys for Christ church.

The church's pastor, the Reverend Kenny Norquist, would not comment on the incident except to say that Benny Jones was no longer in their employ. He added that no one else had seen or heard any manifestation of Beth Boothby or Steve Thomson in the church and thinks that Mr Jones must be mistaken. After an initial ghost scare, attendance at the church has returned to normal.

Since it was impossible to verify Benny's statement in any way, and there had been no repetition of the incident, the press soon lost interest in the story.

Benny's wife (and Beth's housekeeper) Vashti still hopes for her employer's return to the home she has kept ready for her at all times. She believes her husband's story, but most folks locally do not. This scepticism might be expected to upset Benny and Vashti, but that is not the case. They conclude that Beth's song was a message from heaven, meant for them alone.

Author's Note

All the characters featured as protagonists in *Cowboys for Christ* (now retitled *The Wicker Tree*), a work of fiction, are imaginary. Any similarity between any of them and any real persons living or dead is purely coincidental. While there are a number of Christian congregations that call themselves Cowboys for Christ churches, both in Texas and elsewhere, the church featured in this novel is imaginary. The Redeemers, an evangelical movement with a notable choir, do not exist although there are many similar American Christian groups working as missionaries around the world.

The Border Ridings take place every year and are celebrated by certain small towns on the Scottish side of the border with England. The fictional Tressock is quite unlike any of these places. Opinion is very divided as to why and how the ritual of townspeople hunting an elected or chosen young man over hill and dale originated. One tradition (of which there are several versions) has it that it stems from the defeat of a Scottish army by the English, during which the Scottish king was killed. A brave young man rescued the royal banner and, although heavily pursued, carried it back to Stirling castle to the widowed queen. A completely different tradition features in this novel but there is not the slightest evidence it has ever taken place.

The author is grateful for the assistance of the following persons, on both sides of the Atlantic, during the research and completion of this book: Neil Baxter, Darren Blanton, Yolanda Jones, Anne Hodgson, Suzanne Kennedy, Marvin Klein, Alistair McIntyre, Robert Marshall, Eileen, Countess of Mount Charles, Tim West, Geoffrey Woods, Rodney Woods.

Robin Hardy, 2006

POLICE

THE
QUEST
FOR THE
WICKER
MAN

HISTORICAL, FOLKLORE
AND PAGAN PERSPECTIVES

EDITED BY BENJAMIN FRANKS, STEPHEN HARPER,
JONATHAN MURRAY AND LESLEY STEVENSON

The Quest for the Wicker Man

ed. Benjamin Franks, Stephen Harper, Jonathan Murray, Lesley Stevenson
ISBN 978 1905222 18 6 HBK £16.99

Filmed in Scotland, The Wicker Man *has been voted the greatest cult movie of all time. The themes of pagan ritual and sacrifice in a small island community have provoked much curiosity into the fascinating origins and background of the tale.*

What were the historical and folkloric sources of the film?
What is the true history of the religious practices and rituals portrayed in the film?
What is the relationship between the film and its real-life Pagan audience?
What are the stories behind the making, casting, and distribution of the film?

The contributors to the collection represent a broad cross-section of experts, academics, and film industry professionals, who have authoritative knowledge in the areas of archaeology, history, literature and paganism. This book traces *The Wicker Man*'s myriad historical and mythological reference points back to their arcane, often surprising, sources, solving the film's ingenious riddles more successfully than the unhappy Sergeant Howie.

The Quest for the Wicker Man offers readers a rare opportunity to explore a single film from a variety of perspectives. Themes which emerge from the contributions include the relationship between Pagan audiences and The Wicker Man; the historical and folkloric materials which served as sources for the film; the film's reception, its musical score, and its representation of cults.

Includes contributions not only by leading academics, but also from Robin Hardy (the film's director) and Gary Carpenter (the film's associate music director). Also includes an interview with Robin Hardy by Jonathan Murray.

The Supernatural Highlands

Francis Thompson

ISBN 978 0946487 31 8 PBK £8.99

This book can be read as a simple introduction to the way of life of the rural and island communities of the Highlands and Islands of yesteryear and in the more recent past. On another level the reader can take the opportunity to obtain new and different sight-lines which might throw new shafts of light into areas of belief which were once dismissed as folklore, or even classed as superstition and therefore not worth the coin.
FRANCIS THOMPSON

An authoritative exploration of the otherworld of the Highlander, of happenings and beings hitherto thought to be outwith the ordinary forces of nature. This new edition weaves a path through second sight, the evil eye, witchcraft, ghosts, fairies and other supernatural beings, offering new insights into Highland and Island culture using beliefs and traditions once easily dismissed.

Excellent guidebook to the Gaelic-speaking underworld.
THE HERALD

Out of the Mouth of the Morning

David Campbell

ISBN 978 1906307 93 6 PBK £8.99

The Celtic lands of Scotland and Ireland carry a rich heritage of legend and lore: myth comes to life in tales of feisty saints, elite warriors, powerful fairies and ordinary folk. Master storyteller David Campbell eloquently unfolds these tales for our times. They are a reminder of our primal relationship with the land and the connections between all things. The author skilfully traces the carrying stream of Celtic consciousness from its origins in ancient landscapes and tongues, to the men, women and stories of today. Deftly weaving the ancient with the modern, he illustrates the essential nature of the folklore of the Celts in today's Scotland.

This Celtic collection is drawn from various age-old sources, lovingly and lyrically retold by a master storyteller. SCOTLAND ON SUNDAY

The Quest for the Celtic Key

Karen Ralls-MacLeod and Ian Robertson
ISBN 978 1842820 31 5 PBK £8.99

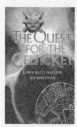

Full of mystery, magic and intrigue, Scotland's past burns with unanswered questions, many asked before, some that have never been broached.

All are addressed with the inquisitiveness of true detectives in this collaboration between medieval Celtic historian Karen Ralls-MacLeod and Scottish Masonic researcher Ian Robertson.

What are the similarities between Merlin and Christ?
Did King Arthur conquer Scotland?
What is hidden in the vaults at Rosslyn Chapel?
Why is the lore surrounding Scottish freemasonry so unique?

Encompassing well-known events and personae, whilst also tackling the more obscure elements in Scottish history, *The Quest for the Celtic Key* illustrates how the seemingly disparate 'mysteries of history' are connected.

A travelogue which enriches the mythologies and histories so beautifully told, with many newly wrought connection to places, buildings stones and other remains.
REV DR MICHAEL NORTHCOTT, Faculty of Divinity, University of Edinburgh

The Quest for the Nine Maidens

Stuart McHardy
ISBN 978 0946487 66 0 HBK £16.99

When King Arthur was conveyed to Avalon they were there.

When Odin summoned warriors to Valhalla they were there.

When Apollo was worshipped on Greek mountains they were there.

When Brendan came to the Island of Women they were there.

They tended the Welsh goddess Cerridwen's cauldron on inspiration, and armed the hero Peredur. They are found in Britain, Ireland, Norway, Iceland, Gaul, Greece, Africa and as far afield as South America and Oceania. They are the Nine Maidens – the priestesses of the Mother Goddess.

From the Stone Age to the twenty-first century, the Nine Maidens come in many forms – Muses, Maenads, Valkyries, seeresses and druidesses. In this book Stuart McHardy traces the Nine Maidens from both Christian and pagan sources, and begins to uncover one of the most ancient and widespread of human institutions.

On the Trail of Scotland's Myths and Legends

Stuart McHardy

ISBN 978 1842820 49 0 PBK £7.99

Scotland is an ancient land with an extensive heritage of myths and legends that have been passed down by word-of-mouth over the centuries.

As the art of storytelling bursts into new flower, many of these tales are being told again as they once were. As *On the Trail of Scotland's Myths and Legends* unfolds, mythical animals, supernatural beings, heroes, giants and goddesses come alive and walk Scotland's rich landscape as they did in the time of the Scots, Gaelic and Norse speakers of the past.

Visiting over 170 sites across Scotland, Stuart McHardy traces the lore of our ancestors, connecting ancient beliefs with traditions still alive today. Presenting a new picture of who the Scottish are and where they have come from these stories provide an insight into a unique tradition of myth, legend and folklore that has marked the language and landscape of Scotland.

... a remarkably keen collection of tales. SCOTTISH BOOK COLLECTOR

Stuart McHardy is passionate about the place of indigenous culture in Scottish national life.
COURIER AND ADVERTISER

Highland Myths and Legends

George W Macpherson

ISBN 978 1842820 64 3 PBK £5.99

The mythical, the legendary, the true – this is the stuff of stories and storytellers, the preserve of Scotland's ancient oral tradition.

Celtic heroes, fairies, Druids, selkies, sea horses, magicians, giants, Viking invaders – all feature in this collection of traditional Scottish tales, the like of which have been told around campfires for centuries and are still told today.

Drawn from storyteller George W Macpherson's extraordinary repertoire of tales and lore, each story has been passed down through generations of oral tradition – some are over 2,500 years old. Strands of these timeless tales cross over and interweave to create a delicate tapestry of Highland Scotland as depicted by its myths and legends.

I have heard George telling his stories... and it is an unforgettable experience... This is a unique book and a 'must buy'.
DALRIADA: THE JOURNAL OF CELTIC HERITAGE AND CULTURAL TRADITIONS

The Glasgow Dragon

Des Dillon

ISBN 978 1 842820 56 8 PBK £9.99

What do I want? Let me see now. I want to destroy you spiritually, emotionally and mentally before I destroy you physically.

When Christie Devlin goes into business with a triad to take control of the Glasgow drug market little does he know that his downfall and the destruction of his family is being plotted. As Devlin struggles with his own demons the real fight is just beginning.

There are some things you should never forgive yourself for.

Nothing is as simple as good and evil. Des Dillon is a master story-teller and this is a world he knows well.

The authenticity, brutality, humour and most of all the humanity of the characters and the reality of the world they inhabit in Des Dillon's stories are never in question.
LESLEY BENZIE

It has been known for years that Des Dillon writes some of Scotland's most vibrant prose.
ALAN BISSETT

Des Dillon writes like a man possessed. The words come tumbling out of him... His prose... teems with unceasing energy.
THE SCOTSMAN

Monks

Des Dillon

ISBN 978 1905222 75 9 PBK £7.99

Ye must've searched out solitude in your life. At least once.

Three men are off from Coatbridge to an idyllic Italian monastic retreat in search of inner peace and sanctuary.

...like hell they are. Italian food, sunshine and women – it's the perfect holiday in exchange for some easy construction work at the monastery.

Some holiday it turns out to be, what with optional Mass at five in the morning, a mad monk with a ball and chain, and the salami fiasco – to say nothing of the language barrier.

But even on this remote and tranquil mountain, they can't hide from the chilling story of Jimmy Brogan. Suddenly the past explodes into the present, and they find more redemption than they ever bargained for.

Bad Catholics

James Green

ISBN 978 1906817 07 7 PBK £6.99

It's a short step from the paths of righteousness…

Jimmy started off as a good Catholic altar boy. Growing up in Irish London meant walking between poverty and temptation, and what he learnt on the street wasn't taught by his Church. As a cop, though some called him corrupt and violent, his record was spotless and his arrest rates were high.

It's a long time since he left the Force and disappeared, and now Jimmy is trying to go straight. But his past is about to catch up with him. When one of the volunteers at the homeless shelter where he works is brutally murdered, a bent copper tips off a powerful crime lord that Jimmy is back in town. However, Jimmy has his own motives for staying put… and can he find the killer before the gangs find him?

The first in the thrilling new Jimmy Costello series.

Stealing God

James Green

ISBN 978 1906817 01 5 PBK £6.99

An explosive sequel to *Bad Catholics*, the first in the Jimmy Costello series.

Jimmy Costello, last seen at the epicentre of a murder investigation and a gangland turf war, is now a student priest in Rome. Driven to atone for his past sins, Jimmy is trying to leave the hardbitten cop behind him, but the Church has a use for the old Jimmy.

When a visiting Archbishop dies in mysterious circumstances, Jimmy is hand-picked to look into the case. With local copper Inspector Ricci, Jimmy follows the trail from the streets of the Holy City via Glasgow and back to Rome, where they stumble on dark forces that threaten everything Jimmy hopes for. But who is really behind their investigation – and are they supposed to uncover the truth, or is their mission altogether more sinister?

Eye for an Eye
Frank Muir
ISBN 978 1906307 53 0 PBK £6.99

One psychopath. One killer. The Stabber.

One psychopath. One killer. The Stabber.

Six victims. Six wife abusers. Each stabbed to death through their left eye.

Six victims. Six wife abusers. Each stabbed to death through their left eye.

The cobbled lanes and back streets of St Andrews provide the setting for these brutal killings. But six unsolved murders and mounting censure from the media force Detective Inspector Andy Gilchrist off the case. Driven by his fear of failure, desperate to redeem his career and reputation, Gilchrist vows to catch The Stabber alone.

Digging deeper into the world of a psychopath, Gilchrist fears he is up against the worst kind of murderer – a serial killer on the verge of mental collapse. Can Gilchrist unravel the crazed mind of the killer?

Eye for an Eye is the first in the DI Gilchrist series.

Rebus did it for Edinburgh. Laidlaw did it for Glasgow. Gilchrist might just be the bloke to put St Andrews on the crime fiction map.
THE DAILY RECORD

Hand for a Hand
Frank Muir
ISBN 978 1906817 51 0 PBK £6.99

An amputated hand is found in a bunker, its lifeless fingers clutching a note addressed to DCI Andy Gilchrist. The note bears only one word: Murder.

When other body parts with messages attached are discovered, Gilchrist finds himself living every policeman's worst nightmare – with a sadistic killer out for revenge.

Forced to confront the ghosts of his past, Gilchrist must solve the cryptic clues and find the murderer before the next victim, whose life means more to Gilchrist that his own, is served up piece by slaughtered piece.

Hand for a Hand is the second in Frank Muir's DI Gilchrist series.

A bright new recruit to the swelling army of Scots crime writers.
QUINTIN JARDINE

Luath Press Limited

committed to publishing well written books worth reading

LUATH PRESS takes its name from Robert Burns, whose little collie Luath (*Gael.*, swift or nimble) tripped up Jean Armour at a wedding and gave him the chance to speak to the woman who was to be his wife and the abiding love of his life. Burns called one of the 'Twa Dogs' Luath after Cuchullin's hunting dog in Ossian's *Fingal*. Luath Press was established in 1981 in the heart of Burns country, and is now based a few steps up the road from Burns' first lodgings on Edinburgh's Royal Mile. Luath offers you distinctive writing with a hint of unexpected pleasures.

Most bookshops in the UK, the US, Canada, Australia, New Zealand and parts of Europe, either carry our books in stock or can order them for you. To order direct from us, please send a £sterling cheque, postal order, international money order or your credit card details (number, address of cardholder and expiry date) to us at the address below. Please add post and packing as follows: UK – £1.00 per delivery address; overseas surface mail – £2.50 per delivery address; overseas airmail – £3.50 for the first book to each delivery address, plus £1.00 for each additional book by airmail to the same address. If your order is a gift, we will happily enclose your card or message at no extra charge.

Luath Press Limited
543/2 Castlehill
The Royal Mile
Edinburgh EH1 2ND
Scotland
Telephone: +44 (0)131 225 4326 (24 hours)
Fax: +44 (0)131 225 4324
email: sales@luath. co.uk
Website: www.luath.co.uk